AMBROSIA

C.N. CRAWFORD

For those who want faeries to take you out of this dull world,
and dance upon the mountains like a flame.

(Also for those who don't mind that I stole these phrases from
W.B. Yeats)

SUMMARY OF FROST

Torin is the King of the Seelie and is plagued by a number of curses. In *Frost*, we learned that his kingdom, Faerie, was cursed by the Unseelie long ago. The Seelie refer to the Unseelie as "demons" because they are enemies, and also because the Unseelie have some animalistic features, like horns and wings. Faerie is cursed with long winters and dark magic.

Torin realized that he must find a queen to stop the creeping winter. In the ancient Seelie tradition, a Seelie queen is chosen through a series of brutal trials.

But Torin has another curse, too. The Unseelie condemned him to kill anyone he loves. Worst of all, he cannot tell anyone about the curse, and his potential bride doesn't know why he is looking for a bride he cannot love.

In Torin's words:

The demons had cursed us. After the conquest, the

demons condemned us to endless winters until we learned how to keep them at bay with the power of a queen and a throne. The demons cursed us again with the Erlkings, who arrived every hundred years to spread their icy death.

And when we'd tried to make peace with them one final time, they'd cursed my entire family. They'd blinded Orla. They'd sentenced my parents to death. And they'd condemned me to murder any woman I loved.

Years ago, Torin killed the one woman he wanted to marry, Milisandia. Because of that curse, Torin's plan was to find a bride he cannot love. He considered Moria, a burgundy-haired princess and surviving sister of Milisandia. Beautiful as she is, he does not love her.

But when he met Ava, he formed a new plan.

Ava is a fae who was found abandoned as a baby. She was adopted and raised by a human mother, Chloe, and she has lived her life among humans. Her best friend is a human named Shalini, a software engineer who retired early and quickly grew bored of her unemployed life.

At the start of *Frost*, Ava came home to find her human fiancé in bed with another woman. She went out to get drunk, and she swore off men for good. When Torin wandered into the bar for a whisky, she drunkenly insulted him. Torin decided that she would make the perfect bride for him—a woman he cannot love. He offered her fifty million dollars to compete in the trials and to rig the outcome with him. In return, he would also be paid an enormous sum of money by the TV station broadcasting the trials. Because of the long winters, the grain stores and food supplies in Faerie have run thin, and his people are at risk of starving.

As the trials went on, Torin helped Ava train for the brutal duels, building on her already strong fencing skills. But as they spent time together, passion started to simmer between them. Torin worried he was at risk of falling in love with her, of killing someone he loves all over again.

After Ava won the final duel, disaster struck. Torin touched her arm, and his curse took hold, freezing her body with his frost. His blast of magic destroyed his own throne and sent Ava tumbling onto the queen's throne. It is the magic of the queen's throne that brought her home.

Except it wasn't a home she recognized.

When Ava looked at her reflection, she found copper horns growing from her head. It turns out that Ava is an Unseelie—a *demon*—and a natural enemy of the Seelie.

𝕊 I 𝕊
AVA

I gazed into the puddle of water on the forest floor, staring at the deep bronze horns jutting from my head: small and devilish, curved out and up to the sky. My eyes looked dark and murky, the slate green of a stormy sea. Dirt was smudged on one cheekbone, and I wiped it off with a shaking hand.

When I'd fallen through the icy portal into this place, my hair had shifted from lavender at the ends to a pale green. My clothing had changed, too. I now wore a damp, seafoam green dress that clung to my body, soaked through by the portal's water. The forest's damp earth stained my little white shoes and the hem of the gossamer dress.

With a shiver of horror, my gaze shifted back to the horns. My pulse ratcheted up.

Demon.

That was the Seelie term for the Unseelie.

Once, Torin had said, "A king is supposed to show that he has the power to defeat the demons." A tapestry hung in the Great Hall of his castle, and it depicted an ancient Seelie king severing the head of a demon with golden horns.

Horns that looked a lot like mine...

Dread sank its talons into my heart. Would Torin drive a blade through my throat if he saw me?

Ava Jones didn't have these horns. They belonged to the new me, a demon with a forgotten name.

I reached up to touch one of the curves, running a finger over the tip. It was disturbingly sensitive, sending a shudder through me. Sharp as the point of a fae sword. For a moment, my mind blazed with an image of the horns tearing through someone's gut...

I shuddered again. Underneath the glamour of ordinary Ava Jones, a monster was waking.

When I pulled my finger away from the point of my horn, a scarlet droplet glistened on my finger. I stuck my finger in my mouth, tasting copper.

I breathed in, trying to calm myself. The scent of the forest filled my nose, rich and primeval: moss, soil, and undertones of sweet almonds. The scent tickled something in the darkest recesses of my memory. Mist billowed around me, obscuring my reflection in the puddle of water.

Leaves rustled, and I jumped to my feet, remembering a terrible, blood-chilling fact I'd forgotten in my distraction: there was a spider behind me, a freakishly large spider.

I whirled around. A spider the size of a dog crawled closer, all six of its iridescent eyes locked on me.

I started to back away carefully, my little shoes

drenched by the puddle. The spider scuttled nearer, mouth open to display its long, pointed fangs.

As I edged away, I silently cursed the magic of this place for supplying me with a pretty dress, but not a sword to defend myself. There were the horns, of course —but I wasn't ready to get that close.

The spider skittered closer, and I turned and sprinted in the other direction.

Hiking up my dress, I raced through the mist. Gnarled tree roots jutted from the damp earth beneath my feet, and I took care not to trip.

I could hardly see where I was going in the fog, and the thick brush scratched my arms and legs. I splashed through muddy puddles and swatted branches away from my face.

Panicked thoughts flitted through my mind as I tried to make sense of my current situation. Exactly what had happened in the past hour?

I was supposed to be Queen of the Seelie now.

I should be sitting on a throne, replenishing the kingdom with my magic, saving it from the frost and famine. I should be Torin's wife—at least for show. I should have fifty million in my bank account. But Moria had showed up in my room with a story about a murdered sister and a premonition of my death. She'd been certain that Torin would kill me, too. Gleeful about it, really.

My heart splintered.

And maybe she was right. Because from what I understood, a Seelie king was honor-bound to slaughter an Unseelie like me.

I fled through the forest, Torin's words ringing in my skull: *Monsters...demons...even speaking of them could draw their twisted attention.*

A low, hissing noise sent fear crawling up my spine. I glanced back. The monstrous spider was gaining on me. I ran faster through the mist, my lungs burning. Thorns scored my bare arms with angry red lines. In the distance, I heard the rush of a river, and I ran toward the sound. If I followed the river, it might lead to a village or settlement.

Any moment, I expected the spider to pounce, the feel of its hairy legs on my back followed by the burning pain of fangs sinking into my neck.

When I stumbled over a root, I whirled my arms to steady myself. Snatching a fist-sized rock from the ground, I spun and hurled the rock at the spider's eyes. The creature jerked back with a screech, and I sprinted away again.

As I reached the roaring river, the setting sun tinged the fog with a rose gold light. White water rushed over snags of driftwood and tumbled down a gentle slope into a clearing. A cool spray misted over me. When I searched the fog, I didn't see any movement.

I followed the narrow path beside the river. Further into the woods, the forest hues shifted into vibrant, enchanted shades. Green leaves blended to maroon, then bright red, and the tree trunks ranged from indigo to midnight blue. As night fell, the light was darkening to twilight shades of violet and periwinkle.

I hurried along the edge of the river bank, over slippery rocks and gnarled roots. Night was closing in, the shadows thickening and lengthening around me. I sucked in a deep breath, trying to imagine how I'd navigate this place in total darkness.

Making my way down the path, I came to a massive tree that loomed out of the murk, the trunk a midnight blue. The branches of the tree arched over the river, the crimson leaves shot through with moonlight high above me. The huge tree blocked the path, thick roots twining down the slope to the river.

I slipped around the tree. Thick boughs shielded the moonlight, and shadows enveloped me.

I shivered, and someone caught me from behind, pulling me into the darkness, one arm wrapped around my waist in a vise-like grip and a hand clapped over my mouth. Fear surged in my veins.

I struggled, slamming my attacker hard with my elbows and trying to rip through his jaw with my horns. The scents of wet rock and soil filled my nostrils, and as my eyes adjusted to the darkness, I realized I was being dragged into a cave.

Leaning down, my captor whispered in my ear, "Please be quiet, Ava."

I recognized the deep, honeyed baritone of his voice, at once dangerous and alluring. The oaky scent of the Seelie king wrapped around me, skimming over the jagged edges of my fear. I was trapped in the steely grasp of the man who might want me dead.

The question still clawed at my mind: was he going to kill me? Because that was the job of a Seelie king.

"Ava." His powerful arm pinned me in place. "I need you to be quiet. Someone was following you."

I went still, no longer struggling against him, and my muscles gave in. Slowly, I caught my breath, and he lowered his hand from my mouth. My heart still thrummed like a hummingbird's. Fear, or simply the effect Torin always had on me? I wasn't sure.

Whatever the case, he wasn't letting me go.

"What are you doing here?" I whispered. "How did you get here?"

"I followed you through the portal," he murmured. "And right now, I'm trying to save you from a demon." Torin's breath warmed the shell of my ear, and his muscled arm remained clamped around me. "He's been tracking you."

Had he not noticed that *I* was a demon?

My heart pounded faster. In my panic, I hadn't seen the other Unseelie. "And why aren't you letting go of me?"

"Because I can see that you're an Unseelie, and now I'm questioning everything." A razor's edge slid through his silky voice, and fear skittered up my spine. "Were you sent to destroy my kingdom, changeling?"

My jaw tightened at the accusation, and I wriggled around to face him. Except he wasn't letting me go—so I found myself staring right up at his piercing blue eyes, pressed against the wall of muscle that was his chest. His forearm remained locked firmly around my lower back like an iron bar.

"Sent on a mission to destroy your kingdom? Don't be ridiculous, Torin." It came out sharp and a little too loud, echoing off the stone. "If this was all part of a Machiavellian master plan, do you think you would have found me in a bar drunk and covered in curry sauce?"

He arched a black eyebrow. "Lower your voice, changeling," he whispered. "But if it wasn't your intent, you really have done a remarkable job of destroying my kingdom. My throne is cracked. My power is gone. Faerie lays encased in ice, and I have no queen to heal it. Famine and cold will creep over my kingdom, and I am trapped in the Court of Sorrows itself, where I'm guaranteed a gruesome execution if I'm caught. It does seem a bit convenient for the demons, doesn't it?"

Demons. There was that word again, coming out of his perfect mouth. But how could he possibly think I was a spy?

"There was no plan," I said through clenched teeth. "I haven't lied to you." My voice trailed off. I was still trying to wrap my mind around this. "And I want the fifty million dollars you owe me."

The corner of his mouth quirked. "You can't be serious, changeling."

"We signed a contract. As a fae king, you can't break it."

"You're not a Seelie. The contract is void."

I was still looking up at him, pressed tight against him. "That's not a real rule, though, is it? It wasn't in the fine print."

"Is this really your concern right now?"

"Your kingdom will be fine. Just find yourself a proper Seelie wife. I'm sure you'll manage." I wished my tone hadn't sounded quite so acidic. "But you still owe me."

His arm was tight around me, and I could feel the pounding of his pulse through his clothes. "You know, I really shouldn't be anywhere near you."

"Then maybe you should let me go," I said evenly.

"It would seem that I have to."

2

TORIN

Insanely, I didn't want to let her go. Even in the gloom of the cave, I could see the gentle curves of her copper horns. She was an ancient enemy of the Seelie, fiendish horns and all—the evidence was right before my eyes—and I'd followed her to the Court of Sorrows.

The only bright spot in this situation was that I'd felt the weight of Queen Mab's curse lift. The moment I'd pulled myself from the portal, breathing in the air of the Unseelie realm, the curse had released its icy grip on my chest. It was a strange sort of certainty, a weightlessness I'd never known before.

Why was the curse gone? I had no idea. But without it weighing me down, I could give in to my desires...I could touch Ava. I could kiss her deeply and pull the hem of her dress all the way up to her waist. It was in the nature of the fae to give in to lust, to seek pleasure above all else—

Except that the person occupying my every waking thought was a demon.

Had she lured me here? I didn't know. The moment I'd seen a stranger following her—an armed Unseelie with horns and wings—I'd had to keep her safe.

"I can't stay here, Ava," I whispered. "I have a small amount of magic left, I think. I might be able to open a portal."

If Queen Mab captured me, I'd be quite literally flayed alive. She'd find a way to draw out a painful and humiliating death for me. And yet, somehow, my attention was transfixed on the Unseelie before me. She stared up at me in the shadowy cave with big green eyes.

"Any idea how to get us out?" she asked.

Us. "I might have enough magic left to create a portal. But you can't come with me back to Faerie, Ava." Here, the curse had lifted. But at home? I'd simply kill her the moment she came near.

Her eyes narrowed, then she fluttered her long, black eyelashes. "You'll really deprive me of Moria's charming company?"

"Whatever our deal might have been, your kind can never again set foot in Faerie."

A war was raging between my mind and body, but I knew I couldn't take her with me for two very important reasons. One, I'd nearly killed her. Thoughtlessly, instinctively, I'd reached out for her when she turned away from me. The icy curse had snapped out of my body, and winter had started to claim her. Two, she was a demon, and a demon had cursed our land with brutal frost and long winters. My subjects would rip her to shreds; they'd destroy the kingdom before letting an Unseelie wear the crown. Who could blame them? We'd suffered for centuries.

It didn't stop my body from craving this particular demon. She was somehow more alluring in her current form—wild, ruthless, and seductive at the same time. My pulse raced at her nearness. Just a moment ago, I'd felt her heart beating against my body through the thin, damp material of her dress. A caress that would have been deadly back in Faerie...

My gaze moved to her perfect mouth, full and slightly parted. I wanted to taste the lips of a demon, to make her moan with pleasure. *Fuck.*

A low, rhythmic sound rattled outside, interrupting my mental battle. The noise sent a chill racing up my spine.

"It's the spider," Ava whispered.

I picked up a rock and stepped out of the cave's mouth. Six dark eyes gleamed in the dusk as the spider crawled slowly down the trunk of the huge tree, fangs dripping with venom. My blood pounded in my skull. I didn't want this thing anywhere near Ava.

As the spider leapt, I darted forward and smashed the rock hard against its head. The spider fell to the ground, and blood coated my hands and body. I dropped the rock. Midnight blue ichor spattered my white shirt, and I pulled it off. I crossed to the river and discarded my shirt, then cleaned my bloody hands in the cool currents.

I scanned the dark wood for movement. Apart from

the wind rushing through the leaves and a strange bird-song, I couldn't sense a thing.

When I stepped back into the cave, Ava frowned at my chest. "Did the spider steal your shirt?"

"Most women wouldn't complain."

"I see the breaking of your throne hasn't damaged your ego."

A ragged truth snagged at my thoughts underneath all my attempts at rationalization. I should leave her here and get myself home—but I could not. "I'll make sure you are safe here, Ava, but I can't take you with me to Faerie. And I don't have enough magic left in me to open two portals." Only a glimmer of magic sputtered in my chest.

Her jaw clenched. She looked too angry to speak, and her dark green eyes flashed. "Who was following me?"

"A large Unseelie with silver horns and dark wings, armed with darts. But I didn't see him just now. I think we may have lost him in the fog and darkness."

She crossed to the cave mouth, peering out into the shadows. After a moment, she turned back to me, a line etched between her eyebrows. "How will you know if and when I'm safe?"

Fuck knows.

I scrubbed a hand over my jaw, my mind roiling like the wild river outside. Maybe the Unseelie would welcome her with open arms. She was one of their own, a long-lost daughter of the Court. I'd return to my kingdom as soon as possible. I'd fix my throne, restore my power, and marry...*someone*. Moria, maybe. There was no way I'd fall in love with her.

A queen only needed to fulfill her role, to bring the spring again. The granaries were nearly empty, the cattle had been slaughtered for meat, and the kingdom had run out of money.

I was king of the Seelie, and my life was an absolute fucking shambles.

"I'll watch from a distance to see how the Unseelie react to you. If they accept you, then I'll quietly return to my realm and try to restore it. I think you'll be better off here than in Faerie."

She took a deep breath. "Why so desperate to pull me into a cave, then?"

I ran a hand through my hair. "Because that demon was armed. We'd be better off finding someone harmless. Someone we could kill with our bare hands if necessary."

Her eyebrows rose. "Sounds like we're in for an interesting evening, then."

She turned and slipped out of the cave into the dark forest.

I followed her, watching the intoxicating sway of her hips as she stalked between the trees. The deeper we walked into the woods, the more vibrant red the leaves became. Pierced by the moonlight, they looked like blood spatters.

How much had I angered the old gods by willingly jumping into that portal? The Seelie's anointed king was letting his people freeze to death to keep a demon safe.

The old gods had chosen me to lead the Seelie.

Before my coronation, the Horned God had transformed the male nobles into stags, and I had proven my strength by defeating every one of them. Then, covered in blood, we'd marched to the Sword of Whispers for the final test of the gods.

Only a trueborn high king could lift the sword. It was forged by the old gods in the land of the dead. Made of Fomorian steel, it could cut through stone. If I held it to an enemy's throat, he confessed his sins. And when a trueborn high king grips its hilt, the sword whispers. On the battlefield in a king's hand, the blade whispers of death and valor, of ravaged bodies and the songs of gods. That is how I'd known the old ones had chosen me.

So what the fuck was I doing right now?

She turned back to me with a frown. "What are you brooding about?"

"The Sword of Whispers," I muttered absentmindedly.

She sighed. "Are you delirious?"

The corner of my mouth twitched. She wasn't entirely wrong. Any king who used the sword would start to hear voices.

But my thoughts about Ava were their own kind of madness, and she'd already rendered me senseless.

3

AVA

Starlight streamed through the tree branches as we followed the river down the slope. The more we walked, the more it seemed as if we were approaching some kind of civilization. Between gnarled trunks, ruined stone arches appeared, covered over with climbing red flowers.

Torin walked behind me, and I stole a few glances at his bare-chested, athletic form. The moonlight seemed to shine off his spiky tattoos, making them look like blades. A little part of me appreciated that he was here, making sure I was safe. Another, much larger part of me rebelled at the fact that he would probably be leaving to marry someone else. He needed a queen, and it wasn't like I was an option anymore.

The thought of him sitting on his repaired throne with someone like *Moria* at his side...

I wasn't raised in these worlds, fed on the enmity between the kingdoms. What was the point of dragging out mutual hatred over millennia?

I glanced at him again, feeling a crack in my heart when I took in his physical perfection. "Who will you marry?" Not sure why I asked when I didn't really want to know.

"Who I marry doesn't really matter, Ava. The main thing is that I need to return and fix my throne as soon as possible. Without my throne intact, I have no power whatsoever," he said quietly. "Maybe Moria or Cleena. Either of them would be perfect. Though frankly, I suspect that my greatest love of all will always be myself. And can you blame me, changeling—"

I whirled, interrupting him when I pressed my hand to his chest. "Not Moria. She hates you. She blames you for killing her sister."

"I *did* kill her sister."

"*Why?*"

"Her name was Milisandia, and I buried her in the Temple of Ostara." He took a deep breath. "It was an accident that I have regretted every day since. I haven't been able to tell anyone until now. Only my sister knew." His sorrowful blue eyes searched mine. "I killed her, Ava."

I stared at him, my heart twisting. I wasn't sure he'd understood that Moria was unhinged and dangerous. She'd murdered Alice, for fuck's sake. "Torin, I don't think she believes it was an accident."

His eyes flashed, and he held a finger to his lips. His gaze went to something over my shoulder. "I can smell another Unseelie."

I inhaled deeply, breathing in a new forest scent. Under the loam and moss and almond-scented mushrooms, a briny scent floated on the wind. As I concentrated, a distant song carried through the forest. Here, the river's flow had grown gentler, more of a burbling than a rush. In the quiet of the night, the forest life around me seemed to have a faint hum to it, like soft woodland music.

I turned back to the path. A faint blue glow beamed between ruined stone vaults further down the river.

The song seemed to call to me, luring me closer. I took the lead as Torin hung back, his footfalls nearly imperceptible. We kept hidden behind the cover of dense ruddy foliage, and I peered through it at the blue light.

I spied the source: large, glowing blue fireflies that floated through the air above a murmuring stream. And there, resting her arms on the river bank, was an Unseelie woman. Her shimmering white hair draped over bare bronze shoulders. She wore a small cap made of bright red feathers and a sheer green veil over her face. She didn't look particularly vicious.

As I craned my neck, I caught sight of iridescent scales that glittered over her shoulder blades.

I turned to Torin, and he whispered, "A merrow. Not dangerous, I think. She can't leave the water."

I inhaled deeply, trying to pick out the scent of any other creatures. I didn't smell anything.

The merrow had started singing again, a quiet, beautiful song that harmonized with the intoxicating melody of life around us.

With a deep inhalation, I pushed through the foliage, the slick leaves brushing gently against my skin.

The merrow turned to look at me and fell silent. She cocked her head, curiosity shining in her violet eyes.

I smiled hesitantly. "Hello."

She sniffed the air, and she spoke in a lilting, unfamiliar tongue.

"Sorry, I don't understand."

She sniffed again. "Cromm. Isavell." She smiled. "Mab."

She seemed friendly enough. I smiled back and touched my chest. "Ava. Mab...that's the queen? Sorry, is your name Isavell?"

She smiled at me, eyes shining. "Isavell."

Gods, I felt like an idiot. I looked like an Unseelie, but I didn't speak one word of the language.

Isavell, if that was her name, giggled. She raised herself from the water, showing off a silvery sleeveless dress that clung to her body, damp with river water. She really looked enchanting. Maybe the Unseelie weren't demonic at all. Maybe they'd been demonized by their enemies over the centuries, but they were actually very sweet.

I wondered if Torin had decided I was safe by now.

I was trying to decide what to say next when Isavell pointed at a flowering tree. I took a tentative step closer, and she smiled at me encouragingly. Little purple berries grew between the flowers. When I pointed at them and raised my eyebrows, Isavell nodded.

Maybe she wanted a snack?

I gathered a handful of berries and brought them over to her, crouching down at the edge of the river. She put one in her mouth, smiling at me. Then she gestured.

She wanted to feed me one? Something more intimate than I was used to with strangers, but maybe this was how the Unseelie made friends.

It didn't seem like a Court of Sorrows.

I opened my mouth, and she popped a berry in. When I bit into it, sweet, tangy juice exploded on my tongue. I knew the warnings about eating the food or drinking the wine in Fae realms, but I was one of the fae.

As I crouched by the riverbank, we shared the rest of the handful of berries. When we'd finished eating, purple juice stained my palm. I stood, wanting to ask her what I'd find if I kept walking. Would I find a town? A city full of beautiful, snack-eating fae?

But I didn't know her language, so I pointed down the river and raised my brows.

The merrow sniffed the air again, her smile slowly fading. Did she sense the presence of the Seelie king? Dark shadows slid through her eyes, and her lip curled to expose brutally sharp canines.

I staggered away.

She threw back her head, and her feathered cap fell into the water. She opened her mouth and let out a loud, wailing song with one word I recognized: *Isavell*, followed by the word *Morgant*.

My pulse quickened.

This didn't seem quite as friendly anymore, and I ran back into the foliage. From the other direction, footfalls and cracking branches echoed through the night. My heart slammed. I was being hunted.

Before I could fully comprehend the danger, a sharp

pain pierced my shoulders, and another plunged into my lower back. Immediately, the air was sucked out of my lungs as agony shot through my muscles and bones. I heard Torin call my name as I fell to the damp earth. He scooped me up in his powerful arms, held me tightly against his bare chest, and ran.

My muscles spasmed as a toxin spread through me, and I struggled to keep my arms around his neck. The darts tore at my skin.

"That was a mistake," Torin said, stiffening, and dropped me to the ground.

Pain shot through my back, and I rolled over on the mossy earth. With blurring vision, I scanned the forest floor for Torin. Darts jutted from his bare back like St. Sebastian, and he was struggling to push himself up on his arms.

On his hands and knees, he crawled toward me and snatched the darts from my flesh. I moved to help him, but a boot slammed into him, pinning him to the earth, and someone yanked me up from behind.

4

AVA

I rolled over, staring at the man whose boot was pressed into Torin's back, a towering fae with broad shoulders wrapped in bronze armor. He wore a crown of gilded scorpions that rested against his horns, and long white hair draped down his back.

I swallowed hard.

"Wait." My mouth had gone dry, and I could no longer think clearly. "Let him go. He doesn't belong here." Could he understand me at all?

Black wings spread out behind him. They were gauzy and thin, like butterfly wings. He might have been beautiful if not for his expression. He looked ready to beat Torin to death.

He glanced at me, narrowing his amber eyes. Slowly, he lifted the boot off Torin's back.

Torin flipped over, snapping the darts, and grabbed our attacker's leg with both hands, twisting the Unseelie's ankle in one direction and his knee in the other.

The white-haired Unseelie fell to the ground, the sound echoing through the forest.

But the stranger was only down a moment, and neither Torin nor I could stand. More Unseelie closed in on us. Dressed in furs and armor, leather, and moss, they shouted in their strange language.

An Unseelie with antlers grabbed me by the arms and jerked me to my feet. "Morgant," he said, addressing the fae with the scorpion crown.

Panic started to crawl up my mind as I thought of what would happen to Torin here in hostile territory.

My body vibrated with pain from the toxins, and I wanted to curl into a ball somewhere and vomit. But I couldn't because Morgant was pulling me onto a horse. Tossing me facedown over the animal's back, he sprang up behind me and started down the forest path.

Lifting my head, I glanced back, horror hitting me like a fist. Tied to a rope, Torin was being dragged behind the horse.

I no longer cared about anything except finding a way to get him out of here. Unable to look at him, I turned away.

The forest thinned, and a distant castle came into view, rising from the rocks and mist. It loomed high above us, the base of it twisting like gnarled tree roots that blended into a gothic fortress.

The poison slid through my veins, blurring my vision. I screamed until my throat went hoarse and a fist slammed into the back of my skull.

I LAY ON A CROOKED FLOOR, MUSCLES BURNING AND my head pounding. Moonlight cast cold light over my room, a strange sort of cell. Half of the walls seemed to be made of bluish bark that shot upward toward the sky, hundreds of feet in the air. The other half were made of stone, an iron door inset into the wall.

Pinpricks of silver dotted the darkness overhead, little rays of light for a cell both narrow and impossibly tall. In here, I had only shadows for company.

I ran my fingers over the place on my back where the darts had pierced me, wincing at the cramping of muscles whenever I moved. I tried to swallow, my throat parched.

"Torin?" My voice came out as a rasp.

The only response I got was the echoing of my own voice off the walls.

I dropped my head into my hands, trying to hold down my rising nausea. I didn't know if Torin had even made it here alive.

If he had? Maybe he'd been able to open a portal to escape.

If he stayed here, the Unseelie would tear him apart.

With my head in my hands, I retched, but nothing came up. If the Unseelie really were monsters like Torin said, what the fuck did that say about me?

My throat was sandpaper. "Torin?" I tried again, breaking into a coughing fit.

I rose from the floor and hobbled over to the iron door. In desperation, I slammed my fist against it. "Hello?" I shouted. "Torin? Anyone?" The more I shouted, the more desperate I became for water. My throat felt like I'd swallowed broken glass.

Panic carved through me, and I turned back to my narrow, towering cell, my gaze flicking to the moon-light-pierced canopy above. As my eyes adjusted, I could make out the ruddy hues of the leaves.

If I'd been able to scale these walls, I could get out through them. But the stone and bark were too smooth for fingerholds.

My throat burned, and rushing water was all I could think about now, how soothing it would feel running down my throat.

I slumped against the bark and closed my eyes. I licked my dry lips and thought of Torin trying to run with me in his arms—then I envisioned us plunging into the river, where crystalline water streamed into our mouths.

If I couldn't have any actual relief for my thirst, I'd have to manage with fantasy.

5

AVA

Thin rays of gold beamed over me, and I woke curled on the floor. I'd been drifting in and out of consciousness for days, I thought. If I ever made it out of here alive, I'd never take food or water for granted again. I'd be forever awed by modern miracles like supermarkets and showers.

At every moment—even while I dreamed—a single question flickered like a glowing neon sign: *What is Torin doing now?*

As I lay on the floor of my prison cell, my mind slid back to the night he'd shown me the view of Faerie from a snow-covered cliff. He'd given me sips of whisky from his flask, and we'd looked out over a breathtaking view of a frozen lake and the dark mountains that swept around it. Snow had frosted the black slopes, and dark castles jutted from the rocky horizons. Golden windows glittered in the distance, thousands of cozy homes. This memory was now my new fantasy. My new escape.

Maybe that's where he sat now, sipping whisky. How amazing would it taste sliding down my throat? And the snow, too. I'd kneel and lick it from the earth.

I'd started to drift off again—just for a moment—when I heard the creak of iron against iron. My eyes snapped open, and my gaze flew to the door. I'd nearly tasted the snow, nearly felt it melting on my tongue, and now the illusion had been ripped away. I hoped it would be replaced with actual water.

When the door creaked open, a trickle of fear scratched at the recesses of my thoughts. Morgant stood in the doorway, dressed in deep green leather. A ray of daylight glinted off the gold of his scorpion crown.

He carried a stone cup, but his icy expression made my stomach curdle.

I tried to stand, but my muscles were too weak, so I leaned back against the tree bark.

"Water," I rasped. Whatever scant ability I'd once possessed to charm or cajole a person had dissipated days ago.

If I were human, I'd be dead by now.

Morgant gave me a grim smile and knelt next to me. His amber eyes narrowed. "I'll give you a sip if you give me the information I want." He gripped me by the throat. "You smell horrible."

As if my current disgusting state was a choice.

"How did you come to be in the company of the Seelie king?" He spoke in an accent with rolled Rs.

I didn't yet know if they still held Torin captive, and I wasn't about to confirm his identity to the man who might flay him alive. "The Seelie what?" I asked.

His fingers tightened on my throat. "If you want water to live, you will answer my questions. Our kind does not lie."

My gaze lifted to the light piercing the tree branches above. It *had* to rain here occasionally, surely. It just hadn't yet. "I don't know what you're talking about."

With his hand around my throat, he held up the stone cup above my mouth. He let a single drop fall onto my lips, and I licked it, burning for more.

"The thing is, traitor, he is speaking to us. And he doesn't seem to care for you at all."

I stared up at Morgant, a dawning horror lacerating my thoughts. All this time, I'd been imagining he'd taken his portal out of here.

"My name is Ava, not traitor." Was Torin really here in the dungeons—or was this a bluff? Because if they were torturing him...

My thoughts swam with darkness.

Morgant's lip curled. "The Seelie king tells me that he loathes you. That he will return to his kingdom and marry a beautiful woman named Moria." He cocked his head. "He has no loyalty to you. I believe he finds you repugnant, slovenly, and utterly lacking in discipline and sophistication."

Ouch.

"He said," Morgant continued, "that he chose you to compete in his trial for a queen only because he hates you. Because he did not want a real wife. He said he could never love you."

I stared at the floor, and my vision went hazy. Ever

since I'd come home to find Andrew entwined with Ashley, my heart had been slowly icing over. Now, the cold seeped right down into my veins and arteries, spreading its frozen mantle through my chest. With Morgant's words, the final glistening sheen of ice crept over my heart.

"He's not the king, though," I said dully. "He's lying to you."

Morgant released his grip on my throat and smacked me hard across the face. The blow dizzied me, pain shooting through my temple. I fell to the cell's floor of rough bark and laid there, not bothering to get up.

If I ever recovered my strength, I was going to rip this bastard's spine out of his body.

"If you are trying to protect a man who loathes you," he said from above me, "I must say I find it rather... what is the word in your tongue? Pathetic. It is also grotesque to me that you are so weak. No magic. No power. No honesty or honor. You are nothing like a true Unseelie. We do not lie. And we know who he is. The Queen knows who you are."

I flicked my gaze to his. "That makes one of us, because I have no clue. Care to fill me in?"

"She has not yet told me." His powerful hand clamped around the back of my neck in a crushing grip. He lifted me into the air, bruises forming beneath his powerful fingers. I kicked behind me, swinging my legs as hard as I could. It was like kicking a stone wall, one I could barely reach.

"Where is your magic?" he barked. "An Unseelie should not be so helpless."

He dropped me, and I fell to the floor, curling up into a ball. Before I had time to answer, Morgant kicked me hard in the ribs, and pain shot through my side. The feel of bruised ribs was blinding, and my thoughts went dark for a moment.

I hugged my legs to my chest, trying to protect my body, my ribs. "I don't have magic. I'm a common fae."

"There are no common Unseelie." His furious voice boomed throughout my cell. "We all have magic. But you? You are broken. You spent too much time among their kind."

My mind felt hunted. If I was "broken" like this monster said, he certainly wasn't *helping* the situation by dropping me on the floor and kicking me in the chest.

"If I had any magic," I gasped, "I would use it." It came out sounding like a plea.

"And in that case, I might respect you. But since you have nothing to fight back with, you must give me some answers to survive. Isn't that right? Because the Seelie king hasn't told me what he was doing here. And he tells me his army is strong, but he gives me no specifics." He knelt next to me, brushing my hair off my face while I clutched my ribs. "You mean nothing to him whatsoever, Ava Jones. There is no reason for you to protect our enemy king. So tell me about his magic in Faerie. Tell me about his army. If you do, you get a meal and water. If you don't, I may break your arms. Or I may rip open the holes where my darts pierced your shoulders. You can choose."

"They have legions of soldiers. And powerful magic. They will come after their king here if you don't release him. They will slaughter all of you." I had no idea if any of this was true. If Torin was in the Court of Sorrows' dungeon, his kingdom would be frozen, starving, half dead.

He bared his teeth, his canines sharp. "Are you trying to make threats? I'd advise you not to make your situation any worse," he said in a low, gravelly voice. "I'd advise you to do as you are told."

"I really don't know anything about magic. I grew up around humans. If the queen knows who I am, she should know that much." The effort of speaking was exhausting me.

"How did you get here?"

I rolled flat on my back, staring up at the leaves. "Some kind of magic I didn't understand." This, at least, was true.

He held up the wooden cup. "Open your mouth if you want to drink."

Hating myself for my pathetic state, I opened my mouth, sticking out my tongue. Morgant let one tiny drop of water drip onto my tongue at a time. I licked them up until Morgant pulled the cup away again.

"What did it look like? And feel like? The magic that brought you here."

Water. "It was...flashing lights...and a spell..." The effort of making up a convincing lie was clearly beyond me, and Morgant smacked me hard again, a pain so sharp that a bright light burst behind my eyes.

"Do not touch me again," I hissed with as much ferocity as I could muster.

Morgant stood, amber eyes boring into me. He held the stone cup above me and dumped it onto the oaky floor by my head. "You lived among the humans and may not know how resilient the fae are. Physically. Your mind may break. You may pray for death as you starve. As you go mad with thirst. But death will not come so easily."

"You're a fucking animal," I muttered. The words tripped off my tongue before I could stop myself. As soon as they were out of my mouth, I knew I'd made a terrible mistake.

Morgant whirled, and pain ripped through my shoulder where I'd been pierced by the arrow, but he wasn't even touching me. I writhed on the floor as his excruciating magic rent the back of my shoulder.

"Do you know the gifts Briga blessed me with?" he snarled. "The ash goddess has chosen me as a healer. I can rebuild broken bones and torn skin and muscle. But the magic that heals can also rip a body apart."

Sharp tendrils of magic pierced my muscles like talons. I couldn't utter a word, just inhuman screams.

"And here I am," he hissed, "with exquisite control over my magic, and you with none. You, howling like an animal. I know that is what the Seelie call us. Animals. Demons. But we respect animals here, the majestic creatures of the forest. In Faerie, they eat them. And do you know what I think? The Seelie should not use the word as an insult when they are more brutal than the animals themselves. When the Seelie spit at fae like you. Pathetic. Unable to summon a single strand of magic."

When he pulled his agonizing magic from me, it was like a predatory beast releasing his claws from his prey.

My entire body was shaking, and nausea welled in my stomach.

"If you want to get out of here alive," he said sharply, "perhaps learn to use your magic. That is the best advice I can give you."

He moved out of my line of vision, and I heard the door creak open, then slam shut.

I pressed my face against the floor and shivered uncontrollably. That neon light kept blazing in the back of my mind, blinking with thoughts of Torin. I was sure now he was locked in here somewhere, battered worse than I was.

And clearly, I was delirious from dehydration, because I was starting to see things...seeing the vines and leaves rising around me, reaching for me—

A pounding sound interrupted the vision. A booming noise in my skull?

I lay back on the floor, head pounding. Heart like ice.

BOOM. BOOM.

But even as the noise hammered on, I let my eyes drift shut. First, I thought of winter—of a frost encasing the world in white. Ice that crept over a kingdom...

Then I dreamed of the tree coming to life, shifting away from the stone walls. It was creeping, moving across the forest, setting us free in a symphony of wooden creaks and groans. Red leaves fluttered through the world around us like blood drops, and Torin and I walked free.

Desperation and pain were fragmenting my mind.

And this was why they called it the Court of Sorrows...

⚜ 6 ⚜
AVA

Every time I woke, the pain seared my back, and I regretted regaining consciousness. So I'd fall back asleep, dreaming of cool lemonade, strawberry milkshakes, and mangoes...

Always in the background of my dreams, I heard Torin screaming my name, and the dreams would slide into nightmares—a landscape of sharp icicles, a frozen tundra where Torin needed my help, and I couldn't find him.

My eyes snapped open. The pain in my shoulder had changed, less a sharp laceration and more of a burning sensation. Swollen.

I reached back with my left arm and winced. The skin was hot and sore to the touch. Infected.

Fuck. Even if the fae healed better than humans, we could still die of infections.

"Ava!" Torin's voice again.

A hallucination, I thought.

Thirst raked at my throat, and I could hardly wet

my lips enough to respond, my "yes," coming out more like "ehhh?"

"Ava!" A distant sound. Muffled, but unmistakably Torin's.

My heart hammered. "Torin?" I rasped.

I tried to crawl over to the wall that was the source of his voice, but collapsed.

"Ava!"

"I'm here!" I tried to shout, but the words wouldn't come out, and I realized that tears were streaming down my face. I was glad Torin wasn't here to see me completely fall apart.

"I'm here!" I managed to say, my voice breaking.

He was shouting something at me through the stone, over and over. But the walls were too thick, and I couldn't quite make out what he was saying. The words echoed in my mind until I no longer had any idea what was real.

"You've been screaming for days," he shouted.

I blinked. For days? I must have been screaming in my sleep. What was he really worried about—me, or that I'd betray each one of Faerie's state secrets to his enemies?

I swallowed, my throat arid as a desert. "Why are you still here?" My voice sounded ragged. I wiped the tears from my cheeks. "Go home, Torin."

Silence fell, then I heard his voice again, calling my name.

My thoughts slid out of focus, and I couldn't understand anything he said.

Every part of my body was too hot and too cold at the same time.

I stared at the floor and dimly recognized the wet sheen of water that had collected between the gnarled roots. Had it rained? I crawled forward a little and licked the rainwater, tinged with the taste of soil.

⚜

A DOOR CREAKED IN THE DISTANCE. I BREATHED IN air thick and heavy with dirt. I had no idea how long I'd been on the floor, facedown.

I turned my head and found Morgant looming in the doorway, staring down at me. He carried a pewter cup, but given our relationship so far, it was probably not going to be a source of relief.

He knelt next to me, and a twinge of fear flickered through me. How much longer would I last here?

A cool, soothing magic spilled over my back, then slid into my muscles. It felt like clean water pouring into my body, washing away the pain and toxins. A poultice of magic, a balm for my fever.

"Your wound became infected," he muttered.

I wanted to say something like "no shit," but I'd learned my lesson about mouthing off to him.

"That was not my intention."

I let out a long sigh of relief, arching my back a little. For the first time in ages, I was able to move.

"I waited too long to heal it," he said. "You will have a scar. But the infection is gone. Did you learn any magic?"

When he pulled his magic from me, I turned onto my side and slowly sat up. I reached behind my shoulder, my fingertips brushing over rough ridges of skin. Scarred, yes, but no longer painful or hot to the touch.

I looked up at him, waiting to see what new horror he had in store for me, but he only handed me the pewter cup. I put it to my lips and drank deeply, then took a breath, trying to pace myself.

"Don't drink too quickly. It will make you sick," he said, as if reading my own thoughts.

Light poured between the tree boughs, rich and honeyed, flecking his white hair with gold. I hadn't realized it was daytime. The world really could be pretty when you weren't writhing with pain on a dungeon floor.

"Is this where you pretend to be the good cop?" I asked.

His eyebrows drew together, and I realized he had no idea what I was talking about. "I felt it through the castle that your blood had been poisoned. Without healing, you would die." A muscle twitched in his square jaw. "It is in my nature to heal, but sometimes, it is the duty of an Unseelie to do things that hurt others. And that hurt us. When we grow strong, it burns."

"Mmm."

"Are you ready to tell us about the Seelie king now?"

As long as I never admitted to knowing him, Morgant couldn't press me for details. "Who?"

He stood, staring down at me, and pulled a small piece of bread from a little leather bag at his waist. "If you want to live, eat this. But not too quickly. I won't be back for a while." He looked up at the leaves above us. "You will have more water soon enough."

He turned and left, slamming the door behind him. I listened as the metal bolt slid into place, locking me in.

I WOKE TO A BOOMING SOUND AND THE FEEL OF rumbling walls. The sound made me shudder until I realized it was something I needed desperately—a storm.

From above, cold water trickled down my body, soaking my green dress. My eyes snapped open, and I instinctively opened my mouth. Rainwater slid down my throat, slaking my thirst. Light flashed above, and thunder rumbled through the tower walls. I made a cup with my hands, collecting rainwater, and sucked it down greedily.

I kept filling my hands, drinking as much as I could. The rain soaked into my skin.

I sat against the wall, letting the water run over me. Shivering, I hugged myself. But the rainwater seemed to be washing away the stench of my cell, drawing it down into the tree's roots. I wished to God I had a cup or something to collect water in, but Morgant had taken it with him.

Since this might be my only chance for a shower in the near future, I stripped off my gown and my underwear. I scrubbed myself in the rain, then picked up the dress and cleaned it as best I could. Morgant had done this on purpose, leaving me without clothes or soap, while he looked pristine in his green velvet and a golden crown. Another control mechanism, so I'd have to take back what dignity I could.

When I'd finished scrubbing my clothes, I hung them to dry and curled up against the wall.

Hammering echoed through one of the stone walls, and I froze. Was I still hallucinating?

Morgant's words played in my mind, again and again.

If you are trying to protect a man who loathes you, I must say I find it rather pathetic.

7

TORIN

I slumped against the wall with my head in my hands, a broken king. I only knew that I needed to get Ava out of here.

Rainwater pooled on the floor, mixing with the blood from my feet where Morgant had used his "healing" powers to rip them open beyond recognition.

Since I'd been locked in here, with poison coursing through my body, I'd been unable to summon enough magic to open a portal. Even if I could, I wouldn't leave Ava.

At first, the worst part of my imprisonment had been when Morgant had slammed an iron pipe into my throat, or maybe when he'd knocked me unconscious, chained me up, then waited until I woke to rip the muscles in my feet with his magic. Bad, but not the worst. The worst had been hearing Ava screaming and not being able to do anything about it.

I touched my throat, and it pulsed with a dull pain.

Drops of rain still spilled from the tree's canopy

high above and slid down my bare chest. I let my head fall back and the drops soothe me like a gentle blessing from the old gods.

Since I'd spoken to Ava through the walls, I'd tried calling her name a few more times, but I didn't think she could hear me.

My mind kept drifting into a fantasy, one where I carried her into my room and laid her down on my bed. There, under an expansive glass ceiling, an apple tree grew. If Ava and I were together there, we could eat as many apples as we wanted, the sweet juices dripping down our throats. I could almost taste it...

I let out a long, slow breath. Even if by some miracle, I got us out of here and we took a portal back to Faerie and my beautiful room, I could kill her with my touch.

I saw my sister's face in the hollows of my skull. I'd had so many conversations with her in my head in the past few days. If I saw Orla now in person, I would tell her I wanted to bring Ava home. She'd remind me that I couldn't. She'd remind me to keep Ava at arm's length. She'd remind me that I'd nearly killed Ava already with a frost spreading over her skin.

I winced at the pain in my broken body.

I glanced at my forearm. Under my skin, the bones were slowly healing where the demon had broken them. Without my magic, I didn't heal as quickly as I normally would.

With a grunt, I forced myself to stand on my bloodied feet. Every time I had enough energy, I tried opening a portal again. What I desperately needed was the Sword of Whispers.

But it was easier to summon magic at my full height, to open my chest to the ancient power of the old gods.

I flexed my fist, imagining the Sword of Whispers in my hand now, carving through the stone walls to get to Ava. A drop of water slid down my temple.

If the old gods had chosen me as their anointed king, they wouldn't simply leave me here to die, would they?

I scrubbed a hand over my mouth, remembering Ava trying to crawl for me when we'd been ambushed. She'd been attempting to get the darts out of my back.

Twilight was falling, and the faintest tinges of violet and gold shone through the scarlet sky above. We called this time the gloaming, when a fae could travel more easily between worlds. This was the best time of day to appeal to the old gods.

My magic flickered, burning a little brighter, the color of dusk.

My body ached, and I leaned back against the wall, resting my head. I could imagine Ava leaning against the other side of the same wall with her beautiful, curved horns.

In my dreams, I often had the antlers of Cernunnos, as I had before the coronation. The stag could travel between the worlds. I glanced up at the flecks of mauve twilight between the red leaves, and the flame of my magic rose a little more.

Cold magic slid through my veins, and the image of the Sword of Whispers ignited like a beacon in my thoughts. I'd only used it once before, and it had etched its permanent mark on my soul. I hadn't allowed it to drive me mad.

Centuries ago, King Caerleon had personally executed one traitor after another using the Sword of Whispers. When he ran out of traitors, he found new ones, more and more, until he simply stalked the streets of Faerie. He'd dabbled in dark magic, raising a ferocious dragon named the Sinach from the mountains. When King Caerleon grew bored of killing by sword, he used the Sinach to roast people, and Faerie had descended into a violent and bloody age known as The Anarchy.

I'd never wanted to use the sword. But now? This was the perfect moment.

A cool wind rushed through the cell from the boughs above. Even though it was still warm in my cell, snow began to swirl in the air. I felt the last of the gods' magic ignite in my chest, and I whispered the words to create a portal. Like a stag, I'd shift between realms. Cool air slid around me, and the snow started falling more heavily.

An icy wind swept the snow through the air and whirled before me, a vortex of white that slowly opened to expose a dark gap in the center. My heart slammed against my ribs.

My chest unclenched. Thank the gods, the opening was twelve inches across and beamed with a pale blue light, just large enough for what I needed. I reached through the opening, my arm brushing the edges of the portal, hard and cold as ice.

I spied the sword, an obsidian hilt and a scabbard of black leather. Legend said the death god had created the sword, hiding one of his arrows in the pommel and carving his hounds upon the dark stone hilt. As I gripped it, I felt his shadowy power course through me.

I pulled the sword and the scabbard into the Court of Sorrows with me, and the portal closed again.

With the sword in my hand, the intoxicating voices of the gods whispered around me in their divine language. I closed my eyes with a whispered thanks to the old gods in their native tongue, a language spoken by gods and kings alone.

I'm coming for you, Ava.

Gripping the hilt in both hands, I swung the sword, slicing through the thick walls, one after another. I carved doors for myself. To her.

Until at last, I saw her, waking from a deep sleep. She was covered in dust from the stones.

And literally nothing else.

❦ 8 ❧
AVA

I was sure a nightmare had come to life as the walls started shaking and a sharp blade pierced the stone, hacking an opening through the thick wall.

Debris filled the air, and the sound of steel against rock echoed around me.

In the bloom of dust, I caught a glimpse of a muscled arm and golden skin, tattoos swirling over a bicep that I recognized.

My heart leaped. Was this real?

Torin appeared in the opening, his tattooed chest coated in gray dust. He looked down at me, his pale eyes beaming with an unearthly light.

Maybe it was the dehydration and general delirium, but he looked so much like a god towering above me that I held my breath. He was a bruised and bloodied god, but a god nonetheless.

How was he still so strong after the past few days in here?

His gaze slid slowly over me, and I remembered that

I was still completely naked. I'd left my dress to dry after cleaning it.

My heart thudded, and I hugged my knees to my chest.

The Seelie king sheathed his sword. "We're getting out of here, Ava."

Sword in hand, he faced the tree trunk and closed his eyes, brushing his fingertips reverently along the blade. Then, with a wide arc, he hacked at the trunk. I gaped in disbelief as the blade slid right through the thick oaken walls, and otherworldly voices echoed in the air.

Whispers...

A lump rose in my throat, and I winced. Why did the sword in the trunk feel like I was watching someone get stabbed?

I reached for my dress, my muscles shaking from weakness. As I clutched it in my fingertips, Torin scooped me up and carried me out into the night.

The shock of freedom danced wildly in my chest, and adrenaline sparked through my nerves. I'd been so certain I would die in there. I couldn't believe we were out under the stars. I clutched the dress over myself. No time to put it on.

From the castle, horns blared.

"Are you all right?" Torin asked. "I heard you screaming days ago." He was trying to move quickly, but I could tell his gait slightly favored his right side. "What did he do to you?"

"I'm fine. You're the one he really hates. Torin, are you limping? I can run on my own."

"We'll get a horse from the paddock," he said, ignoring my question. His gaze drifted down my body again.

I tugged the top of my dress up, trying to cover myself. I wasn't being modest; this didn't seem like the ideal time to distract him.

"Torin. Morgant claims you find me repulsive and slovenly, but I feel like you're not keeping your eyes on the mission."

"I only said that to get him to leave you alone. I didn't want him to think we were allies. Apparently, it didn't work." His breathing was labored, and he held me tightly. "We're almost there."

I turned to see a small paddock where horses grazed surrounded by a stone fence. A cacophonous throng of crows swept over us, cawing wildly under the night sky.

"I'm not letting them get you again," he said, almost to himself. His velvety voice was like a balm against the ravages of the last few days. "I'm getting you away from the fucking demons."

"Awkward that I'm one of them," I muttered.

With me in his arms, he clambered over the stone wall. For a moment, his dark eyelashes lowered, and he met my gaze. "It doesn't appear that they agree."

He let me down in the grass, and I grasped for the hem of my dress to slip it on—but Torin pulled it out of my hands, turning back to the horse.

"What are you doing?" I hissed.

"We don't have much time." He laid my dress over the back of a white horse, folding it. "And trust me. You will want something between you and the horse when we break into a gallop. The dress is all we have."

He scanned the wall and grabbed a halter and lead rope that had been slung over the stone.

I hugged myself and cast a glance back at the castle, my pulse quickening. Steel glinted in the starlight. The soldiers were coming after us already.

Torin spoke to the horse in Fae and fashioned reins out of the lead rope. As if enchanted, the white mare knelt before him, folding her front legs in front of her.

"Get on," Torin said. "Now."

I glanced back at the castle looming over us. Dark stone towers pierced the sky, rising from twisted midnight roots, half stone and half tree, with dark boughs twining the towers and blooms of cascading red leaves. It was as if a castle had grown from the soil, and the earth was reaching up to drag it back. The enormity of it made my stomach plummet.

I slid onto the horse, straddling my own dress, and gripped her white mane. Turns out Torin was right. I really did want something between myself and the horsehair, because this was already weird and uncomfortable enough.

What was the opposite of a bucket list? Because whatever that was, "riding a horse naked" was on mine. And yet, one glance back at the oncoming soldiers told me this was not the time to worry about the method of transportation.

Torin mounted the horse behind me and slid his arm around my waist. With his free hand, he grabbed the reins.

When he spoke again in the Seelie language, the horse rose to her full height.

Torin gave a light kick, and we took off, galloping through the middle of the paddock and then leaping over the stone wall. The cool night wind whipped at my hair and my bare skin.

My heart raced as I clung to the mare's mane for dear life. Still, Torin's grip around my waist was like iron. And after a few moments, it started to feel exhilarating. After far too many days withering in a dungeon, it felt like I'd come to life again.

Though it was also a situation for which I would have greatly appreciated a sports bra.

Once I was certain that Torin wasn't letting me go anywhere—that his powerful arm around me was a vise of security—I released the mane with one hand and tried to hold my boobs in place.

Gods, it felt amazing to be out here, finally free.

Horns blared from the castle, and the sound floated over the starlit kingdom. My gaze trailed over the rolling hills to our left, dotted with little stone buildings, and the flecks of warm light that beamed from their windows. In the distance, a circular fort stood on the top of a slope, bathed in silver light. And even further over the horizon, a dark mountain range stood against the sky, its peak illuminated red.

The horse sped into a line of trees. Above us, moonlight pierced the red leaves.

As we swept over the path, the forest wrapped around us, concealing us under its canopy. Torin guided the horse onto a narrow path off the main route. Mist twined around us as we galloped deeper into the forest, and Torin steered the horse to a trail that wended between the trunks.

"Oh, my gods. You did it, Torin." Everything had happened so quickly that I'd nearly forgotten about the actual escape. It almost seemed like part of a dream. "How, exactly, did you get a sword that could cut through walls?"

"A gift from the gods to their anointed king. I was able to open a portal large enough to pull it through. I couldn't keep it open long enough to get us out." I felt Torin shift behind me, and his breath heated my neck. "What the fuck happened to your shoulder? Was it the demon's magic?"

I shook my head. "Yes. That's probably when you heard me scream. Then it got infected, and Morgant came back to heal it."

"Did he take your dress from you?" A steely violence laced his voice. "I already want to rip his lungs out and hang him from the castle gates, but if he forced himself on you, I will find a slower method of death."

"No. I took my clothes off to wash them in the rain. I really have been craving a bath. And food. So much food." I leaned back into Torin. "Oh, God, I kept dreaming about ice cream."

"I was dreaming about apples," he said quietly.

I turned my head back to him, and my face brushed against his. Something about the feel of his warm cheek against mine made me aware of my utter nakedness all over again.

His thumb rested just over my hip bone, and it

brushed over my skin once, like he was trying to soothe me.

With my thighs, I clenched tightly to the horse. "Any idea where we are going?" I asked.

"Not really. But I want to get us away from the castle and maybe find some shelter. Then I want to find the Veiled One. And I'll feed you apples."

He sounded slightly delirious, but I was drooling anyway. "Apples," I repeated. "Wait. Back up. Who is the Veiled One?"

He breathed in deeply. "According to the legends, she's an oracle who lives among the Unseelie. They call her the Veiled One. She's like the Unseelie counterpart to our oracle, Modron. Modron can only see the past, and they say the Veiled One can see the future. Some say the crones are old gods, or spirits of the land itself. I don't really know what they are, but if anyone can tell us how to get out of here, it would be her. I just don't exactly have any idea where to find her. And when we do find her, I don't know if she might murder us."

"She has powerful magic?"

He inhaled sharply. "I believe so."

My muscles burned from the exertion, racing as we were at a breakneck speed. "Do you see any signs of shelter?"

"I'm not looking for that yet. If we find our way to a river, it will help to hide our scent from trackers."

The air was cooler now, and goosebumps rose over my bare skin. I nestled back into Torin for warmth and heard a low murmur rise from his throat.

His fingers were tight on my waist.

Around us, moonlight pierced the canopy, streaming down to the dark forest floor and dappling it with silver flecks.

At last, a river rushed between the trees, sparkling with light.

"There we are," Torin murmured, guiding the horse into the water.

The horse galloped into the shallow stream, and cold spray washed over me. I licked my lips, my throat still burning with thirst. The rain had been nice, but not nearly enough. Every drop of river water was a blessing from the gods.

Torin's steely chest warmed me from behind. With me secure in his grasp, my muscles slowly started to relax and melt into him. For the moment, at least, I felt safe with him. But when it came down to it, we were probably still stuck in this world. What were the chances of finding this veiled woman? And if we did, would she help us?

It felt like chasing smoke.

But as long as Torin had hope, I'd keep my dark thoughts to myself. I couldn't bear to see the look on his face if I told him I thought we could be trapped.

❧ 9 ❧

AVA

A briny wind swept over us, nipping at my exposed skin as we raced through the river. From the salty taste in the air, I thought we must be near the sea. A thick fog billowed around us.

When Torin reined in the horse, the sound of rushing water roared like a waterfall nearby. "Ava, that might be an abandoned house over there."

A gust of sea-kissed wind swept over us, sweeping away some of the fog. Between the tree trunks, I could make out a stone structure that overlooked the cliff, a small cottage with darkened windows.

Torin helped me off the horse, my feet sinking into the cool water. I snatched the dress off the horse and pulled it on.

Torin was already kneeling to drink from the river, and I joined him. I cupped my hands together, scooping it up. The life-giving river streamed down my throat, running down my chin and dress. Oh, gods, no wonder people worshipped rivers in the old days.

I was still drinking when Torin stood. "I'm going to make sure it's empty before we go inside," he said. "Bring the horse closer to the house in case we need a fast escape."

I waded out of the river after him, watching him stalk into the clearing, his sword slung at his waist. When my gaze slid down to his feet, my heart cracked at the sight of his lacerated heels.

With the night air growing colder, I hugged myself tightly, leading the horse out of the river and into the clearing. After days in the bleak cell, the house looked cozy as hell. Dark, but the idea of a place with a soft bed seemed like absolute heaven. One side of the house overlooked a jagged cliff that sheared off into the glittering sea, and the forest arched protectively over the back. A rounded door gave the home a cozy appearance. In the moonlight, I could see that the house had been painted sky blue long ago, but the paint looked worn down by the sea winds. Red leaves littered the ground in a carpet of claret.

I took a step closer to the cottage, watching as Torin drew his sword and climbed the steps to the front door.

I turned, my gaze skimming over two crooked tombs outside the house. As I moved closer, I took in the brutal, beautiful carvings on the stone, twisting, interlocking designs, coiling serpents of blue and purple. Runes marked the names of the ones buried there, but I couldn't read them. Cobalt vines with blood-tipped leaves crawled over the tombs, as sinuous as the carvings. Whoever had been buried here, someone had loved them enough to take great care with their burial, etching their names for eternity.

Overturned tin troughs stood by the side of the house, which suggested there must have been farm animals here at one point. I found a post, too, for the horse, and tied him up.

As soon as I'd finished, a rustling in the branches pulled my attention back to the forest.

My heart raced.

From the shadows, an enormous insect with spindly limbs of beaming silver loomed over me. My jaw dropped. The thing was as big as a horse. Not a spider this time, but what exactly was it? Before I could get a good look at it, it dropped to the forest floor and disappeared into the forest once more. I let out a long, shaky breath, but tension still coiled my muscles.

My relief was short-lived. In the next heartbeat, the creature rose up on its back legs, its head beaming in the moonlight. My heart froze as it towered over me like a metallic praying mantis.

It lunged for me, one of its massive scythe-like arms slashing at my head. I dove out of the way and rolled to my feet, sprinting away from it and into the salty wind. "Torin!"

I reached the edge of the sheer, dark cliffs and had nowhere else to run. I stood in long seagrasses and whirled to face it. Luminescent compound eyes stared at me, a pair of enormous fangs twitching and spasming hungrily in its mouth. Its blade-like arms flexed.

Finally, Torin slammed the door open and drew his sword.

The mantis stopped moving, its head swiveling to assess the new threat. As Torin slashed at the mantis's torso, the creature leaped away, driving me to the very edge of the cliff. From behind, a gale whipped sea spray at my back. I glanced back at the sheer drop off the cliff. Far beneath me, the ocean churned. My breath caught in my throat.

The mantis lunged at Torin. He swung his sword, slicing one of the creature's arms, and the thing screeched in pain. A sliver of dread twisted through me as I wondered if the soldiers would hear its cry.

Torin swung again, and the insect darted away, lightning-fast. My heart skipped a beat. The mantis could easily jab its remaining arm straight through Torin's body.

My mind had started to go blank, filled only with the rush of the ocean and the low, musical hum of the nearby forest. With the wind whipping over me, I ran around the mantis, putting myself between the creature and Torin.

"Ava!" he shouted, but I ignored him.

My instincts had crystalized around one idea: I would keep Torin safe, and the forest would aid me.

As I stared up at the mantis, my mind bloomed with images of the earth coming to life, bending to my will. Of the long seaside grasses rising to pull the mantis into the sea...

I let out a roar, a furious scream from deep within

that the wind caught and carried over the roiling waves. Red leaves ripped from the tree's branches, tumbling in the gale, whipping at the creature's face.

The mantis stumbled back and back again until it plunged over the side of the cliff.

❧ 10 ❧
AVA

I stood there, shaking, and stared out over the rocky cliffside. A loud crack echoed over the sound of the waves. The mantis had crashed below.

Torin was staring at me, his brow furrowed. "That was...interesting. Did you scream him over the cliff?"

My body crackled with electricity, but that was just the fear left in my nerves, right? I didn't know if I'd summoned magic or if the wind itself had forced the monster off the cliff.

I caught my breath, nausea rising in my stomach. "Is the house empty?"

He nodded.

The battle fury started to leave my body, but my legs still shook. "Good."

"I'm going to make us some food," he said, "and you a hot bath."

My throat tightened. When he'd first smashed through the wall into my cell, I'd thought he looked like a god. He was every bit as beautiful now, but my gaze slid down over his bruised arms and bloody feet. Shades of red and purple stood out sharply on his skin.

I inhaled sharply. "Your feet are bleeding. We can make bandages from my dress."

"We're both in rough shape, aren't we? But that is the beautiful thing about a fae body. It heals." He turned away, raking his hand through his hair as he walked into the house.

I arched an eyebrow. A good king was a caretaker and protector of his people, and I was starting to get the impression Torin needed to feel like a protector more than he needed to look after his broken body. I had the distinct sense that if he wasn't looking after someone, he'd feel shattered. I'd have to be careful about how I phrased things.

"Torin?" I called out.

When he turned to look at me again, I reached behind my back. "Morgant healed my shoulder, but I still feel a little twinge of something. Did you see anything in the house that could be a sort of antiseptic or ointment?"

He turned to look at me from the doorway, and his eyebrows rose. "Just a twinge?"

"Very small. But it wouldn't hurt to disinfect it so it doesn't get worse."

"I didn't see anything inside." He pointed to the purple-berried tendrils that climbed over the graves. "But the leaves of Eventide ivy are practically magic. They grow in Faerie, too. If you grab some of those, I can crush them into an antiseptic oil that will work wonders for your shoulder."

I gave him a small smile. "Thanks."

By the graveside, I plucked handfuls of glossy, deep blue leaves until my hands were stuffed with them. When I got inside, Torin was already kneeling before an enormous stone hearth, fiddling with a metallic fire starter. As it sparked, I caught glimpses of a cauldron that hung in the fireplace, one shaped like a large teapot with a handle and spout. A large bucket stood next to it. About five feet away from the hearth stood an enormous copper tub. It seemed a weird place for a tub, but I supposed that without running water, it would be the easiest place to get a hot bath.

I dropped the leaves onto the kitchen table and surveyed the dim interior. Apart from the streams of moonlight through the windows and the dull glow of small flames, there wasn't much light in here. I breathed in the scent of dried herbs. After a few moments, my eyes adjusted to the shadows, and I was able to find my way around a little.

My footfalls creaked on the floorboards as I explored the space. Two heavy carved wooden doors led to other rooms. One was a bathroom with a stone toilet and little else. The other was a bedroom with a narrow four-poster bed. Dark wooden beams crisscrossed white walls, and white curtains hung over mullioned windows.

When I returned to the kitchen, Torin had managed to stoke the flames in the hearth. The fire bathed him in gold, and the light wavered over the giant copper tub.

I pulled a candle from one of the sconces in the wall

and leaned down next to him to light it. With my guttering candle, I lit the candles in the other sconces, and soon, the little room danced with rusty light.

Now I could see the room more clearly. Knotted pine shelves jutted from a wall, each one piled with clay dishes and cups. A layer of dust covered everything, but it still looked cozy and homey.

Torin caught my eye. "Sit down, Ava. I'm going to get some water from the river. You wanted a bath."

A bath sounded divine, but it was a struggle not to roll my eyes. The idea that he should be running in and out of the house on his injured feet while I sat on my ass was absurd.

He stood, and I could tell by the way he walked, back straight and stiff, that he was in pain.

"I need to heal my back," I called out to him, trying to hide the irritation in my tone.

He picked up the bucket and went outside anyway.

I pulled a stone mortar and pestle from one of the shelves. Dropping the leaves into the mortar, I mashed them into a bluish pulp, an oily sheen forming on top. I poured the oil into a smaller bowl.

Torin pushed through the door again, ramrod straight, and poured the water into the cauldron.

I dipped my finger into the oil. It stained my pinkie sapphire, and I rubbed it onto my back, feeling absolutely nothing because my injury had healed. "Ahh," I said loudly, pretending relief. "That's better. Torin?"

He paused on his way back to the door with the bucket and turned to look at me, the firelight sculpting his chest with gold and shadows.

I cleared my throat. "I have a whole bunch extra here if you need any. I don't want it to go to waste."

I crossed over to him and handed him the oil. Torin's pale eyes glinted with amusement, and the corner of his mouth twitched. "I know what you're doing, and I have survived worse, changeling. You don't need to make a fuss over me."

"All I care about right now is food," I lied. "And we'll eat sooner if you can walk faster. If I don't eat, I could die. And that would be on you, king."

A small, rueful smile curled the corner of his lips. "I can't have that." He took the oil from me. "But you can sit down now. I'm getting us bathwater."

I bit my lip, trying to layer a little desperation into my voice. "I'd actually feel better if I could move, Torin. I was cooped up for so long in a cell, being confined in here is the last thing I need. I'm *desperate* to feel my freedom. And also, I believe you promised me food? I am absolutely starving. So I'd prefer if you didn't delay it by wasting your cooking time fetching water." Before he could object, I snatched the bucket off the warped floorboards and strode into the marine-tinged air.

If Torin had any sense, he'd be cleaning and healing his feet right now. But maybe Morgant had beaten the sense out of him.

Outside, I kept my senses alert for the sound of oncoming soldiers, but I only heard the mournful call of an owl, the rush of wind through the boughs, and the waves crashing against the cliff. I knelt at the riverside to fill the bucket from the burbling stream.

Gods, it felt amazing to be out of that dungeon. I

really did crave the freedom to walk around, even if my muscles screamed at me.

Rising on aching legs, I carried the bucket back to the house, the weight of it dragging on my arm. As I approached the faded blue door, Torin stepped outside, a lock of his dark hair falling in his face. This time, his muscles looked relaxed, his hands in the pockets of his dirt-stained pants. Clearly, he'd used the healing oil, and I felt a little twinge of pride that I'd helped him. "I'm going to get you food, changeling. Like you said, I don't want you to starve to death on my watch."

A smile ghosted over my lips. "I'm ravenous."

In and out I moved, filling up the bucket and pouring it into the giant teapot contraption to boil, then dumping the hot water into the tub.

But I wasn't about to fill this bath twice, was I? It would be just about large enough for two.

As I dragged the water in and out of the house, Torin returned with a pheasant and juniper berries. While I filled the bath, he plucked and salted the meat, then rubbed it with herbs and old port from one of the cupboards. He speared the pheasant on a spit to roast in the fireplace.

At last, the tub was filled with hot water, and steam coiled from the bath. The smell of the roasting pheasant made it difficult to concentrate on anything but what it would taste like, mouthwatering and succulent.

Torin turned the pheasant on its spit, his sharp jawline and high cheekbones cast in the warm glow of the hearth.

"Torin," I said, "you are getting in this tub with me."

He glanced at me over his shoulder, his expression unreadable. "I...what?"

"That took over twenty minutes. I'm not filling it again. And I'm not dealing with the guilt of taking the only bath. We were both tortured in the cells. We'll both take a bath, facing in opposite directions."

His eyes danced. "If you really want to see me naked, changeling, you could just ask."

"It's not like that." I closed my eyes. "We will each face the opposite direction. I'll face left, you right. It's only practical."

"Whatever you want, changeling."

❧ 11 ❧
AVA

We faced away from one another, and I reached down for the hem of my dress. The green material was beyond filthy at this point. Even though I'd already been naked around Torin all the way here, it felt very different now in the calm and quiet of the house. And when I pulled the dress off, I was acutely aware of every inch of my bare skin. The hearth warmed one side of my body, and I glanced behind me at the tub.

"No looking," I said, more of a reminder to myself than to him.

"That will make it difficult to get in the tub," he said quietly.

Behind me, I heard the rustle of his clothes as he undressed. An unbidden image of Torin naked rose in my thoughts, and I imagined every sculpted, iron-hard curve of his muscles.

It really was difficult to find the tub without looking, so I stole a glance over my shoulder at the tub.

Awkwardly, I climbed back over the rim, mentally congratulating myself for getting the temperature exactly right—hot enough to turn my skin pink, but not hot enough to blister. I slid down, sitting cross-legged in the water.

I heard Torin slip into the bath behind me and the sharp intake of his breath. The water rose higher, and the steaming water lapped at my skin above my breasts.

"Gods, Ava. Are you trying to boil us alive? Is this hell?"

"Do your subjects know you're such a delicate flower?" My muscles relaxed, and I folded my arms over the edge. I should be actively washing my hair and body, but I just wanted to let myself melt. And I was intensely distracted by the fact that Torin was crammed into the tub close to me, trying *very* carefully to keep his body from touching mine.

Next to the tub, I'd piled neatly folded clothes— trousers, boots, and clean white shirts that I'd found tucked away in a wardrobe. My gaze skimmed over the garments and back to the Seelie king. From the corner of my eye, I glimpsed a warrior's body, the dark tattoos that climbed vine-like over his finely cut muscles. His shoulders flexed, and shadows and firelight sculpted the chiseled contours of his back. I let my gaze trail over the angry plum-colored bruises on his spine, fury curling through my chest. Morgant had really done a number on him.

Sighing, Torin leaned forward, his arms folded over the front of the tub as mine had been moments before.

The heated water was a balm for aching muscles, and the sultry air was soothing to the lungs.

Maybe it was the excruciating, heartbreaking loneliness of that time spent in the cell, but I had a hard time tearing my eyes away from him.

With the scent of roasting meat and rosemary wafting over me, I found my primal desires were getting confused. Did I want to care for him, devour him, or straddle him? I was no longer sure.

Maybe some combination of all three.

He caught me watching him, and my cheeks burned,

"Ava," he said softly, "I thought we were supposed to be facing away from each other."

I turned sharply, my cheeks flaming. "You wouldn't have known I was looking if you hadn't looked." Did I sound childish? Maybe.

Behind me, I heard the sound of water rushing off Torin's body into the bath as he washed himself, then his feet on the wood floor. I felt a twinge of disappointment, but I didn't want to leave the water. This bath right here was heaven.

I kept my eyes firmly locked on the floor while he dressed.

A minute later, Torin knelt next to the fire. The clean white shirt I'd found stretched over his muscles, several sizes too small, as he turned the pheasant on its spit.

My mouth watered, my stomach hollowed out with intense hunger. "The pheasant must be done by now?"

I honestly would have eaten it raw. Completely raw.

Another rotation of the spit. "Not quite yet. We

haven't eaten in days, so we might as well make it a good one."

"If you make me wait any longer, I could end up cannibalizing you. I think I'm getting in touch with my demon side here, Torin."

"Sounds strangely tempting." His eyes glinted as he turned to look at me. "I *suppose* I could give you a few of the berries, but the rest I'm using in a port sauce—"

I flashed my canines at him. "I will start with your shoulders, Torin, tearing out chunks of your beautiful muscles with my teeth."

A smile flickered over his lips, and he stood. "Not long ago, you were fretting about the state of my feet. Now you want to eat me alive." He handed me a small wooden bowl with purple berries.

"I contain multitudes." I popped a berry in my mouth and bit into it. *Heaven.* Had I ever tasted anything so sweet? "I'd share these with you, but I'm afraid the Seelie and Unseelie are ancient enemies."

"Good thing I'm fully capable of waiting for the real meal." The velvety murmur in his tone made my blood heat.

The berries stained my fingers purple. "If Morgant comes for us tomorrow and we die an excruciating death at his hands, we have to make sure this was a good night."

"And that's why I'm not rushing things, changeling."

"So, if we find this veiled woman, and she can tell us how to return home, how long will you wait to consummate your marriage with...whoever it is you plan to marry?"

He shot me a sharp look, then stood and crossed to the kitchen table. "I'm going to focus on the important work of making the port sauce."

As he ground up the berries, he seemed rattled. I turned all the way around in the bath to get a better view of him. I couldn't help it. I really liked looking at him.

"While I'm sure the port sauce requires all the concentration your pretty little head can muster," I said, "you will be needing royal offspring. Who else is going to grow up and slaughter the sacrificial victims at Beltane if you don't produce an heir?"

The corner of his mouth twitched. "You know, it really has been a very long time since we've sacrificed one of your kind at Beltane. The clans would be delighted."

"A demon would be perfect. Horrible creatures. Can I recommend Morgant for that role?"

A smile flickered over his lips. "I think he is the queen's son. Her remaining son, anyway."

"That was my impression."

I finished the last of the berries. By now, the bath had made me pink. "Turn around, Your Highness. I'm getting out."

He did as I asked, averting his eyes.

I hadn't found any towels, but I had unearthed an old wool blanket, so I dried myself off, then pulled on a white button-down shirt that reached halfway down my thighs and a pair of tiny blue shorts. I hadn't been able to find any trousers that would fit me.

Once I was dressed, I thought I should help the

dinner effort, so I pulled plates from the old shelves and slid them onto the table. "And I'm pouring the port. And whatever is going on with that pheasant, we're eating it, because the berries are gone, and the pheasant would taste better than your muscly flesh."

With a sigh, Torin started to pull the pheasant off the metal rod. "You must take care not to eat too quickly. After days of starvation, if you overindulge, you'll make yourself sick."

Golden light wavered around the cozy room, and I crossed to the table to pour port into glasses. "Look at us, all domestic, just a Seelie king with a fondness for human sacrifice and his demonic enemy. Breaking bread together like a couple of old pals."

Outside, thunder rumbled across the landscape.

"You're really hung up on the human sacrifice thing, aren't you?"

"Kind of a quirk of mine." I turned around, and to my absolute delight, I was staring at a perfectly roasted pheasant, the crisp skin a rich buttery color. Actual drool dripped from my lips, and I wiped the back of my hand over my mouth. "Because of this, all is forgiven with the human sacrifice."

Torin slid the bird onto the table, and I hurried over to the wooden bench.

At one point, I *did* have manners, but they'd died in the cell several days ago, so I simply ripped off one of the thighs and started gnawing it like a caveman.

"Slowly, little demon."

Never in my life had I tasted anything so divine. This was the food of the gods, rich but delicately spiced. Where did Torin learn to cook? I would have imagined a king would never have to bother. Of course, he really did seem to like looking after people, and cooking was the perfect way to do it.

The heat seared my tongue, but I couldn't get enough.

"Ava," Torin said quietly in a warning.

"Fine." I forced myself to slow down and took a sip of the port. I sighed. "It's almost like being home, isn't it?" But something rang false about it, like I was trying too hard to ignore everything that had happened in the dungeon. And with the words out of my mouth, all the horrors of the past week slammed back into my thoughts. The utter lack of control. The pain of my infected shoulder, and the wild desperation of thinking I was dying alone, that no one would come for me. Even if I'd been born here and this little cottage was cozy, this horrible realm was nothing like home. Sharp talons of homesickness found their home in my heart, piercing me until I hardly wanted to eat anymore. I stared at the table, trying to school my expression. Where was that cheeriness I'd been able to muster a few minutes ago?

"What do you usually eat in that bar?" Torin sipped his wine. "The one where I met you? Is that a regular spot for you?"

I blinked at him, struck by the banality of the question when my thoughts had spiraled off on such a wild tangent. When I caught his eye, I had the impression that he'd been able to precisely read the look on my face or had detected the slight crack in my voice when I'd said *home*. And he must have realized how desperately I craved normalcy at that moment.

Shocking, how easily he could read what I needed.

"Yes," I answered at last. "I went there a lot with Shalini. Taco Tuesdays, especially. But I was usually broke, so I got nachos. They were cheaper." Never in my life would I have guessed my voice would one day crack with emotion at the word *nachos*, but here we were.

"Nachos," he repeated slowly. I had a feeling he had no idea what they were, but he was trying to play along. "Will you have this again when you return home?"

"With Shalini." I blinked, trying to clear the tears from my eyes. "But this food is amazing, Torin. I feel confident in saying it's the best thing you've ever done." I licked my fingers—a disgusting habit, and something I never would have done if I hadn't been starved for a week.

Lightning flashed, and a few moments later, rain started to hammer against the window. Outside, a storm picked up.

"Where do you plan to sleep, by the way?" I asked.

"Out here."

"On the floor?" As soon as the words were out of my mouth, I realized I'd have to approach this carefully. The truth was, I didn't want the guilt of a battered hero sleeping on stone while I had the cozy bed, but I couldn't just come out and *say* that he needed looking after. He'd immediately reject it.

I frowned at him. "I'd feel better if you and I were in the same room. For one thing, I might need you to protect me from another monster. And also, I'll get cold."

His blue eyes glowed brighter. "First the bath, and now you're inviting me to bed?"

"For safety reasons. I know you're saving yourself for marriage, but I'm sure you can restrain yourself around me."

"First of all, I said no such thing about saving myself. Second, I can restrain myself, changeling." A lazy smile curled his lips. "But you, on the other hand? I saw how you looked at me in the bath. Beautiful muscles, I think you said."

I pulled another piece of meat off. I hadn't managed to find any cutlery. "Oh, bless your heart. I was looking at you as food. Just like I think this pheasant has beautiful thighs."

He arched an eyebrow, pinning me with his intense gaze under thick black eyelashes. The warm light danced over his sculpted cheekbones. "Fine. Bed it is."

☙❧

I CRAWLED UNDER THE COVERS, SINKING INTO THE most comfortable, downy-soft bed I'd ever seen. My thigh muscles felt cramped and exhausted, but my body was cocooned in softness, melting into the bed itself. And with the rain pattering against the window, my eyes were already starting to close.

But they snapped open when I heard Torin enter the room, his dark hair ruffled. Still, he somehow looked model-perfect in the silvery light, and he'd already taken off the small shirt. In fact, now he was wearing nothing but one of the pairs of shorts I'd found, shorts that were *extremely* tight. Low on his hips, they showed off every inch of his cut abs.

Was he doing this on purpose to prove something? Given the devilish look in his eyes, I'd say yes.

I closed my eyes, his words from Faerie echoing in my mind.

Because if it were you and me, in the oak grove on Beltane, I would have you screaming my name. Calling me your king. I would have your body responding to my every command, shuddering with pleasure underneath me, until you forgot the human world existed at all...

He ran a hand through his hair as he approached the bed, his eyes locked on me in a way that made heat swoop through my belly.

I rolled over, determined to sink into the bed and fall asleep.

My eyes drifted closed, but I knew the truth. I wasn't going to get a moment's sleep with Torin next to me, nearly naked. *If we get out of here, he's going to marry some judgmental Seelie princess*, I reminded myself.

I tried to picture him walking down the aisle with Moria by his side. How stunning they would look together.

I pulled the sheets up around my chin.

As soon as Torin slid into the bed, his delicious oaky scent wrapped around me, and I felt his heat, his power radiating off him.

When his bicep brushed against my back, my pulse started to gallop at full speed.

And of course, the Seelie king noticed.

"Your heart is racing," he murmured.

"Anxiety."

To my surprise, he pulled me in tightly to him, his chiseled arms wrapped gently around me. I could feel his heartbeat, a rhythmic thud against the thin material of my shirt.

I was acutely aware of how little I was wearing and the feeling that every inch of my bare skin craved his touch.

"Ava, you are safe with me." He brushed my hair back from my face, then lightly brushed his fingertips over my temple. "That animal left a bruise on you."

A little sliver of guilt twisted through me because he was being so surprisingly kind, and it wasn't anxiety making my heart race. I would have thought with all his intense self-regard, he would have seen right through the lie.

His body curved around mine, and my muscles went soft against him.

He breathed in sharply. "What do they feel like?"

My mind spun in a billion directions, none of them appropriate for two people who firmly agreed we could never be together. "What does what feel like?"

"The horns."

"They're a bit sensitive, I guess. In the cold wind."

"What happens if I touch one?"

"Nothing, I think." But as soon as I said it, I knew it was wrong, because just the thought of it sent a hot shiver through me.

He slid an arm free and reached up. One languid

stroke up the curve of my horn left a sensual trail of heat in its wake, making my eyelashes flutter. Molten desire swept through me, evaporating the thoughts from my mind. I found my hips pressing back into him, and I heard his breath catch.

My back arched, and I turned to look at him. "Are you seducing me?"

He lowered his lips closer to my ear. "My demonic friend," he purred, "if I wanted to seduce you, you'd be moaning my name right now. But I'm not trying, am I? Because you're a pretty little demon I could never have."

"I'd be moaning your name right now?" I stared at him, and my gaze slid down to the sensual curve of his lips. I hated how much I wanted to taste those lips again. "I can't tell if you think this highly of yourself or if it's all part of your kingly performance."

"Oh, it's genuine and very much warranted."

My mouth twitched. "That's just what everyone tells you when you're the king. Like how Henry VIII was supposed to be the greatest sportsman of the era." I wrinkled my brow. "Do you think maybe it was just that everyone was too scared to tell him the truth, given his habit of cutting off heads? Maybe all those nice Seelie ladies at Beltane didn't want to piss off the High King. Maybe you're the Henry VIII of fucking."

He propped up on one arm and gave me a slow, wicked smile, his eyes darkening. A shadowy, sultry heat radiated off him. "Now *that*," he murmured into the crook of my neck, "sounds like a fucking challenge, changeling."

12
AVA

"The thing is, changeling," he whispered, his breath warming my throat, "if by some chance I don't make it out of the Court of Sorrows, I can't die with you thinking I'm the Henry VIII of fucking. And I will make you moan my name." His low, silky voice caressed my skin, sending a wicked thrill through me.

Moonlight slanted in through the window, silvering his heartbreakingly beautiful face. I couldn't let myself love him, but I ached for him. The look he was giving me was molten, with a dangerous undercurrent in his unearthly blue eyes.

He reached up again, gently caressed my right horn, going slowly from the tip all the way down. As he did, he searched my face, watching my mouth open, my eyelids lower and flutter with the forbidden pleasure of it all. Under the thin fabric of my shirt, my breasts peaked, and heat slid up my spine.

"That's cheating," I breathed.

"But how could I resist seeing that look on your beautiful face again?" His voice had gone husky. He leaned down and grazed his lips over my neck, then his teeth over my throat. His tongue swept over my skin, tasting me, and the rest of the world fell away. My thoughts narrowed to the worshipful strokes of his tongue.

One of his hands slid across my abdomen, then inside my shorts. From one hip bone to another, his fingers traced like he was memorizing my contours with his touch. Oh, *gods*, his languid strokes were igniting my body with need.

As my breaths grew shallow, my hips moved back into him. When they did, I could feel the large, hard length of him against me. His obvious arousal only made me more desperate for him. The thin cotton fabric felt excruciating on my skin, and my body heated with the torturous desperation to pull it off me. All my nerve endings felt full, aching for him.

When I moved my hips back into him again, he let out a low moan. Sucking in a deep breath, he gripped my shorts in his fist, and I had the distinct impression he was about to lose control of himself. To rip them straight off and plunge into me—

He'd never had to restrain himself this much when we'd been fighting. Then, it had always seemed so easy for him to maintain complete control, every one of his moves carefully calculated. But now I could feel the strain of his arm muscles and the steel of his chest.

His mouth moved from my throat, hand still clenching my shorts in a death grip. I felt his breath warming my back, exactly in the place where Morgant had ripped my shoulder open. Gently, Torin's fingertips trailed over the scar. "It doesn't hurt anymore, does it?"

His lips replaced his fingertips, and his kiss sent warmth radiating from the point of contact where his mouth met my skin. In between kisses, he murmured, "I will eviscerate that man someday. Do you know that?"

"No thinking about the future." Flushed, I lay on my back so I could look at the heartbreak of his beautiful face more easily.

With me, Torin wasn't able to let himself go completely. Not when he knew it would be ending.

A ghost of sorrow crossed his perfect features. "Ava. I thought of you all the time in my cell. How much I wanted you next to me, your limbs entwined with mine."

His words stunned me, this version of Torin with his guard dropped. Under the intensity of his gaze, my chest flushed.

When I tried to remember what I'd been thinking about in that prison cell, it was all muddied in my thoughts. Just sharp flashes of desperation and a glimpse of what I must have looked like licking rainwater off the floor. I'd felt so wildly helpless there, but with Torin? It didn't matter if we were technically from enemy factions. I was safe with him.

I touched the side of his face, tracing his high cheekbones.

Torin must have seen my expression change because he asked, "What are you remembering?"

I let out a long breath, trying to smile. This wasn't taking the direction I'd been hoping for. "Nothing that I want to. Maybe your job is to take my mind off that dungeon."

"Ava, you know we can never be..." A jagged edge ran through his words.

He needed something from me, but I wasn't sure what it was. All I knew was that a moment ago, he'd been so close to touching me exactly where I wanted him, and now I was remembering things I'd rather leave buried. I felt the moment teetering on a knife edge, like I was about to lose what I so desperately wanted.

"I think you should just kiss me," I said. "Why worry about two weeks from now? We could be dead tomorrow."

A pained expression flickered across his divine features, but it was gone in an instant, replaced by a seductive curl of his lips, a heated expression in his eyes.

I'd sworn off men, and him specifically. But now? I was desperate to feel something crack through the icy numbness in my chest. Being close to Torin was like lava melting through black rock.

Responding to my command, he leaned down and claimed my mouth with his. His lips brushed mine lightly, like a question, and my response was to open mine to his kiss, to sweep my tongue against his. His muscles went taut, and I drank him in—his smell, the feel of him against me. The way he kissed me, as though he'd been imagining it for months.

Sparks danced over my exposed skin.

As he kissed me, he slid his hand under the hem of

my shirt, caressing my hips, moving slowly over my ribs. Under the crisp white shirt, my nipples went tight with anticipation. He slid his hand down again, traveling to my hips. The way he touched me made my muscles coil tightly with the certainty that he knew exactly how to make me shudder with pleasure.

"I want to take my time to savor every moment, Ava."

Slowly, teasing me, he swirled his fingertips under the band of my shorts. A wild ache built at the apex of my thighs. I yearned for him.

But he was taking his time, and he traced circles over my hipbone with a languorous stroke. My breath hitched, and he shifted his body, his hips between my thighs now. He kissed me slowly, savoring me, one hand sliding to cup my ass, and I moved my hips into him.

His fingers slid into my hair, gripping it, tugging it just a little as he kissed me. And with every languid stroke of his tongue, my body begged for more. With a nip to my lower lip, he pulled away from the kiss.

"I love the taste of you." His voice came out husky, almost desperate.

I needed more contact from him, my bare skin against his. I started unbuttoning my shirt, and he glanced down to watch me, his eyes glowing with heat. As I pulled the shirt off, his gaze slid down me like a sultry caress, lingering on my bare breasts. My breath went shallow as his eyes rose again, pausing on my lips. A wildness shone in that pale blue, a primal desire that looked barely restrained. The Seelie king was about to come undone.

Leaning down again, he kissed me with the desperate fervor of a man who thought he could die tomorrow and only a kiss could save him. He moved his hips against me, hard and slow, and liquid warmth pooled in my core. With my breath hitching, I raked my fingernails down his back, my teeth grazing his shoulder, a hint of my threat from earlier.

His hand slid into the band of my shorts, and he tugged them down. "Take these off." His voice shifted, the low, commanding demand of a king used to getting what he wanted.

He leaned back, watching me pull them off. He could have tugged them down himself, but he wanted to watch me do it, and the feel of his eyes on me made me pulse with need for him.

A primal expression shone in his eyes, and heat radiated through the air around us. "If I could have you always around me naked, Ava, I would be a happy man." He stared at me, drinking me in. "In fact, it's a king's privilege to be surrounded by beauty. And it's a king's privilege to indulge his wickedest desires."

He slid down, his abs between my thighs. He closed his lips over my nipple. His tongue swirled and licked, making me want to cry out. I moved my hips against him, letting him know exactly how much I needed him.

"Demon," he murmured against my skin. But this time, I loved the sound of that word on his tongue, the reverent, husky timbre.

My back arched, and I stifled a cry as he stroked and licked my breast with a pace that was frustratingly indolent. Desperately, I wanted him inside me.

One of his hands moved down my body, gentleness twining with a dark possessiveness as he cupped my sex, slick with arousal. "For tonight," he whispered, "this is mine."

At his words, my thighs opened wider for him, and I moved against him, growing desperate for release as his fingers glided in and out.

"Torin," I breathed, raking my fingernails down his back once more. "I want you. Now."

He released my nipple from his lips, peering up at me. And to my immense frustration, his fingers stilled as well. "A Seelie king hurries for no one. Especially when he has his absolutely bewitching enemy in bed, naked and wet for him."

Gods, he was an unrelenting tease, and I couldn't stop myself from moving against his hand. I was so close now, but I needed more of him. "Take off your clothes."

Ignoring my demand, he sucked at my nipple again, and my toes curled.

He was touching me exactly where I needed him, his fingers moving expertly as a crescendo of pleasure coiled in my core. Heat spread across my chest, and he raised his mouth to mine again. He kissed me deeply, stroking his tongue against mine. I moaned against his mouth, my muscles going taut, then softening as shudders racked my body. As my orgasm rocked through me, my thoughts fragmented. A carnal, dark pleasure pulsed through my body, rolling waves that made blood rush to my core.

As I rocked against him, my mind bloomed with a color, the divine, pale blue of Torin's eyes.

When I opened my eyes again, I found him staring at me like he was entranced. With his hand still between my legs, he kissed me once more.

Flushed, I caught my breath. Torin wrapped his arms around me, and I breathed against the glowing skin of his throat.

Torin, without a doubt, made it his mission to look after those he cared for.

※

BLINKING, I WOKE IN THE NIGHT, FEELING TOO COLD, missing Torin's heat.

When I turned to look at him, I found him sitting on the edge of the bed. He rested his hands over his knees, and his head hung down.

"Torin?"

He turned to look at me, the mournful blue of his eyes piercing the dark, his hair rustled with sleep. In the moonlight, he was all contrasts—shadowy tattoos against pale skin, pale eyes, and hair dark as jet.

"Just a bad dream," he said quietly. "You know, Ava, I only told Morgant that I didn't care for you because I didn't want them to use you against me. If they knew you were important to me...I don't really want to imagine what they might have done."

The first golden blush of heat started to thaw the ice in my heart. "I'm not sure he believed you. He seems infuriatingly good at detecting lies."

My breath caught as he held my gaze for another minute, and then he turned away again. He ran a hand through his hair. "When we trained in Faerie, I feel like I got to know your every move, changeling. How you thought. How you breathed. And you're not really an Unseelie. You're not from this cursed place."

"What was your bad dream about?"

"I was dreaming about my mother. I have vague memories of her when I'm awake. But when I sleep, I dream of her vividly. And I don't know if the dreams are based on memories or something my mind conjured. I think this was a memory." His voice sounded ravaged. "This time, I was standing by her bedside, watching her die. The curse had made purple veins crawl over her skin. I loved her, but I thought she looked like a monster as she was dying. I remember being so angry that she wouldn't get up to look after me because I think I knew she was all done looking after me. And I didn't really know who else to be angry with. So...those were her last moments with me. Me, being an absolute brat."

A lump rose in my throat, and I moved closer to him. I wrapped the blanket around him and slid my hand around his broad shoulders to keep it in place. "I'm sure she wanted you there. Even if you were being a brat."

He leaned into me. "The thing is, I know I'm a king in the enemy's territory. I need to get out of here, and I need you to go as well. But I *really* can't stop thinking about what it would be like to hunt down Queen Mab and Morgant, and end both their lives."

I shook my head. "And then what? Then you die in a foreign kingdom. The Seelie and Unseelie go from a cold war to a hot war, and everyone dies."

"Of course, you are right, changeling." He turned, sliding back into the bed with me.

He folded himself around me, and when his breathing started to grow heavy again, his heartbeat slowing, my body melted into his.

13

TORIN

Morning light slanted through the window over the kitchen, highlighting the steam curling out of two mugs.

Ava had found coffee beans in this house, which felt like a miracle. She now sat with her hands curled around a mug, staring into the fireplace. "I like it here."

I had no desire to leave, either. Here, I could touch Ava like I wanted to. On the other hand, at any moment, we could be hunted down, shot with darts, beaten, and then executed. I'd be killed as an enemy of Unseelie, and she'd be slaughtered as a traitor to her own kind. It wasn't exactly a perfect situation.

I sipped my coffee, and the caffeine was already lighting up my mind. My muscles tensed with eagerness to move, to get her to safety.

In my stolen clothes, I rose from the table. "We should get on the road." I crossed to the hearth and poured a pitcher of water onto the flames, extinguishing them.

I turned to look at Ava, her hair lit up by pearly light from the window. With her eyes closed, she stretched her arms over her head in a lazy, feline movement.

My chest tightened.

Was I an idiot for climbing into bed with her last night? Obviously, I was. And yet, I don't think it was a call I could have refused.

She looked at me, blinking. "Any idea where we find this Veiled One?"

I had only the vaguest memory of hearing about her. And truthfully, I didn't even know if she was real. I only knew the legend: an immortal, eyeless crone living on a snowy, fire-licked mountain who foretold the future for the Unseelie.

Would she help us? Was she still on a mountain? And was she even real at all?

Fuck knew.

A sharp tendril of regret coiled through me. I should have *tried* to bring Ava back to Faerie. I should have done my best to open a portal when I still could.

I rubbed my eyes. "We need to look for a fire-licked mountain."

Her eyebrows rose. "Do you mean a volcano? I think I saw it in the distance. East of here. When we get out of the forest, we'll have a better view."

"Ava, I can't promise we will find her, or that we will get what we want from her even if we do."

She shrugged. "I don't have any better ideas."

IN THE DAYLIGHT, IT HADN'T TAKEN LONG TO FIND our destination. From the waterfall, we'd spotted it in the distance, a dark, snowy mountain that overlooked a kingdom of stone and red leaves. From a distance, the mountain summit resembled a ruddy jewel resting atop the peak. Wisps of smoke rose into the dark sky, tinged with red light.

And as soon as I saw it, an ember of hope started burning in my mind. If I could get to this oracle, I could get Ava the fuck away from the Court of Sorrows.

Ava was seated astride the horse in front of me. She leaned back, and I breathed in her scent, the smell of the wild Unseelie forest and the air after a storm. I closed my eyes, savoring this moment. Because when I returned to Faerie, my changeling could not come with me.

🧿

WE'D BEEN RIDING FOR A FULL DAY. ON THE ROCKY path, the skies were darkening, violet streaked with pumpkin, and the dying rays of sunlight pierced the canopy of leaves above us.

The air smelled of smoke and ash, and the horse's hooves crunched over black rocks on the path. "Ava," I whispered, "how do you know if a volcano is going to erupt?"

"Let's just hope it doesn't."

As the path became too rocky and steep—sleek black rock, covered in snow—we slipped off the horse. I let Ava walk ahead of me in case she fell in the dark, and we continued on foot.

Close to the top of the mountain, shadows gathered around us, and the air grew cool. Ash and snow covered the rocks and dark, bare boughs. Beneath the thin dusting of white, black lava scored the mountain.

"Are you worried about what's happening in Faerie?" Ava asked as she hoisted herself up the rocks.

It was strange how little I'd been thinking about it. Before now, my entire life had one purpose: to look after my subjects and make my kingdom thrive. Here, in the heart of my enemy's land, my thoughts were distinctly distracted.

The cooling air stung my cheeks. "I can't imagine what's happening, but I hope Orla declared herself regent and took the throne..." My voice trailed off. "But I never thought she was strong enough to sit on it. Perhaps she appointed someone else as regent in my absence."

"You'd better hope it wasn't Moria." Breath misted around her.

My chest tightened. "If there is no queen on the throne, I'm afraid everyone will be dead by the time I return."

As we neared the mountain's peak, the trees grew smaller until only snow and ash remained. From here, on a narrow, icy path, I still didn't quite have a view of the summit. But when I turned to look back down the mountain, the blood-red forest spread out far below us.

Ava steadied herself on a rocky wall to our left, and we followed the curving trail that swept up to the peak.

When we reached the summit, red-tinged wisps coiled above us, and an orange glow warmed the air from the crater. Sprays of molten lava rose from the volcano's depths, shooting into the air.

But my gaze was on the impossible, gravity-defying structure above us, a narrow castle that sat atop a craggy column of black rock. Like a strange flower on a stem of stone, the fortress was bathed with red from the fires below. Rickety ropes made of vines led up to the castle's entrance. A cold wind whipped over us.

"This is amazing," Ava whispered, staring up at it.

I exhaled slowly as hope burned brighter in my chest. If anything around here was the home of a weird old mountain hag, this bizarre castle must be it.

And right now, this was our one and only chance to escape and return Ava to the mortal realm, where she belonged.

Everything hinged on what happened next.

"Ava," I said quietly, "let me go in first."

She turned to me, a puff of breath escaping her mouth. "Fine. I'll be the lookout."

I hoisted myself up the vines. The icy wind whipped over me, making the snow whirl around me in vortices. My heart raced with anticipation. A few thorns stabbed my fingers, and I kept my eye on the dark entry above. At last, I reached the door and hoisted myself up. Moonlight pierced narrow open windows, and ash dusted the floor inside.

Lanterns jutted from the walls, made from fae skulls with unlit candles inside. Lightning flashed, illuminating the walls, a bas-relief carving of a veiled woman with antlers, her body surrounded by gnarled, leafy designs. A chill rippled over me. At least I knew I was in the right place.

My gaze slid over the Unseelie words carved into the walls, over and over. The same words, and for a moment, I thought I understood the foreign language. From somewhere deep in the recesses of my soul, the words rang out.

I burn.

My breath caught, and I turned away from them, unnerved by whatever magic danced all over this place. I only needed the lady of the castle to appear.

A well stood in the center of the hall. How could she have a well in this place? I peered over the edge and saw a void that made the hair rise on the back of my neck.

Outside, the mournful sound of an owl pierced the air. I crossed to a stairwell, sniffing the air. It smelled of dogs in here. Wolves, maybe.

"Torin!" Ava's voice made my heart slam, and I raced back to the door.

When I peered out, I found her trying to climb the vines. An arrow shaft jutted from her back. My blood turned to ice as Morgant swooped up behind her, his black wings pounding the night air.

Sword in hand, I leapt from the entrance. When I landed on the rock, pain shot up my legs, but it hardly registered. I was too late. Morgant had pulled Ava away and was carrying her into the air.

As I raced down the rocky path, Unseelie surrounded me, armed with swords and bows. My heart beat like a war drum.

I forced my thoughts to go quiet, like a blanketing of snow.

An Unseelie demon with long black hair and fangs stood at the front, gripping the hilt of his sword. "Where did you think you were going?" he asked. "No one enters or leaves except by the pleasure of the queen, and you, Seelie dog, will be strung up before the castle gates and eviscerated at her pleasure."

I gripped the Sword of Whispers, focusing on the dark-haired fae. I didn't have time for panic, and I didn't have the luxury of making a single mistake. I was vastly outnumbered. At least I'd trained for this.

An Unseelie with long white hair and antlers aimed an arrow at me. "Drop your sword."

A third stepped forward. "If you make this easy, we might make your death quick."

I clenched my teeth. That promise didn't sound particularly likely.

The white-haired archer shot an arrow that glinted in the moonlight as it soared for me. Time seemed to slow, and I blocked it with my blade. The dark-haired one screamed and ran for me with his sword raised, but his battle cry had given me the opportunity to ready myself for his attack. I slashed left, blocking his attack, then carved back again toward the right, slicing through his gut. The Sword of Whispers sang to me as blood spilled on the black lava.

You are death. The final rattle. You are the cold, silent shadows at the end.

The white-haired soldier arced his blade, swinging for my stomach. In one swoop, the Sword of Whispers carved through his weapon. A soldier slashed at me from above, and I drove my blade into his groin, crippling him. I whirled, spinning my sword to adjust my grip, and dodged out of the way of a battle ax. When I righted myself again, I cut my blade through the man's throat. He dropped to the ground, and his ax clanged on the rock.

I pivoted, bringing the Sword of Whispers down through a man's shoulder, the blade carving him in half.

I was trying to keep an eye out for the archer as I fought, but he'd slipped into the shadows. I'd always thought of archers as cowards, attacking from afar.

I whirled, driving my blade through the neck of my next attacker, then shifted to slice it through the chest of a demon with antlers.

As I readied my sword for another attack, excruciating pain slammed into me from behind. An arrowhead plunged into my flesh next to my lower spine, and I fell to my knees.

My blood roared in my ears as I tried to keep my grip on the sword. Another arrow pierced my shoulder blade, and I fell forward onto my hands. Blood spilled into my mouth. I clutched my sword as tightly as I could, but lost my grip on the hilt.

❧ 14 ❧
AVA

The journey up the mountain had seemed long and slow. The one back down?

Fast and brutal, a race on horseback over black, rocky terrain. Lying as I was facedown over a horse, my muscles jolted with every bump. At least Morgant had the decency to pull the arrow out of my back before he bound my hands.

Pain shot through me where the arrow had pierced my back. Morgant held me, one hand gripping my arms and the other on the horse's reins.

Given the amount of blood flowing from me, if I were mortal, I'd be dead by now.

I closed my eyes, thinking of Torin. I'd seen him jump from the castle, and I bitterly regretted calling out to him. If he'd stayed inside, could he have hidden from them? Perhaps, but that wasn't his style.

I desperately wanted to know whether he'd found the Veiled One. Maybe he already knew how to get out of here.

When I opened my eyes, I watched as the castle came into view, stone and crooked trees twisted together under a vault of stars.

"Back to the dungeon, then?" I said through gritted teeth.

"If you vex me."

"And if I don't vex you?"

Instead of answering, he kicked the horse, spurring him onward to the castle's entrance.

At last, Morgant reared his horse to a halt. He slipped off first, then yanked me to the ground by my bound arms. I fell hard, landing on the side where the arrow had pierced me. I didn't want to give him the satisfaction of a scream, so I managed to strangle it.

He pulled me up by my wrists.

I could ask him again where he was taking me, but I knew he'd never answer me.

Inset into the fortress were enormous gothic black doors, and they groaned open as we approached. He pushed me into a hall of carved dark wood. Candlelight writhed over a mossy floor, and vines hung from a vaulted wooden ceiling.

Morgant took the lead ahead of me, turning to look at me with grim satisfaction. "I want you to know that we have your great Seelie king. We will break him before he dies. We will rip off his skin and feed it to our spiders. The Seelie kings always say their old gods protect them. We will prove they do not."

I felt my thoughts going dark until they were nothing but a vision of thorny vines rising from the earth to rip Morgant to shreds. But the man was trying to get a reaction out of me, and I wouldn't give him the satisfaction.

After a few hundred feet, we reached a small antechamber with a wooden door inset with green jewels.

Morgant pushed it open, revealing a spiral staircase of dark blue wood. The stairs seemed to be carved from the interior of the enormous tree. Up and up we climbed, my arms still bound and my thighs shaking from exhaustion.

Everything he'd done so far had been designed to disorient me and make me feel powerless—the starvation and dehydration, the isolation. Telling me about how he'd kill Torin. If I felt hopeless, I'd tell them whatever they wanted.

I had no way of knowing if they had Torin at all.

Morgant pushed a small button on the wall. The door swung open. Moonlight shone in through an open-air tower, illuminating dark boughs that wrapped around a stone floor. A long oak table stood in the center.

High above the kingdom, a gentle breeze ruffled my hair. I breathed in the rich air, tinged with herbs and honey. Looking over the side, I could see the ruddy forest canopy a few hundred feet below me, silvered in the moonlight. Above the canopy, shadows moved. As I looked closer, I could see they were giant butterflies swooping over the forest.

A winged archer with flowing black hair and white wings swept through the night sky. I met his gaze, and he aimed an arrow directly at me. My heart stuttered, but he didn't shoot. Another archer swept by, arrow trained on me. I got the message, loud and clear.

I turned back to the open-air tower, and my head started to swim with shadows. I'd lost too much blood, and I faltered.

Morgant's hand shot out, catching me by the bicep. "You are weak."

Quite the observational skills, Tarzan. Might have something to do with the arrow he'd shot in my back.

Gripping my arm, he started chanting a spell, his voice toneless and harsh. His magic slid down my back like warm water, easing the pain. Warmth washed through me, and my muscles relaxed. When he'd finished, he released my arm and unbound my wrists. I rubbed at my chafed skin.

Shadows crept over the mossy stones around me.

"Stay where you are," said Morgant. "The queen wishes to speak to you. But you must not get too close to her. You are being watched."

"I noticed."

"Don't move." Morgant barked, turning back to the door.

I don't know where he thought I would go, not without wings.

Morgant straightened, staring at the stars, and bellowed, "Empress of the Forest, Queen Mab of the Dark Cromm, our great ruler."

He opened the door, and the queen stepped out, every inch of her radiating silver and gold. Her platinum hair hung down her back in waves, and she wore a delicate platinum crown with sharply spiked points. Her pale skin radiated silver light, the same color as the dress she wore, a silver gown beaded with pearls. Only her black gossamer wings stood out.

Her pale gold gaze swept over me, taking in my clothes. Her lip curled. "So. This is the spy."

I breathed in deeply. The queen of the Unseelie stood before me, looking much younger than I'd expected. She could be forty, I supposed, but she hardly looked it.

She narrowed her eyes. "Why would you come here so unprepared? Does the Seelie spymaster want you to die?"

"I'm not here as a spy. I fell into your realm through magic. That's all."

She arched a black eyebrow. "And the king of the Seelie simply fell in after you? This is your story?"

"Yes. There was a magical rift between our worlds, that's all. And he's not the king. His name is Alan."

She smirked. "The king of the Seelie declares that he does not care for you at all. And yet, he took great care to help you escape. I think someone must be lying."

"If you let us return home, you won't ever need to worry about us again."

"Alan." She huffed a laugh. "You are a mendacious one. How disappointing. In the Unseelie kingdom, we do not lie. If you'd been raised here, you would have learned the value of honesty."

I wanted to ask what she thought about the value of kindness, but I had no power in this situation and kept my mouth shut.

She stepped closer to me and lifted my chin, examining my face. She was nearly a foot taller than me, radiating light and power that thrummed over my skin. I could almost see the shimmering magic twisting around her, electrifying the air.

She dropped my chin.

"If you were raised here, you'd feel pain every time a lie fell from your lips. Though if you loved him, perhaps you would do it anyway. Love burns us, doesn't it? And that fire makes us strong." She let out a long sigh. "Do you know how a sword is made strong? Like the Sword of Whispers, for example, that your king once possessed."

I stared at her. *Once* possessed?

"Here in my kingdom, we worship the ash goddess," she went on. "They say the ash goddess Briga has only one eye, her body covered in soot. She sacrifices for us. They say that she's a giant in that mountain you climbed, Mount Tienen. The Veiled One made her home there."

My heart raced faster. We'd been in the right place, then. Was it possible that Torin already had an answer?

Mab smiled. "Briga's flames make us strong and purify us. In her sacred forge, a sword must endure the heat, the pressure, and the hammer as the steel is tempered. Only then can it become strong enough to fulfill its purpose. Love is a forge, too, as the ash goddess teaches us. And that is where Unseelie magic comes from, Lost One. From the pain of love and loss. So, perhaps you'd lie for your king, even if it hurt. Perhaps you'd endure the flames, or sacrifice yourself, as she does. Perhaps you'd come out stronger and truly live as an Unseelie."

Her words had an entrancing quality that made me wonder if she was putting me under a spell.

She arched an eyebrow. "But the question is, would he do the same for you?"

AVA

A chill rippled through me. She was trying to get under my skin, but I wasn't going to give her a single detail about him. "Don't really know him."

"And who, exactly, are you?" she murmured.

There was that question again. "Ava Jones."

"A human name."

I shrugged. "I was raised among them."

"Why? How did you end up leaving this kingdom?"

I shrugged again. "I have no idea. Someone brought me to the human realm and left me there. I thought you knew who I was."

She stared into my eyes, and I felt as if she was examining my soul. Reading me. "I see the humans taught you to be weak and lazy, as they are, that they raised you to bury your own great Unseelie power, so you don't even know it exists." She turned her head back to Morgant. "You can relax. She's hardly a threat. This wretch has been thoroughly defanged. I'm surprised you couldn't see that right away. Maybe that's what happens when an Unseelie can't even speak her own language."

Curiosity sparked. What was this Unseelie power I allegedly possessed?

My mind whirled, and I rubbed my wrists where I'd been bound with rope. The skin was chafed and raw.

She gestured to the table. "Join me for dinner. We do not get many foreign guests here."

Weird. Maybe people didn't like being beaten in a dungeon or something.

Morgant pulled out her chair at the head of the table, and she gestured for me to sit next to her.

I took a seat. My stomach rumbled, and hunger ripped through me. The pheasant had been delicious, but I'd hardly eaten a thing today.

She raised one of her hands. "Morgant, have the servants bring us food and ambrosia." She turned back to me and rested her elbows on the table, her chin propped in her hands.

It seemed a very casual posture for a brutal queen.

I licked my lips. I had no idea what ambrosia was, but my mouth was already watering. The only thing ruining the moment was the knot of guilt in my chest. Wherever Torin was now, I doubted he was about to eat.

The queen narrowed her eyes at me. "I imagine King Torin is still upset that I killed his parents. It was a slow and nasty curse." She smiled at me and fluttered her eyelashes. "And perhaps he's angry about *his* curse. Did he tell you how it works?"

I swallowed hard. I didn't want to answer a single question about him. My strategy right now was simple: say as little as possible.

Mab lifted her eyes to the moon, and they darkened to a deep forest green. "It was fated, though. All of this is written in the stars. For a while, I had lost faith in my destiny. Now, I can see it written once more." The corners of her lips curled, and she dragged her gaze back to me. "And when I am through with the Seelie king, I will have what I want. My heirs will sit on the throne of Faerie for the rest of time, turning it into the realm of the Unseelie once more. It was our land from the start, you know. At least we shared it."

A shudder rippled up my spine. Gods, Torin needed to get out of here *fast*, and I could only hope he'd already learned the key to our escape. There was something particularly fanatical about the way her eyes shone as she spoke of destiny.

The door creaked open, and female servants in black gowns began bringing out a feast fit for a queen: steaming earthenware bowls filled with broad beans, carrots, peas, and sauces that smelled of spices. A woman with black braids carried out a wooden tray with tiny roasted skewers of cheese and tomatoes and a large bowl of rice. A third woman brought a fresh salad garnished with flower petals and a loaf of flat, buttery bread.

"I hope you like the food. Unlike in Faerie, we do not eat corpses in my kingdom."

It took me a moment to realize she was referring to

animal meat. I would not mention the pheasant I'd eaten last night, then.

I had a vague sense that you were supposed to wait for a queen to eat, but it really was her fault I was ravenous, so I started with the bread. When you are truly starving, nothing seems better than bread and butter. As I ate, someone filled our glasses with a pale blue liquid that shimmered under the moonlight—the ambrosia, I assumed.

I scooped the sauces and beans onto the bread, shoveling it into my mouth. Every moment here felt like it could be my last, so why not fill my stomach? The spicy food left a delicious burn on my tongue, and I washed it down with ambrosia.

Gods, what I would do to kill this queen and replace her with Torin instead. He deserved to be here with us, eating the roasted cheese. Oh, gods. The flavor of the cheese was extraordinary, rubbed with ginger and coconut and something delicious that made my tongue burn. I don't know if it was ghost chilies or a spice unique to the Unseelie realm, but the burning grew increasingly intense.

I sipped the ambrosia again. It was cold and fresh and flavored like berries. Immediately, the burning sensation in my mouth faded. Except the queen wasn't drinking the ambrosia, which made me wonder if I was about to get hammered.

I licked my lips. "Might I request some water instead of this ambrosia?"

She pinned me with her gaze. "It's only concentrated black orchid nectar."

"And what does that do to someone who's not used to it?" I speared a lettuce leaf because that wasn't spicy at all.

"Maybe it will loosen your tongue. What does the Seelie king have planned for us? An invasion? Is that what this spy mission is about?"

"My companion and I only want to go home, and if you could help us with that, you will never need to speak to us again." The ambrosia had gone to my head. My body felt warm and tingly, and my cheeks had gone hot.

She drummed her fingers on the aged wood of the table. "Your companion is in chains right now." She sipped her drink, eying me over the rim of her cup. "And if you are wondering if I am lying, I would like to remind you that we don't lie." She raised her hand again. "Morgant! Bring out the shattered king."

My stomach dropped, and my breath went shallow.

I turned to the door, and the air left my lungs as Morgant and an Unseelie with fiery hair dragged out Torin. Blood poured down his chest, and he struggled to keep his head raised.

Darkness flickered inside me, and for a moment, I wondered what would happen if I ripped off the queen's wings and threw her over the side of the tower.

She was testing us, and the best thing I could do now was to keep my mouth shut, my expression blank. She was showing him to me for a reason, trying to see how I'd react.

Torin lifted his head. "Ah. Queen Mab. How lovely to see you again." His tone sounded surprisingly bland.

Almost bored. "The last time I saw you, I suppose you were cursing my entire family."

I swallowed hard. Seems we were done pretending he was a common fae named Alan.

"Is that why you came here with this Unseelie? Revenge?" Her gaze flicked between Torin and me, her amber eyes narrowing. "One of you will die first. I haven't yet decided who it will be. Morgant, do you think either of them can fly?"

Morgant, clearly intuiting it was a rhetorical question, merely raised an eyebrow.

With a sharp movement, Torin managed to rip his arms free. "Are you really this desperate for company, Mab? You don't have any friends, do you?" His gaze flicked up to the skies, and I knew he'd seen the archers.

Moonlight shone from her skin. She inhaled deeply. "I suppose I do need to be entertained. If I were a purely practical person, you'd be dead by now. But I have dreams and visions I'd like to indulge."

Mab was like a cat toying with her prey.

"Listen, Your Highness." My jaw was clenched tight, but I tried to keep my tone friendly. "Why don't you let the Seelie go, and I'll stay here. I'm one of you, but clearly, he doesn't belong here. I'll stay, and everything will be in its right place. Otherwise, I'm afraid you might have the entire Seelie army descending on you to burn everything to the ground."

She let out a hiss, the sound like water dousing a fire. "But there's no queen on the throne of Faerie, is there? It must be in quite a state now. Freezing over.

Dragons circling like vultures, waiting to feast on the icy dead. Did you know that they collect corpses?" Her expression changed as she seemed to warm to this idea, and she beamed at me with a radiant smile. "I think we will keep you both for fun. Won't that be nice, Morgant?"

My fingers tightened into fists. "Let him go."

"Ava," Torin said quietly, like he was trying to calm a wild beast.

A thorny silence spread between us until Queen Mab lifted a finger to her lips. "I think she really cares for him." Her voice was an icy gale that sent a shiver up my spine. "A truly lost Unseelie, so sweet and sad at the same time." Her gaze slid down Torin's body. "I can see *why* she likes him. I may be twice your age, but I'm not blind."

Torin stepped closer to her, and despite his brutalized state, his movements were fluid and graceful. "My dear queen. You really *are* lonely."

Was he flirting with her?

Despite the blood running down his chest, he was still so beautiful that it made my heart stop. Maybe he could *charm* his way out of this?

She put a finger to her lips. "It is lonely at the top, as they say. Are you offering yourself up to me? I've never been with Seelie, nor have I been with a male as beautiful as you are."

Oh, gods. The food in my stomach was starting to curdle.

"Your Highness," Morgant started. "There are security—"

Mab lifted her hand. "When I want to hear from you, I will ask. But I could use your strength, Morgant." She turned to me. "I am still thinking of throwing this wretch off the tower to see if she can fly. Do we think she can?"

"I'd advise you not to do that." Torin's deep, smooth voice cut through the night air, a sharp blade of warning in his tone.

"And once she is out of the way, Torin, what would happen if I took you to my bedroom to see if you could prove yourself to a queen?"

Torin's jaw tightened. "If you go anywhere near Ava," he said smoothly, his tone laced with violence, "I will rip out your spine, Your Highness."

My gaze flicked back to the archers circling over-head, their white wings pounding the air. One more arrow in the right place, and he'd be dead.

The queen's eyes widened. "So you *do* care for her after all. How interesting. A Seelie king cares for his little Unseelie friend." She folded her arms. "Well, if you're going to make threats, you won't be able to stay in my bedroom unchained. Don't you think it would be better if your hands were free?"

What the fuck was she playing at? I bit my lip. She seemed to phrase a lot of things as questions, which had me wondering if she really *couldn't* lie, and the questions were some sort of workaround.

She sashayed closer to him and traced a finger over his collarbone. "Torin, darling. When you first arrived, I thought I knew how I wanted to kill you." Her finger brushed down his chest. "I thought I'd beat you unconscious and seal you up inside a tree so that when you woke, you'd find yourself entombed in oak, and you'd slowly starve to death over a few weeks, feasted on by bugs. Here, we give back to the forest."

Bony fingers of dread wrapped around my heart.

"What is *wrong* with you?" I whispered to myself, no longer able to restrain myself.

"Oh, don't worry." Her finger was moving down over his abs. "That was *before*." She whirled to look at me. "But you know what? I have never wanted to be with a weak man. Don't you think a corpse-eater should prove his worth? Should we see his skill on the battlefield?" Her cheeks glowed with a radiant silver light. "Here is my magnanimous offer. I will let one of you leave the kingdom." She fluttered her long, black eyelashes. "But only after a duel between the two of you. Torin, darling." She slipped behind him, stroking a hand down his muscular shoulders. "Tomorrow, your job is to fight this Lost One before a crowd of my subjects and run your sword through her. If you prove yourself to me in the way that I require, I will let you return to your sad, withering kingdom."

My chest tightened. "You need him to kill me?"

"Don't worry, my little wretch,'" she said soothingly. "If you should stab him, I will allow you to leave. If you want. And I don't even need any extra favors from you. Really, you are a lucky girl." Her amber gaze slid between Torin and me. "Do you know what? My subjects have been bored lately, and I'd love to entertain them. They will be thrilled. They don't have all the frost and starvation to contend with that you do in Faerie, and their lives are so comfortable, it gets tedious." She smiled. "They need *bloodshed*. So, tomorrow, you will both fight. And one of you must skewer the other for it to end."

She bit her lip coquettishly and fluttered her eyelashes at Torin. "But I have never liked to share. When I see something I want, I don't like anyone else to have it. Torin, darling, if I catch you going anywhere near the Lost Unseelie, there will be consequences. Have you ever wondered what it would be like to be castrated? To be ripped apart by horses pulling your limbs in every direction? Would you like to find out?"

Torin wasn't responding anymore. He just stared at her, his eyes darkening to a midnight blue.

The queen gingerly stepped away from him and drummed her fingertips together. She turned to Morgant. "Before you bring them to their quarters, heal the Seelie king. I want him to be healthy before they fight. And since someone will be impaled tomorrow, let them stay in a tower room this evening. Separately, of course." She cut Torin a sharp look. "I have made myself very clear on that point, haven't I? I am commanding you not to go anywhere near each other."

I felt dizzy, short of breath. "And if we refuse to kill each other tomorrow?"

"Lost One." She cocked her head, and her expression was almost maternal. "I plan to throw you off the tower. I think it's merciful, really. You are a traitor, but you are Unseelie. But Torin? As an enemy of our kingdom invading our lands, I believe most of my subjects would say he deserves a very slow, humiliating, and excruciating death. And Lost One, wouldn't it hurt you to watch it before you plunged from the tower walls? Love can hurt more than the worst tortures we can devise."

Her softly spoken words hung in the air like a death knell.

🐾 16 🐾
AVA

My heart was still slamming against my ribs as Morgant led me through the castle with its vaulted halls of stone and vines.

A slow, humiliating, and excruciating death...

Sconces jutted from the walls, made of something that looked like smooth bone. Their warm candlelight danced over Morgant's white hair, his enormous frame, and the wood walls. If it came down to it...

If it came down to it, I would absolutely not be able to take him in a fight. Nor could I take down Torin, so I had exactly zero plans for tomorrow. And even if I *could* stab Torin, I didn't want to.

At least we'd bought ourselves some time, I supposed. More time to find out if he'd found the Veiled One. More time to charm the queen, or whatever it took to get out of here alive.

Morgant's boots echoed off the stone floor, and he turned to look back at me. "You are lucky our gracious queen didn't rip your heart out. She is giving you the gift of a chance. And death by the sword is certainly preferable to anything else she might dream up."

My mouth felt watery, like I was about to vomit. "Let's find out how lucky I am tomorrow. Morgant, where is Torin?"

He bared his canines in a show of aggression, but I had the feeling his heart wasn't really in it. "You must stop asking your questions. I'd advise you to leave well enough alone. The queen ordered you two to stay separate." He cut me a sharp look. "Rest, so you can kill him tomorrow. You may be a traitor, but you were one of us once. And I want to watch you kill their broken king."

My stomach twisted. I was skilled at fencing, yes. But Torin had spent his life training with the best swordsmen of Faerie, fending off challenges from petty kings and their sons for half his life. Slaughtering them to defend his throne. He probably had dozens of deaths at his hands.

At last, we reached an arched wooden door, and Morgant pushed it open. I breathed in the humid air, scented of basil, lemon, and mahogany. Blue wooden arches swooped over me, and steeply peaked mullioned windows were inset into the walls, overlooking the kingdom of stars and red leaves. Firelight on a stone hearth danced over a bed and a claret rug spread on the stone floor.

It was a million times nicer than the dungeon, except for the heavy pall of icy dread hanging over me.

Morgant stood in the doorway and folded his enormous arms. Shadows danced over his leather-clad body and long hair. "Where did you come from?"

Frustration simmered. "I thought you said Mab already knew."

"She has not informed me yet."

"Well, I have no idea. My family could have been glamoured in the human realm for hundreds of years, for all I know." I dropped onto the bed and let out a long breath. "I honestly doubt I'll get any sleep tonight."

The fact that I was even talking to the queen's torturer was a sign of my desperation.

His brow furrowed, and he pointed to a copper bathtub near the hearth. "There are herbs there to calm you before you sleep."

"What can you tell me about the duel tomorrow?"

"If Her Highness wanted you to know any details, she would have told you. She *always* has a plan, and she does not make mistakes. All you can do is rest tonight and kill the king tomorrow." Morgant pointed to a dark wood dresser. "Clothes in there. Your door will be heavily guarded. Do not try to leave." He stepped closer and lifted my chin, his eyes piercing mine. "Do not try to see your Seelie dog, or you will both die. And then I get the pleasure of putting the cur out of his misery. It will be worse than death by a sword. You understand?"

A wintry shadow swept through my mind, and I imagined the vines around us snaking over him, dragging him away.

I swiped his hand away. "Don't touch me again."

The corner of his lip curled. "Maybe you do seem like one of us.

"Why do you hate Torin so much?"

A breeze rushed into the room, toying with his hair. "He sends assassins after us, using fae with the ability to move between worlds. Once, I woke to find a Seelie assassin in my room. I was able to kill him, but my brother was not so lucky. Torin had him slaughtered in his sleep."

Oh. That explains the reception we'd received.

Morgant turned, and the door slammed closed behind him.

I sat in silence, my body buzzing with exhaustion and nerves. I still clung to one thread of hope: that Torin had learned something from that crone. If not, we would need to find a way to free ourselves. We'd turn our swords on the queen if necessary—break free or die trying. Or maybe there would be a loophole of some sort?

"Stab," she'd said. "Skewer." What if I skewered a pinkie? An earlobe? Fae were bound by oaths, weren't they? She'd have to let one of us free if we skewered a little bit of skin. The freed person could summon help from Faerie.

After a few minutes, I poured myself a hot bath and slipped into it, breathing in the scent of basil and lavender. With the fire crackling next to me, my mind started to drift, my vision going hazy. For a moment, it almost looked like the vines were crawling over the stone, writhing like a living thing. My breath caught, and I sat up straight in the bath.

As I blinked, the vision slid away again.

I tightened my jaw. The stress was getting to me. I stepped out of the bath, water dripping off my naked body in little rivulets. The humid breeze swept into the room, raising goosebumps on my skin.

I snatched up a towel, leaving wet footprints on the flagstones as I crossed to the dresser. When I pulled open the drawers, I found neatly folded white night-gowns. I pulled one on and snuffed out the candles in the room.

As I crawled into bed, a shadow's movement on the balcony caught my eye, and I sat up, clutching the sheets to my chest. A silhouette loomed outside my window. Within the next heartbeat, I recognized the athletic shape, the ice-blue eyes that pierced the shad-ows. He wore a shirt now, crisp and white.

Torin.

My pulse roared. Had he lost his mind? With his eyes on mine, he prowled into the room, a finger on his lips.

I flung off the covers and tiptoed closer to him, closing the distance between us until I could feel the heat radiating off him. He brushed my hair behind my ear, leaning down to whisper, "I don't know what's going to happen tomorrow, Ava, and I don't know if it will be possible. But if we have a chance to escape, we must take it. We must use our swords to free ourselves." He brushed his thumb over my cheek. "I don't know how. For the first time in my life, I honestly have no idea what to do."

My heart tightened. "So, I guess you didn't see the Veiled One?"

He shook his head. "The castle seemed empty, as far as I could tell."

117

I sucked in a deep breath. "What about a little stab? I have this feeling that she is *very* particular in how she chooses her words. She didn't say we had to kill each other, did she? What about a little piercing, somewhere harmless? One of us could go free and get help."

He nodded. "Good. Stab me, then."

I shook my head. It made more sense for him to leave, I thought. He was the king. But we didn't really have time to argue about it. "Did you hear what she said she was going to do if she caught you in here?"

He brushed his knuckles against my cheekbones. "I do hope to avoid that fate, changeling. But I had to see you."

"Why?"

"Because I don't want to be without you any more than I have to." Instead of leaving, he leaned in and pressed his lips against mine. He kissed me lightly, but when I ran my hands over his white shirt, feeling the hard muscle beneath, his kiss deepened. I melted into the slow, bittersweet kiss. Right now, I wasn't worrying about the duel or his kingdom, or thinking of anything else in the world except him and the feel of his tongue sweeping against mine, his hands sliding down my nightgown, pressing me close to him.

The rest of the world faded away, the Seelie and Unseelie, and it was just the two of us lighting each other up. It was dawn breaking from within.

I couldn't get enough of him, and I wasn't sure it would ever be enough.

A shout pierced the door, and his muscles tensed. My body froze, panic climbing up my spine.

"Torin," I whispered through heavy breath, "you have to go. Now."

He leaned in close, whispering, "In Faerie, I will freeze anyone that I love, Ava. I will kill anyone that I love. That's what Queen Mab cursed me with. And that's why you can't come with me, my changeling."

His words took the breath from my lungs, and as he stepped away, his mournful blue eyes gleamed in the dark. "Part of the curse meant I couldn't tell a soul. Only Orla ever knew. I killed someone that I loved, Ava. I won't ever let it happen again."

He turned and slipped into the shadows, blending into the night.

I stood still, feeling my heart cracking. I hardly heard the sound of the lock sliding on the door, or the hinges creaking open.

By the time Morgant sauntered into the room, Torin had disappeared.

He frowned at me. "I felt your heart racing. You should go to sleep, Ava."

But my heart still pounded like a hunted animal, and I wasn't sure anything would help me sleep.

❦ 17 ❦
AVA

Morgant led me through a corridor with mossy vaults that soared hundreds of feet high. My footfalls echoed off the stone walls.

This morning, I'd been up at dawn and dressed in simple black clothes for the duel. I wasn't sure if I'd slept at all, but my mind could not stop obsessively raking over whether I'd discovered a loophole.

Skewering, not killing...I'd been running the words in my mind all night.

"Morgant," I said, "the queen seems very precise with her language."

He turned back to me, nodding once. "Just focus on killing the Seelie king."

I wasn't in a fit state for a duel. My mind felt foggy and muted, my nerves crackling with exhaustion and panic.

Morgant led me into a room with towering stone columns on either side and aisles full of Unseelie spectators. Amber beams of morning sunlight streamed in through narrow, towering windows, gilding the crowd of fae with antlers, hooves, and long tails. They were clad in green garments, some of the females wearing gossamer dresses spun like spiderwebs. All eyes locked on me, and whispers rippled throughout the hall. For a few breaths, I let my gaze roam around, taking in the strange beauty of this place.

At the far end of the hall, Mab was sitting on an ornately carved wooden throne that seemed to rise out of the tree roots, her pearled gown spread out at the base. A pale, delicate crown glittered on her white hair.

Torin stood before her. This could have been some sort of strange wedding except for the four archers flying above, arrows pointed at him. Another three had weapons trained on me.

A moss green carpet ran the length of the hall, the distinctive bright red leaves scattered like drops of blood against blue-black stones. Ruddy leaves bloomed from dark vines that crawled over every column and wall. This place was lush with strange vegetation.

As I stepped further into the hall, Morgant drew a rapier and handed it to me by the bronze hilt. He stepped away, arching an eyebrow at me.

From her throne, Mab twirled a scepter made of gnarled wood that snaked around a glowing sphere. She stood and addressed the crowd in the Unseelie language, her words booming over the hall.

A guard with long red hair translated what she said into English. "My subjects. Does anyone have any idea whom this lost Unseelie belongs to?"

Her words sent my nerves jangling with a desperate hope that someone would speak up and this disturbing spectacle might be avoided. A mother and her long-lost daughter reunited would certainly be a distraction, a spectacle so heartwarming that no one would need to see bloodshed today.

I scanned the crowd again, desperately searching for anyone who looked like me. And when my gaze landed at last on a set of coppery horns, my pulse raced faster. The man, broad and athletically built, was maybe old enough to be my father, with copper horns like mine. Black hair, dark eyes, olive skin and tattoos—he didn't look exactly like me, but...

"Dad?" I said, desperately. "Dad!"

His brow furrowed, and he shot a nervous look at a winged woman to his right. I had no idea what he was saying in the Unseelie language, but the tone strongly suggested this woman was his wife, and it was probably a frantic defense of his faithfulness.

My heart sank, and after another moment of awkward silence, the redheaded guard was translating for the queen again.

"No one claims the Lost One," she said. "This duel will follow our traditional fencing rules. No daggers, no running about in circles. If you step off the mossy strip, my archers will shoot you. If you fail to do as I ask, I will throw the Lost Unseelie off our tower walls. I will find a more creative fate for the Seelie king."

This last remark elicited a disturbing ripple of pleasure from the crowd, their eyes gleaming. I closed my eyes, slightly horrified that my own kind were so unrelentingly sadistic.

Then, in English, the Queen called out, "Take your positions. By the end of this duel, I require that you use your sword to pierce through your opponent's heart, neck, stomach, or eye socket, until the sword protrudes from the other side."

The world tilted beneath my feet. No loopholes, then.

"As I have already explained to Torin," she bellowed, "if either of you tries to escape or thinks you can take down a queen, I will have my archers disable you. I will then throw Ava off the tower, and I will execute the Seelie king." She smiled. "Am I clear?"

Fuck.

The queen had just doused the flames of every bit of hope I had. And now, my pulse pounded so hard I could no longer hear my own thoughts. A cold sweat broke out on my brow, and my gaze flicked back to the door, looking for an escape route. But an entire line of guards stood before the wooden doors, arrows aimed at us.

Dread spread its chill over my chest as I moved closer to Torin. If we were going to find any way out of this, we couldn't panic.

Queen Mab smiled. "When the horns blare, it is time to begin."

Torin's pale eyes were locked on me, and he stalked closer to me, gracefully. Somehow, with a slight curl of his lips, and the poised way he stood, he did not seem to be gripped by the mind-bending panic that robbed me of breath.

My gaze flicked over his shoulder, and I wondered if it was possible for us to slaughter her before we were shot.

My heartbeat seemed to echo off the walls and arched ceilings. There didn't seem to be enough air in my lungs, and I could hear every inhalation and exhalation of my breath like the creaking of a rusty hinge.

The horns blared, and I didn't have another moment to think. Torin advanced on me, his rapier and his blue eyes glinting.

How casually he launched into action, attacking my sword. Completely in control of himself, while the bleak horror of our choices splintered in my skull.

Our swords clashed as I parried, simply trying to keep up with him. Was he going slow for me?

At least I was used to a fencing strip, the way I'd trained all along. No cemetery stones in the way, no tree roots. Maybe I should simply focus on staying alive until I mastered my panic.

Torin lunged again, and I parried. He was testing me, trying to feel out how I operated on the fencing strip, but I still had no idea where this was leading.

I will throw you off the tower...

I raised my blade and waited again for Torin to attack. He lunged, and this time, I counter-parried, swiping his blade aside and lunging forward myself. Torin darted out of range, and we fell into the rhythms of the fencing that we knew so well. After all those hours practicing, learning each other's movements and quirks, this felt more like a dance than a fight.

A slow and excruciating death...

As I focused on the two of us, his beautiful face and the graceful way he moved, the memory of our kiss last night, my panic started to fade. As we moved—attacking, parrying, ducking—the world seemed to come alive around us, plants rising from the stones and the red leaves dancing in the air. When he attacked again, I countered. Back and forth we went—attack, parry, attack, parry, attack, parry—as the red leaves lifted into the air, floating in a breeze around us. The world was a symphony of clashing blades and fluttering leaves.

Maybe we could simply dance like this forever.

But as we fought, I struggled, finding the steel blade a little stiffer than I was used to. I could parry okay, but when I counterattacked, it felt slow.

As Torin leaped back, I rushed forward with a series of stabs and lunges, knowing that Torin's speed would be able to keep up with every flick of my blade. Exactly as it was when we'd practiced together, he countered my attack with crisp parries.

"I am growing impatient!" the queen roared, her voice no longer a gentle whisper. "I want blood spilled in my hall."

Her voice pulled me from my focus on Torin, and I slowed. This time, when Torin parried hard, he slammed his rapier into mine, snapping my blade in two. The ember-red leaves around us dropped to the floor, and Torin stared down at my broken sword with horror.

I stared at my fragmented blade, catching my breath. My body buzzed with adrenaline, and with something else—an unfamiliar feeling of power.

Torin turned back to the Queen.

Her lips were pressed into a thin line. "You must continue. Am I clear?"

"Her blade is broken." Torin's voice boomed over the hall. "I cannot fight her like this. That is not a fight."

She stood, her lip curling and her dark wings spread out behind her. "So you concede? Are you choosing your own excruciating death? Would you prefer to be castrated and quartered?"

My breath left my lungs, and a maelstrom of red leaves lifted off the ground around us, whipping in the air. Was my own panic causing that to happen?

I whirled, searching for Morgant as fear burned through my veins.

"I have another sword," Morgant shouted.

Surprise flickered that he would offer this to me without the queen's approval, but he was hurrying forward anyway, handing me his own sword. This one had more supple steel and a hilt of pale gold. "Thank you," I whispered.

He nodded once. I knew he was only giving me this because he wanted to watch Torin die, but I was grateful all the same.

I turned back to Torin, the new blade glinting in the sunlight, sharp as a viper's fang. I breathed in, filling my lungs, trying to marshal that sense of control again.

Torin stepped forward, his eyes locked on mine, and the dance began once more, a graceful minuet of attacks and parries. The world was alive around us, a cyclone of red leaves whipping through the air.

As far as I knew, there was no plan beyond dragging this out as long as possible, beyond savoring every last breath, every last moment together, every step in this strange waltz.

At least, that's what I thought.

But Torin had other plans.

As I attacked in a move I knew he could parry, Torin shifted his body in front of my blade.

The steel blade plunged clear through his heart.

18

AVA

I pulled my sword from his chest, horror punching me in the gut as I stared at Torin's blood dripping off my blade. Faltering, I staggered back again. Torin lay flat on the stones, bleeding out, and I felt the world go dark.

The hall that moments ago had been alive with excitement fell silent with a horrible hush, and I no longer felt as if I had a mind to think with.

Torin's blood spilled onto the moss, pouring from his chest. I stared down at my own sword, my mind refusing to believe what was before me.

It must be a trick. My thoughts went horribly silent. No words could explain my mind-shattering horror as I stared at his blood.

A scream pierced the silence, someone asking him why he'd done that. A distant scream, muddled under the hush.

He couldn't answer.

At last, the reality of it smashed through, and I

rushed to his side, frantically pressing my hands against his chest to stanch the blood, but the sword had gone through his heart, and he did not move. There was no heartbeat. My hands shook uncontrollably.

He'd done that on purpose. I'd seen the look in his eyes for a fraction of a moment, the intent behind that movement. My sword had gone into his chest, but I'd felt it in my own heart, a sharp blade that made it impossible to breathe or think.

Only then did I realize it was me screaming at him, asking him why the fuck he'd jumped in front of my sword. Tears blurred my vision.

But I knew, didn't I? He'd told me. He'd lived with crushing guilt because he'd killed someone he loved.

It was just...

Now he wanted me to suffer the same curse? His blood covered my hands. I didn't think his heart was beating anymore, as the flow of blood was starting to slow.

"Love is a forge in the fiery depths of Mount Tienen," Queen Mab's melodious voice floated over the hall. "It makes us stronger, but the pain is excruciating. Isn't that true, little wretch?"

When I looked up at Queen Mab, at the smug little smile on her face, wrath spilled through me like hot blood. I gritted my teeth, fingers tightening around the sword. Around me, the leaves lifted from the stones and flitted into the air. My body vibrated with hot fury.

Queen Mab's expression was exhilarated, glowing. She was delighting in this horror. Her enemy, the Seelie king, had been slain by the hand of his lover. What a *victory* for the Queen of Sorrows.

A dark power slid through me, charged from the stones beneath my feet. How *dare* she end his beautiful life.

From the stones around us, vegetation came to life, snaking toward the queen. I didn't know if that was my magic or hers, only that I wanted to choke her to death.

But I had to kill her fast. Time seemed to slow down as I raced across the mossy floor. One step, two...

My blade, covered in Torin's blood, was destined for her throat. I didn't care what happened to me anymore, and I was sure I was going to die anyway.

I was closing the distance between Mab and me when an arrow slammed into me from behind, piercing bone.

I heard her voice echoing over the hall. "Lost One, if you're going to take aim at the Unseelie queen, you'd better not miss."

⚜

I WOKE ON TANGLED ROOTS, INHALING THE SCENT OF blood mingling with earth and moss. In the dungeon once more, it was near total darkness.

My fingernails had grown too long. They curled over the tree roots.

I felt strangely disconnected from the lacerating pain in my back. My mind still wasn't able to comprehend what had happened—the sword piercing his chest, his blood spilling onto the moss—but it kept replaying anyway, an endless loop in my thoughts.

It felt as if I'd seen it from a distance, a horror unfolding at the end of the tunnel.

It couldn't have been me who'd stabbed him.

I lay, breathing in the smell of soil.

I couldn't think of a single reason to bother moving.

❧ 19 ❧

TORIN

The blade went in—not as piercing as I'd thought, but like a punch to the chest, followed by a sort of dizzying disbelief at what I'd done.

With the stones beneath my back, I felt myself hollowing out—my bones, my skull. My body filled with cold shadows and the warm scent of her, like burning cedar.

I couldn't survive killing another woman I loved. And what was the point of the two of us dying? Queen Mab would never allow me to live, for all her promises.

Light pierced the arches from above, and I was no longer in the Court of Sorrows, but I saw Ava before me. There she was, standing before the portal of Faerie as a little girl, trying to get back into a kingdom I already ruled as a child. Tiny Ava had tears running down her pink cheeks, and she clutched her Mickey Mouse backpack. She'd loved her mother, Chloe, but no one else in the human world thought she belonged.

My own mother's voice rang in my thoughts, and the vision disappeared with a rippling of waves, like a stone cast into a lake.

You are dying, Torin.

I had to die at some point, Mother.

I'd always taken pride in being able to take care of people, anticipating their needs and making them comfortable. A king and queen were parents to an entire realm. A flicker of icy panic pierced my dulling thoughts because who would be there to care for them now?

But Ava was safe...

When I'd first walked into the bar to find a tiny brunette fae glaring at me, drunkenly staggering, I never could have imagined this was how it would end.

Somewhere in my soul dwelled a phantom life, one where Ava was my wife. One where she slept in the crook of my arm and kissed my neck. One where she peered over coffee at me across a morning-lit table.

In my phantom life, she curled up on a bed to read a book next to me.

But that was as tangible as smoke.

She couldn't be my wife. Though, as my mind hollowed out, I couldn't quite remember why...it was a stupid reason.

Was that the sound of Ava screaming?

My thoughts rushed back, a wild river careening to different memories etched in my mind. I was with my mom, walking after her. Snow covered the fields, but Faerie still had a queen, so icicles dripped onto the path. In some places, the snow had melted away to reveal bright green blades of grass. When my mother turned to look at me, I felt so proud of her for inviting the spring and for being the most beautiful woman in Faerie. But as we walked deeper into the forest, she wouldn't stop coughing, and I hated the noise. Why had I felt like she was doing it on purpose? No one is sick on purpose.

I was falling apart because I knew she wouldn't be able to look after me anymore.

The river of memory veered in another direction, and I was at her bedside, making her a card with a pencil and paper. Someone had convinced me that the magic of wellness could be created through a card.

Another turn of the river.

I was running through the castle hall now, years after Mother died. Orla was screaming, and when I slammed open the door to her room, I found that the fire from the hearth had burned her dress. A nurse was supposed to be looking after her, but the nurse must have fallen asleep. I remember feeling that no one except me was capable of looking after her.

In the Court of Sorrows, I stared at red leaves raining down on me, struck again by the realization that I was dying and that I would never see Ava again, or Orla. Even if my thoughts were about to stop forever, I felt certain I'd miss them horribly.

When I brought Ava to the craggy cliffside overlooking Faerie's valley and pointed out the mountain ranges and tribes, I could never have predicted that one day, I'd intentionally step into the blade of a heartbreakingly beautiful Unseelie.

20

SHALINI

elicate white webs of frost spread over the old panes, obscuring my view of the snowy world outside. I breathed on the glass, fogging it up, and ran my hand over it to get a view of the kingdom.

The cold seeping through the glass made me shiver, so I pulled the blanket tighter around myself to get warm and glanced back at the fireplace. Once again, the blaze had simmered down to embers. I couldn't keep the damn thing lit. The temperature in the castle kept plummeting, low enough for me to see my breath form a mist around my head. Right now, I was wearing three layers: long underwear, pajamas, then leather pants, a shirt, and two sweaters—and a blanket over it all.

My mind slid back to two years earlier, when I was working in an office and drowning in a perpetual torrent of Jira tickets. Every night, I'd work till nine and get takeout curry or pizza for dinner. I'd started to grow

increasingly bored with my life, until the day I'd
marched into my manager's office and quit.

Gerald had been a patronizing fifty-five-year-old
man who'd once gotten drunk at an office party and
claimed he'd had a former career as a "stunt cock" in
Canadian porn. It had been *deeply* satisfying to tell him I
wouldn't be coming back.

I hadn't needed the money. Who in their right mind
worked ten hours a day when they had millions in a
bank account from the last startup?

And the first several months of retirement had been
amazing. Yoga, lunches by myself, endless books, a wine
tour in Sonoma...it had all started with euphoria that
drifted into contentment, then complacency, before
settling into absolute boredom. The amount of wine I
was drinking kept creeping up. I'd pour the drinks
earlier, first at five, then four. And wasn't two p.m.
acceptable when you didn't have anything else to do?

I'd been starting to get desperate for a story I could
tell, an adventure.

And that was how I'd ended up here, in a frigid
castle with temperatures that beyond all expectations
continued to get colder.

That was also how I'd lost my best friend two weeks
ago. And that was why I was still here, waiting for her
return.

I wasn't leaving without her.

I pulled the blanket tighter around me, my thoughts
once again roving over the landscape of Ava's disap-
pearance.

I hadn't been there to see how it had happened, but Aeron had been. Ava had plunged through some kind of magical portal, and Torin had followed after her. Within moments, the portal had sealed with ice, then stone. The king's throne had broken, and a wintry hoarfrost had snapped across the kingdom.

So now, the biting cold seeped into every stone in Faerie, into every piece of fabric and glass. It cooled hot tea before the cups were even filled and stung cheeks and exposed fingers. It made my teeth chatter when I crawled into bed and slid into my body like a phantom when I slept. Here, the cold was an unwanted guest that would never leave.

As I stared between the blooms of frost on the window, a large black and red dragon swept through the stormy skies in the distance, his wings outstretched in the setting sun. A shudder rippled up my spine.

I knew I was safe in the castle—at least, I *thought* I was safe here. But it was an instinctive terror, and the sight of the dragon made my heart hammer faster. I didn't think humans had evolved to mentally cope with the sight of actual dragons.

From what I gathered, dragons weren't normal here, either. No one in the castle seemed to want to venture outside, which didn't do anything to calm my nerves. Supposedly, the dragon was a sign of some sort of dark magic encroaching, or maybe a sign that the dragon was waiting for people to die of the cold so it could roast our bodies and feast. Dragons hoarded things, and the rumors were that this dragon hoarded corpses.

A knock sounded on the door, and I nearly jumped out of my skin.

"Who is it?" I asked.

"Aeron." His voice pierced the oak door.

I let out a long sigh. Maybe *he'd* warm me. I still couldn't get him to share a bed with me—not because he didn't want to, but because of some stupid vow of chastity that made no sense whatsoever. But I could tell he was tempted, lingering around me longer, leaning in to kiss me.

With chattering teeth, I hurried over to the door. I really hadn't seen him enough in the past two weeks. He'd been working nonstop, delivering food to hungry families, trying to keep homes heated.

When I pulled open the door, I found him standing in the hall, clouds of breath puffing from his blue lips. He held a plate with a single piece of bread on it, and it made my heart squeeze.

"Get in here," I said. "You're freezing."

"I thought you might be hungry." My stomach rumbled sharply, and yet I didn't quite feel like eating. Stress had that effect on me.

I sat on the bed with the plate of bread in my lap and the blanket over my shoulders. "What I really want more than bread is for you to get warm next to me. You've been out in the cold all day, haven't you?"

"You need to keep the fire going." Aeron crossed to the hearth. "I don't want you freezing in here by yourself."

"I don't understand how everything changed so fast," I said. "Just a few weeks ago, we were eating entire banquets, and now it's all blizzards and food rations."

He knelt, trying to stoke the fire again. "Torin didn't want to marry until it was absolutely necessary. If Ava had sat on the throne, we'd be enjoying spring right now. Torin had been promised money that we were supposed to use to buy food. The humans offered him an enormous sum for filming the trials, but the contract also required an actual wedding. Without the wedding itself, they're not paying him. The granaries are empty. The livestock have been slaughtered. I've been visiting house after house today. The young and old are getting sick without heat and the right nutrition. People are eating all of their farm animals. The chickens are freezing to death, not laying eggs. Nothing has grown in Faerie for years. We were down to our last rations when Torin disappeared."

A weight pressed on my chest. Someone needed to take control here. "What is Orla doing?"

"Refusing to take the throne. She's certain Torin will be back any day now. And I don't know if she's wrong. She's unfailingly loyal, and Torin never wanted her on the throne. He thought she was too weak, and that the magic would kill her."

He turned back to me. "We are not in good shape. We don't have any more time to spare. And I know Torin wouldn't be allowing this to happen if he had any control whatsoever. If he could be here, he would. I'm just worried that he's..." Aeron trailed off for a moment. "That he's trapped or something."

Worry twisted in my gut. If Torin was in trouble, Ava must be, too.

I slid the plate of bread onto a bedside table. "What is the dragon I keep seeing?"

He crossed to the bed. "It's the curse the demons placed on us long ago. When the frost encroaches, dark magic takes over. The dragon is circling like a vulture, waiting to eat the dead, to feed off our destruction. Our kingdom hasn't seen them in centuries, but I think they're attracted to misery and desperation."

When he sat down across from me, I pulled the blanket off myself, and I wrapped it around both of us until we were cocooned in wool. He took my cold hands in his and rubbed them together, then breathed on them.

When he looked up at me again, his golden hair hung before his eyes, and his cheeks were pink with the cold. Even with the chaos around us, he still had that perfect rakish charm.

"I don't understand what happened," he said. "I keep piecing together what I saw, trying to make sense of it. Moria had come up here to speak to Ava but wouldn't allow me anywhere in earshot. Ava ran down to the throne room to speak to Torin. And then I saw him touch her, and ice spread over her body. But I don't understand why Torin would freeze her with his magic. I suppose it was an accident, but I've never known him to lose control of his magic before."

A disturbing memory threaded through my mind, a tidbit of a conversation I'd overheard.

"How much do you trust Torin?" I asked.

"Honestly, I trust him with my life. I've known him since we were little."

I shifted closer to him.

"I don't trust Moria," I began. "Ava didn't trust her, either, but whatever Moria said to Ava, it was believable enough to make her upset. I didn't hear the whole conversation, but I heard a little. Moria accused Torin of killing her sister. I think Moria's sister might have been the person whose diary we found. She was Torin's girlfriend or lover or something."

Aeron stared at me. "Milisandia. That's what Moria said? Milisandia went missing. But it's treasonous to accuse a king of an unlawful murder. And of course, Torin is not a murderer. He kills lawfully."

"So maybe Moria was lying. But something about that conversation had Ava rushing to speak to Torin, and now they're both gone. What if Torin was trying to cover up what he did?"

Aeron went still. "Maybe you misheard."

Annoyance flickered through me. "I didn't mishear," I said, more sharply than I needed to. When had I last eaten? It had probably been far too long.

He stared at me, a line forming between his eyebrows. "Torin never spoke about Milisandia after she went missing, but I always assumed...well, I assumed she ran off with someone else, started a new life with someone across the mountains. You have to understand, Shalini. I've known him since we were boys. He's not a murderer, and I will not tolerate the accusation."

I bit my lip. "Okay, but when Ava questioned him about it, Torin froze her with his magic." Aeron's fingers were still like ice cubes. "Don't you think that's strange?"

"We live in strange times."

Sorrow tightened my chest. When it came down to it, Torin seemed a million times more trustworthy than Moria.

"So, how do we get Ava back from wherever she went?" I asked. "Isn't there some kind of magic? You must have Seelie witches here who can tell where they are or what happened to her."

Orange light wavered over the hearthstones. Aeron really had done a good job of getting the fire going again.

"Orla sent soldiers to search for an old crone named Modron," he said. "She lives far beyond the frozen Avon River. Modron is said to be as old as Faerie itself, and she might also be the only person who could fix Torin's throne. She's a truth-teller, and she gives us glimpses of what happened in the past."

"As old as Faerie itself?" My eyebrows rose. "How has she stayed alive this long?"

"No one knows. Some say she's a god or a nature spirit. I think she's a Dearg Due who summons humans to Faerie and drinks gallons of their blood. It keeps her heart pumping."

My lip curled. "Really?"

"No one does that at court anymore. It sort of went out of fashion. No one has seen her in decades, I think."

I stared at him. "Moria is a Dearg Due, isn't she? Has she returned to her kingdom?"

Aeron shook his head. "No." His face paled. "Actually, she's been advising Orla. If what you said is true, that she made treasonous accusations against Torin, I should let Orla know right away. We'll get them back," said Aeron with more confidence than his furrowed brow suggested. "I'm sure Modron will help us learn the truth. And I have complete faith in the king."

The cold bit at my skin, and I nodded. "You know, it's impossible to get warm in here, even with the fire. This isn't a normal cold. But where I come from, they say body heat is the best way to warm another person."

"Is that right?" He raised his eyebrows, and a sultry look ignited in his eyes.

My gaze brushed down to his beautiful lips, then back up again. How could anyone be so perfect looking?

His eyes danced with a seductive promise. "Every day, I think of giving up my vow."

He slid his hand around my neck, pulling me closer. With the touch of his lips against mine, embers rose to molten heat inside me, until I found myself pushing him down onto the bed.

He kissed me back, deeply, and it felt like the kiss of a man who'd been thinking about this intensely, every moment of every day.

As my hand slid under his uniform, feeling the heat of his hard abs, he moaned into my mouth.

"Wait," he whispered. "I can't."

Gods damn it, Torin.

A loud knock sounded at my chamber entrance, and I caught my breath, my gaze reluctantly sliding to the door. I tried not to groan audibly with exasperation.

Sighing, I noticed that someone had slid a letter

under the door, which was weird. I didn't feel important enough to get letters here, just a human who'd overstayed her welcome by several weeks.

Aeron kissed my throat, his lips hot against my skin. "Are you going to get the door?" he murmured against my neck.

"Hang on, Aeron. I'm coming right back to you."

Painful as it was, I forced myself away from him, my heart racing. What if this was news about Torin or Ava?

I picked up a cream envelope with maroon calligraphy on the surface. It was addressed to *Shalini*.

When I opened it, I found an invitation, inscribed with the same maroon ink and ornate decorations around the borders.

Dear Shalini,

We have succeeded in locating Modron, and our soldiers are returning with her as we speak. In the meantime, we have been working hard to keep every family fed and clothed through the cursed frost. This terrible tragedy that has befallen our kingdom is not an accident of nature, but the scourge of the demons' evil curse. We ask that you not blame King Torin for his absence in this time of need. We have only one true source of blame, and it's the demons who have haunted and tormented us for centuries.

While we wait for the arrival of Modron, we request the presence of all members of the court in the throne room tomorrow night at dusk so that we may discuss our current situation and discover how to work together.

It was signed by Moria and Orla. My stomach twisted, heart hammering.

I wasn't sure I was ready to find out what had

happened to Ava, and I knew I didn't trust Moria to get to the truth.

Deep in my bones, I knew Ava was in trouble.

With a pang of regret, I realized I almost wanted to stay in the safe cocoon of ignorance with Aeron for just a little longer.

❧ 21 ❧

AVA

"In Faerie, I will freeze anyone that I love, Ava. I will kill anyone that I love. That's what Queen Mab cursed me with. And that's why you can't come with me, my changeling."

My eyes snapped open, and cold grief spread through my chest. I still lay on the roots in the dungeon, flat down on my front. Once again, my back was ripped open. I don't think I'd slept for longer than twenty minutes in...however long I'd been in here.

Every time I fell asleep, I saw Torin again, as if he were alive before me.

I don't want to be without you any more than I have to.

I turned my head, looking up. Faint silver light pierced the canopy high above me.

This was a different cell than the one I'd been put in before, the one where Torin had carved through a wall. There was less light, and it was more cramped. My gaze trailed over the five bowls of food someone had delivered to me. They were feeding me this time, but I hadn't bothered to eat.

I had no appetite whatsoever, either because of the infection or because I'd killed the man I loved. *Torin.* The memory of it was like a thousand rocks pressing on my chest, crushing my ribs.

My normal life seemed a million years away. I could hardly remember what Faerie looked like, let alone the apartment I'd shared with Andrew.

The human world seemed a distant gray dream, vague and unreal. I faintly remembered a room with white walls, and a kitchen downstairs. A blue comforter. The bar I'd gone to with Shalini every week...

It felt like another planet altogether.

My memories of Faerie were a little more vibrant— the towering dark castle, the snowy valleys, and the mountains. But it hurt to think about it. Mostly, I thought of Torin.

The Seelie king and the four cramped walls around me were my universe right now.

Wincing, I reached behind my back. The skin felt hot and swollen. Infected again. I sat up, and my thoughts swam, my stomach tightening with nausea. Every inch of me felt sensitive to the touch, my body alternating between hot and cold.

I closed my eyes, delirious. My brain kept forcing me to relive those moments with the red leaves swirling around us and the vines that seemed alive snaking over the columns.

For a moment when we'd been fighting, I'd imagined the leaves and vines were responding to me, but I must have imagined it. I was disoriented by pain and fever, losing touch with what was real and what wasn't.

The sound of the lock shifting pulled my attention up, and the door groaned open. Morgant's enormous frame filled the doorway. If I'd had the energy and the strength, I would have attacked him, except I wasn't sure I could stand. Warm light beamed into the room from the torches in the hallway. Morgant frowned at the food on the floor.

"Why aren't you eating?"

I wasn't giving him the satisfaction of answering, so I simply stared back at him.

"Are you trying to die in here?" he asked sharply. "Because in Mab's kingdom, the Empress of the Dark Cromm has the privilege of choosing when her prisoners live and when they die. And she chooses how they die."

I cocked my head, keeping my mouth shut.

He sniffed the air. "Something smells rotten."

I gave him a grim smile. "Well, Morgant, that would be me. I do realize that thinking isn't your greatest strength and you probably don't have more than two brain cells to rub together, but when you lock someone in a tiny cell for several days at a time, they will start to reek. And you know what, Morgant? I really don't give a fuck."

"Why?" he said sharply.

"Why what?" I shot back.

"Why don't you care?"

I stared up at him, my fury rising. "You and your queen have done everything in your power to make it clear to me that I have no control. You control when I have food or water. You control if I live or die. And you forced me to kill a man I was falling in love with."

"You do have control. You have magic you refuse to use. Did you know you can heal yourself?" He crouched down, staring at me like he was investigating an alien specimen. "Do you want revenge?"

At the question, the tiniest spark of brightness lit in my chest. Of course I wanted revenge. I wanted to murder him and his queen, but I wasn't in any position to exact it. I bit my lip. "Is the queen your mom? Or are you her consort? Or both?"

His lip curled. "She is my mother."

"I see you inherited the black wings and the twisted soul."

"We *all* have black wings in the royal family," he said sharply. "Some are just too stupid to use them, and you know nothing of my soul."

"Okay."

He sniffed the air. "Your back is infected again. You refuse to heal yourself."

When I didn't respond, he gripped me by the shoulder and forced me around so he could look at my back. I was wearing the same grimy, blood-soaked black clothes I'd been in for days, and the lack of bathing opportunities in here probably explained why it had become infected so quickly. I grunted as he tore at my shirt, exposing my infected shoulder.

"Do you mind?" I snapped. "You don't have the best bedside manner."

"And yet, there's no one else here helping you, is there?" he said quietly.

I closed my eyes. If Torin were alive, he would help me. I swallowed the bitter thought as Morgant brushed his fingers over my infected skin. The pain made me wince, but in moments, Morgant's soothing magic rushed over my skin, cleansing it like warm water.

Why was he healing me? What else did these people want of me?

When he finished, I rolled my shoulder, breathing deeply. I turned back to face him, my dirty hair hanging before my eyes. "Why are you here?" I asked.

"Eat your food," he barked.

He picked up one of the metallic bowls from the floor, one filled with rice and vegetables, and shoved it at me. I stared down at it, nearly hysterical with the thought that these people took pride in being vegetarians while they clearly delighted in sadism.

This felt like another power play. He was ordering me to eat because I didn't want to, and he simply wanted me to know that he was the one in control. I met his gaze, falling silent again.

"The Unseelie are not weak," he said in a low voice.

I cocked my head. "And I'm not one of you. You people disgust me."

It all happened in a flash, his powerful arm shooting out and gripping me by the neck. One moment, we were on the floor, and in the next, he stood, lifting me by the throat, choking me. "You have more power than you think, Lost One, and the only way for you to survive is to learn how to use it. I want you to survive.

But strength only comes through pain. Do you understand?"

He dropped me on the floor, and I fell hard, the pain jolting up my tailbone.

What doesn't kill you makes you stronger.

So, I'd been brutalized by a muscular fae Nietzsche.

"You stabbed the Seelie king," he said. "You are one of us now. Every Unseelie has magic, but you are no good to us until you can summon yours."

He turned. The door slammed behind him, and I heard the bolt slide shut. Did they really think I would be one of them? That I would lend my magic to their kingdom, even if I could summon it?

But a single thing Morgant had said burned in my mind. A little kernel of light in a landscape of shadows. A glimmer of meaning in my life.

Revenge.

People didn't need comfort to thrive, or pleasure; they only needed to find meaning.

I closed my eyes, and the ghost of Torin's voice whispered in my skull.

I don't want to be without you any more than I have to.

His words were a light beaming from my chest.

When I opened my eyes again, the red leaves from the prison floor had risen into the air.

❧ 22 ❧

SHALINI

I clutched a cup of cold tea in my gloved hands as I walked through the hall. By my side, Aeron exhaled deeply, and a cloud of frozen breath puffed around his head. He leaned closer to me, whispering, "I tried to ask about fixing Torin's throne. Moria seemed remarkably uninterested in making that happen."

"There's something very wrong with her," I said to Aeron through clenched teeth.

We walked into the throne room, my heart hammering. He knew how nervous I was about finding out what had happened to Ava, so he'd made me a cup of tea out of some kind of soporific herbs. It had gone cold almost immediately.

The Seelie throng packed the hall from one corner to another, every aisle and alcove full of fae waiting to learn what had happened to their king. The room hummed with anger and tension, a rising vibration of desperation. It was the nervous energy of a panicked and hungry mob, and it set my teeth on edge.

Until I'd read the letter yesterday, it hadn't occurred to me that people would blame Torin for going missing. But of course they did. It was his job to take care of them, and he wasn't showing up. In their time of greatest need, he'd gone missing. Whether he had a good reason didn't matter—in Seelie, a king must be strong and able to protect his people. A king had to defend his crown from all threats, or he wasn't fit to rule.

Right now, I didn't care if people thought I was a rude human who'd overstayed her welcome. Ava was my best friend, and I wanted to hear what was going on. So I pushed through the throng to get closer to the front, ignoring their grumbles.

I made my way through the crowd and spied the king's broken throne. Ice encased the queen's throne and what was left of Torin's, and icicles hung from the stone arches above.

I glanced at Aeron. His mouth was pressed into a tight line. I sensed he was as nervous as I was, but he didn't want to admit it.

At last, Orla pushed through a wooden door behind the thrones and shuffled onto the icy dais with Moria close behind her.

The two of them could not look more different, and it was immediately clear who was actually in charge. Orla looked frail, shaking in a black fur coat. She seemed even smaller than she had the last time I'd seen

her, like the stress of all of this was physically dimin-
ishing her.

Moria, on the other hand, seemed almost untouched
by the cold. She wore a deep red silk dress that showed
off her porcelain cleavage. She wore long black gloves,
and her lips were painted a deep red. Her burgundy hair
was swept up on her head, and a cloak in a matching
color covered her shoulders.

She lifted her chin, staring out at the crowd. "Thank
you all for joining us in our time of tragedy. We are the
Seelie realm, and our people have ruled this land for
thousands of years. During times when our kings and
queens have not been able to lead, we have always
joined together, with the guidance of the kingdom's
princesses and petty kings."

Orla lifted her face, her pale eyes not quite meeting
the crowd. "Modron is now on her way, and she will help
us learn the truth." Her voice sounded thin and reedy.
"While we await her arrival, Moria thought we should
hear from you all. Please tell us what you are facing now
as the frost takes over our kingdom."

The room was quiet, the silence punctuated only by
a few coughs and chattering teeth.

After a minute, someone from the back shouted, "I
found my mother lying on the floor in her house. Her
skin had turned black with frostbite."

"My babies won't stop coughing, and I can't keep the
house warm enough," a woman called out. "We need
someone to sit on the throne. I'll bloody do it if no one
else is willing. Seriously. Can I do it?"

"My children are starving," barked a brawny man.

"How long do you expect this rationing to go on? We've never had to ration before. And pardon my expression, but where the fuck is the king when we need him? Maybe he could come here and tell my children to their faces why they can only have one meal a day."

"Get someone on the throne!" A woman's shriek echoed off the high, vaulted stones. "If our king can't look after us, he's not our king."

Technically, wasn't this treason? Torin was still king, and calling for his replacement should have been a serious crime. But he wasn't here, was he?

Moria opened her arms. "Thank you, Seelie friends. We will face this together. In a few days when Modron arrives, we will get answers from her and develop a plan."

Orla looked at her with a furrowed brow. She seemed uncertain, but she wasn't speaking up.

Moria gestured to her. "Princess Orla and I would like to emphasize once again that the cause of all of the misery and tragedy that has befallen us is the demons and the demons alone. I know you are frustrated with King Torin, but it was the demons who cursed Orla and killed her parents. It was they who cursed our kingdom. They are the reason your children are starving. They are the reason your parents are freezing to death on cold hearthstones. Please save your wrath for them. The demons are why you've had to kill your livestock until there's nearly nothing left, and why your children grow weak instead of strong. We have always feared them. We don't even call them by their true name, but we were strong once, and maybe it is the demons who should fear us. Maybe we should not be so afraid to call them by their names, because what is so great and terrifying about being an *Unseelie*?" Venom dripped from her tone.

A murmur of assent rippled through the crowd. As I looked around the hall, the crowd seemed completely enraptured.

Moria raised her hand. "My sister, Milisandia, always said it was the *Unseelie* who should fear us," she went on, pacing over the icy dais. "Before she went missing, she warned me that the day would come when we would need to fight them. She always said we must make war on the Unseelie and their treasonous allies within our court. They attacked our royal family, cursing them all. They have cursed our kingdom for centuries, saddling us with famine, with cold. So do not blame King Torin when you can see your children's ribs and their gaunt cheeks. He may not be here, but he is not an Unseelie, is he? He doesn't love them, does he? He would not leave us here to die in a famine unless he had a very good reason. And we must stand together against our ancient enemies."

Something wasn't adding up about her speech. On the surface, it seemed like she was trying to protect the king from their anger at his absence, to give them another scapegoat. And the people you called *demons* for the past several hundred years were a perfect scapegoat.

Except I happened to know that she hated Torin.

Why would she want to protect the man she accused of murdering her sister?

AVA

Even in this little prison, the seeds of my revenge were starting to bloom—my one and only reason for being. The meaning that illuminated my life.

I didn't think I'd ever get back to my old life, or that I'd see Shalini again. But I *could* try to kill the queen, and that was enough to bring a smile to my face.

And Morgant was right. Every Unseelie had magic —even me.

Rays of light shot through the leaves high above, dappling the gnarled wooden floor with flecks of gold. As I stared up at the branches, I pictured Torin's sorrowful blue eyes as he sat on the bed next to me. When he was thinking of his mom. For some reason, my magic worked best when I was thinking of him.

I felt the power move up my body. Tendrils of warmth sprouted beneath my feet, curled up my legs and thighs, and spilled into my stomach and chest. When I was using my magic, I didn't feel alone because

I felt the tree's life, its consciousness. I imagined the branches shifting and moving above me, letting in more sunlight.

I could feel its soul.

The boughs over my head groaned, parting, and sunlight washed over me. I tilted my head back. The warmth felt glorious on my skin, a gift from this tree where I made my new home.

I breathed in deeply, soaking in the rays. Tingles rippled down my shoulder blades.

And yet—

Even with this power, I still felt as if something about my magic was trapped inside me. My power was magma locked under the frozen earth.

When I heard the sound of metal sliding against metal, I pulled the magic back inside me. The tree branches shifted into place, filling the room with shadows once more. A few leaves fluttered down onto the cell floor.

Morgant pushed the door open and hefted a little copper tub into the cell. He dropped it onto the floor, along with a pair of fresh clothes and a bar of soap.

"Has the Queen decided I'm allowed to wash now?" I asked.

"I didn't ask her."

"Then why are you taking it upon yourself to make me more comfortable?"

"Because you are one of us," he said.

A bolt of guilt shot through me. I was one of them because I'd killed Torin.

"You could have healed him, couldn't you?" I asked.

Morgant shrugged. "Who am I to defy the Queen's explicit orders?"

My jaw tightened. "You and your mother have a real fucked-up relationship."

"Her methods can seem brutal," he said, "but she has the best interests of her family at heart. The Seelie have been trying to invade our kingdom for decades now. Torin sent an assassin who killed her son. My brother. Mab is the reason we remain a sovereign kingdom. But our success depends on her ruthlessness in protecting us. Without her, we'd be overrun by the Seelie."

A lump rose in my throat. "She told me if I killed the king, I would be released. I thought you all were bound by oaths."

His amber eyes pierced the darkness. "Perhaps that's what she intended at the time before you tried to kill her. But you are alive for one reason only, and that is because someday, you might be useful to us."

He yanked the door open and slammed it behind him. I heard the lock slide into place.

Sighing, I turned back to the thorny plants that climbed over the tree trunk and the stone walls. I imagined Morgant standing there in the hall, watching as Torin died before him.

Under my control, the vines started to move and rise. I closed my eyes, feeling my thoughts mingle with those of the tree that had become my home, relaxing in the warmth of sunlight on its canopy. From where I lay, I could feel the roots burrowing into the earth, twined with a delicate network of mycelium and fungi that spread beneath the kingdom. I breathed in, exhilarated. Every living thing here was connected, interacting. Communicating.

But a heavy burden pressed on the tree. The stones were crushing its boughs, trapping it beneath their weight. Power surged through me, but my chest felt weighted down with rocks.

My eyes snapped open, and I gasped for breath.

I wasn't sure why it mattered, but I kept wondering what they'd done with Torin's body. I had a horrific feeling they'd make a spectacle out of him. That's what fae kings did, place their enemy's head on a pike and hang their body from the castle gates.

A vanquished enemy.

I had no idea what Seelie burial traditions were like, but I knew they'd want the king's body back, and that he deserved a burial alongside his parents. My chest felt tight thinking about it. How many days had passed? I didn't want to remember him as a corpse, but I felt responsible for getting him home to Faerie.

Morgant thought I could be useful to him. But I had other plans.

One day, when I'd mastered control of my magic, I would free the tree and wrap these thorny vines around his throat.

❦ 24 ❦

SHALINI

My nerves were crackling as I stood in the front of the hall, waiting for Moria to step onto the frozen dais once more. Modron—the truth-telling crone—had arrived earlier today. It was never men tasked with living in caves and foretelling the future, was it? It was the crones of the world, the supernatural gossips and tea-spillers.

Silence fell over the hall, broken by scuffing feet and rustling cloaks and furs. Coughs echoed off the ceiling. Cast by wavering torches, shadows flitted over the room. It wasn't the most festive atmosphere.

As we waited, fevered whispers rippled through the hall. At last, Moria stepped onto the dais, heels clacking on the ice. She hugged herself in a show of vulnerability. "We starve here in Faerie with no leadership, cursed by the Unseelie. And if we want to move forward, we must know what happened to King Torin. We have summoned Lady Modron so we may learn at last what has befallen our Seelie king."

My heart was beating a million miles a minute as I waited to find out what had happened to my best friend. I found myself leaning into Aeron, and he wrapped his arm around me.

Dressed in gray with a silky veil over her face, the old gossip shuffled into the room, one arm linked with Orla's. I wasn't quite sure who was leading whom. They both looked frail and likely to slip on the ice.

Through the thin fabric of her veil, I caught a glimpse of Modron's bony white face. It was strangely skull-like, and a shiver rippled up my spine. One of her withered hands gripped a gnarled walking stick. Her long, silvery nails curled around the wood, and it cracked the ice with each thud as she crossed the dais.

At last, she stopped, and Orla stepped away from her.

Through the veil, I glimpsed her eyes, large and cavernous. "You wish to learn what has happened to your king. And his bride." Her voice was a hiss that somehow managed to fill the entire hall and sent a shudder down my spine. "You wish to see the past." A low, disturbing chuckle rose from her chest. "I used to live among you. None of you alive remembers those days. But once, I was here at court. Easier to have me out in the wild, though, isn't it? Until you need me." Another low gurgle of laughter.

Get on with it, woman. It all seemed a bit passive-aggressive for what we needed right now.

She lifted the veil, giving us a view of her aged chin and her long white teeth, which were disturbingly sharp as blades. Her lips were dark and glistening. She grinned, then took a deep breath. When she exhaled again, a cloud rose from her mouth, a thick fog that filled the air above the dais. And slowly, figures began to take shape within the cloud.

A beautiful woman with pale white hair sat on a throne made of tree roots, with black wings spread out behind her. And there, before the throne, stood Torin, holding a sword.

I swallowed hard. Torin stood there like he was her protector.

For a moment, I had no idea what I was looking at. But the furious reaction of the crowd quickly gave me a clue.

When I glanced at Aeron, I saw horror etched across his features. I leaned closer to him, whispering, "Unseelie?"

His eyes were firmly on Modron as he nodded. "I don't understand," he said, sounding dazed. "He's standing before the throne of Queen Mab."

My pulse raced. I was getting the first inkling of the plan Moria had been weaving, the threads she'd been twining together to form a monstrous tapestry of betrayal.

She gaped up at the image, her hand covering her mouth.

"What is it?" asked Orla.

Oh, *gods*. This was terrible and awkward. Orla couldn't see the vision, and she was left there in the dark while everyone gaped at her brother standing before the enemy queen.

"He's with Queen Mab!" Moria shrieked in a

mimicry of shock. "Standing before her throne. He's protecting her."

The vision evaporated into the air above the thrones, and a new one took shape—a face that made my heart thump. Ava's pretty features emerged, except now, she had two curved, coppery horns rising from her head. Her eyes had turned green, and she leaned back into Torin. The two of them were on horseback on what looked like a mountain path, and a forest of blood-red trees spread out behind them. As Ava leaned back against Torin, you could see the look of rapture on his face, his eyes closed as he savored the moment.

Shouts of rage filled the air, shouts of *traitor* and *demon whore*, and I wanted to shrink into the shadows. Were these visions real?

Though I was thrilled to see that the two of them were unharmed, my stomach twisted at the sight of her horns. I didn't give a fuck if she was Seelie or Unseelie, and apparently Torin didn't, either. But the crowd around me wanted blood.

I leaned into Aeron's shoulder and whispered, "Are you sure this is real?"

The stricken look on his face told me he was. He'd gone completely pale, staring at Modron. I sensed he wanted to protect his king and the king's sister, but he didn't want to leave my side, either.

A scarlet current of danger and violence hummed through every stone in the room, making my muscles go tight.

"He's left us for the bloody demons!" someone

screamed. "And we're leaving the throne open for this bastard?"

A dreadful feeling was crawling up my spine. Moria had crafted her speeches for this moment, hadn't she? She'd whipped up the mob into a furor, then showed them the most damning evidence.

Moria's hands went to her cheeks as she stared at the images. "But—this doesn't make sense, does it? Why would our king join the Unseelie?" Her tone sounded more histrionic than Hannah G. on season four of *Hitched and Stitched* when she faked a brain aneurysm to get Cole into her hotel room.

"My sister was once his intended bride," Moria went on, "and no one hated the demons more than she. Torin wouldn't have murdered Milisandia, would he?"

Of course, I'd already heard her beliefs on this topic.

"Modron!" she shouted. "Please, tell us what happened to Milisandia! Please."

It was a performance with all the sophistication of a thirteen-year-old belting out songs in *I'm Really Rosie*, but these people had never sat through bad musical theater, and they didn't know the difference.

"No," Orla shouted. "That's not why we're here."

But Modron wasn't listening to Princess Orla. With a low, rattling sound, Modron breathed another cloud into the air, and the gray mist took shape above the dais. In the fog, a beautiful woman appeared with hair red as blood draped over a white cape. She stood in a ruined temple dusted with snow. A tear ran down her cheek, and her expression looked agonized.

In the gray fog, Torin took shape by her side, his

expression grim. And when he turned sharply away from her, she grabbed his arm. He whirled back to her, his expression horrified. Ice spread from his body to hers, freezing her from the point where their bodies made contact.

Moria screamed, the sound filling the hall.

"It's not what you think!" Orla cried. "It's not what you think!"

She was shouting this over and over, but without explaining any further, which wasn't particularly helpful.

Dizziness swam in my thoughts as I watched what Modron was showing us next—the king himself, burying a body at the Temple of Ostara. Cracking the wintry earth with a shovel.

Moria turned on Orla. "You knew about this, Princess." Her voice dripped with venom. "You knew before I showed it. What else did you know? Are you also in league with the Unseelie rats?"

But all Orla could say was, "I can't speak of it." She staggered back over the dais, looking fragile.

Why wasn't she explaining?

The crowd was screaming at Orla now, their voices hysterical. She stepped back over the dais. A few guards dressed in blue uniforms like Aeron stepped before the princess. But they looked uncertain now, as if maybe they should not be protecting her.

Aeron's body tensed against me, and he leaned in to whisper, "Get out of here, quickly."

Fury flashed in Moria's burgundy eyes. "Torin is the only one in their family who remained un-cursed.

Maybe the Unseelie spared him because they could use him."

This had all unfolded too perfectly for Moria, hadn't it? All the lurid threads had woven before us into the vision she'd wanted us to see.

Maybe Modron was telling the truth, but that didn't mean it was the whole truth. After twenty-four seasons of *Hitched and Stitched*, I knew selective editing when I saw it.

The visions had been curated.

"I never expected to find that our king has betrayed us," Moria shouted, her voice growing wilder. "I never dreamed that he'd murdered my sister to protect the Unseelie."

A clear lie. She'd already accused him of murdering her sister. But who would believe me, the human friend of the "demon whore"?

"Milisandia wanted war with the demons, and he didn't want it." She strode across the dais, adopting a tremble in her voice that, frankly, sounded deranged. "Now he lives with them. With their queen. And this is why we must be vigilant. Who else among us has Unseelie sympathies? Who knows who else among us might be trying to destroy our kingdom from within?"

But I'd read Milisandia's journal, and she hadn't said a thing about the Unseelie. It was all about how beautiful Torin was, and how he couldn't touch her. There'd been a bit about Moria's premonition that he would kill her and bury her body at the Temple of Ostara. Moria had known this would happen even before it did.

My jaw tightened.

I didn't know what Torin and Ava were doing, but I did know Moria was full of shit.

It was only then that I realized the crowd had turned to me, eyes narrowed with suspicion. Aeron slid his arm around me, his hand shifting to the hilt of the sword.

Around me, the crowd chanted Moria's name as Aeron ushered me out of the hall, his powerful arm around me like a shield.

"Hide, Shalini," he whispered. "I need to get you and Orla to safety."

❧ 25 ❧

AVA

I lay on my back, my throat dry as sand.

Who knew why, but Morgant had given up and stopped bringing me food and water several days ago.

Beneath me, the roots were twisted and gnarled, and I closed my eyes, willing them to shift a little. Mentally, I slid into the tree's mind, feeling the glorious heat of sunlight on a fire-kissed crown of leaves. I drank in the power of light that fed the tree. When I was mentally melding with the tree, I no longer felt the thirst.

Below my back, the roots groaned, smoothing out. I stared at the dark branches high above me, wishing that calling forth rain was within my power.

The newest skill I'd developed was hearing vibrations through the roots and mycelium. Now, I could hear the sounds of footfalls through the castle, movements that sent a faint thrumming through the roots, letting me know when a group of guards marched above.

By the markings I'd made in stone, I was fairly certain I'd been locked in this cell for over a month. With every passing day, my magic grew stronger and more controlled. I could summon vines at will, make them slice through the air like blades. I could twist them into a noose. I could compel the tree branches to groan open. When it rained, I could shift them apart for more water.

All day and night, I'd have conversations with Shalini and Torin. Sometimes, they seemed so real that it felt like they were here.

I could almost hear Torin in the cell with me, calling me *changeling*.

My stomach rumbled. The lack of food had me growing lethargic.

Sometimes, I'd slip into dreams where I was home again, in the little suburban house with Mom. When the dreams started, I'd feel a total sense of calm, of being cocooned in love. It was the homecoming I'd been looking for when I'd fallen through the portal and asked to come home. I wanted to watch movies with Mom or sit at the kitchen table with her in comfortable silence while she read the news. But in the dreams, she'd always step into another room. She'd wander into the kitchen to make dinner, and slowly, the feeling of peace would grow ragged and thorny, and my heart would start to race. Slowly, I'd realize she was never coming back, and I'd feel a sharp hole opening in my chest.

The dreams of Torin might have been worse. In those, I'd find myself next to him in Faerie, in the

Temple of Ostara or overlooking the valley with its icy lake. In every one of those dreams, I'd turn to see his beautiful face. Always in these dreams, he had a hint of that vulnerable, unguarded expression I'd seen just briefly in the little cabin, a rare moment when he dropped the king's veneer of power and control.

And then, against my will, my own hand would plunge a dagger into his heart, and I'd scream.

I heard the lock slide open on the door and sat up. I didn't want to look desperate for water, to let Morgant know how happy I was to see him, but it was hard to hide my relief.

Except when I saw him standing in the doorway, I found him empty-handed.

I arched an eyebrow. "I see you're starving me again."

"It was the Queen's order."

"Why?"

A line formed between his brows. "She said that if you don't have magic, you are no good to her."

"Then why are you here?" I asked sharply.

"The queen plans to throw you off the top of the tower."

I rose on shaking legs, staring at him. "She promised to let me go if I killed Torin."

He'd gone completely still, like a beast of prey, and his amber eyes had darkened to a caramel shade. "She will let you go, as promised. But she will throw you from the tower first."

Darkness flickered through me, and Torin's blue

eyes burned in my mind, framed by black lashes. "What did you do with Torin's body?"

If I could figure out how to return to Faerie, maybe I could wrap him in a blanket and return the broken king.

"We've kept him where everyone can see him," said Morgant.

A hot violence coiled through me.

Behind Morgant's head, the thorny vines writhed and snaked over the stone walls.

Morgant's eyes darted as he caught the movement, and his muscles tensed. I didn't give him a moment longer to think.

Love makes us do terrible things...

I flicked my wrist, and the sharp tendrils snapped around his throat, drawing blood. My lip curled back from my teeth as I sent the vines surging upward.

Morgant kicked his legs in the air, and I stepped back. A river of magic flowed into my body, surging from the tree roots upward and washing the fatigue from my limbs.

"Morgant, I plan to make this hurt until you tell me what I want. And if you do tell me the answers I'm looking for, I will let you live. Where is the Sword of Whispers?"

His face had turned beet-red, and his feet slammed against the stones. I flicked my wrist, uncoiling the vines to let him drop on the floor. He fell *hard*, with a crunch. "I learned my interrogation techniques from you, Morgant. Thanks for that." My tone sounded acidic. The vines coiled around his throat again. "How do I get out of the Court of Sorrows?"

He coughed and reached for his bleeding throat. I tightened the noose around his neck again, choking him until his face started to turn purple.

"One more chance, Morgant. How do I get out of this kingdom?"

When the vines loosened enough for him to talk, he said, "The Veiled One, Cala, can tell you. She's here in the castle. The Sword of Whispers is here, too. Everything you want is in the castle. Cala is in the Dusk Tower, to the west." His blood poured onto the ground. "We're not like the Seelie. They live for pleasure. We live for duty. Our strength comes through love."

It was such a startling declaration that I couldn't bring myself to finish the job of directing these plants to rip him in two.

Or maybe it was the small kindness he'd shown me by bringing me a bath and soap.

But that moment's hesitation gave him the chance to rise from the ground, reaching for me, and it happened almost without me realizing I was doing it. The earth began to shake, and stones topped from the walls. The enormous tree that formed half my prison cell was groaning, shifting. The towering cell rumbled around us, and stones tumbled from the walls. Morgant's arms flew over his head, shielding himself.

That was all the time I needed to slip past him and into the castle tunnels, to taste freedom on my lips.

I breathed in deeply, sprinting through the dungeon's corridor.

I hoped I was ready for this because I still felt as though most of my power was entombed by rock, desperate to break free.

Heat and tingles raced down my shoulder blades.

❦ 26 ❦

SHALINI

Ice and snow clung to the trees around the cabin. In the remote forest, everything around me was encased in white. The snow turned the trees into misshapen mounds like frozen ghosts. And the fact that I'd started talking to the frozen ghosts was probably a good indication that I was spending too much time by myself.

In the cabin, I kept imagining that the frozen dead surrounded me. Long icicles hung from the tree boughs like ragged spirits. They glistened in the sunlight, making the boughs bend under their weight, until a frozen gust swept through, sending an icicle crashing to the ground with a hollow thud. Every time that happened, I jumped.

There hadn't been much time to prepare for my trip here. Moria had quickly gone on a rampage, trying to ferret out anyone who might be loyal to Torin. Now, I was stuck here, whether I liked it or not. The only way out of Faerie was with a monarch's permission, and

Queen Moria would sooner execute me than let me leave. Apparently, I was a *demon lover*.

A month ago, Aeron had rushed me to this remote safe house. Orla was kept in a separate location, Cleena in yet another. We were, I think "high profile" targets. Princess Cleena was once Moria's closest friend, but she'd loathed her ever since Moria had tried to slaughter her in the arena. Funny how that can put a real damper on a friendship.

Now, the crackling fire, a single book, and my frozen spirit friends kept me company. The idea that I'd been bored before in early retirement now seemed quaint and ridiculous.

A wild howl carried on the wind, and I hugged myself, shuddering. The mournful cry of the banshee carried on the winter winds.

I swallowed hard. Someone was going to die. And if Cleena didn't gain control of her banshee scream, it could end up being her.

Aeron hadn't said this out loud, but I think we were supposed to know as little as possible about the others in hiding. That way, if any of us were caught, they wouldn't be able to torture answers out of us. Whenever that disturbing thought occurred to me, I'd turn to my frozen spirit friends and ask them to kill me with their icicle hands before I was captured.

Was I losing my mind?

Yes.

The highlight of my day was sitting in front of the fire. Aeron, bless him, had supplied me with an automatic fire lighter, and while I sat in this cabin, he ferried himself among the safe houses, checking on everyone, supplying them with food as best he could. Whenever someone in town would get tarnished with the epithet "demon lover," he'd try to bring them to safety before they were captured.

He wouldn't tell me about the ones he couldn't save, or what he saw going on by the castle, and that told me it was a particularly grim situation. This was, after all, a culture in which people casually said things like, *Oh, Sir Durian, yes, I decapitated his son in a duel*, or *and then we slaughtered the human sacrifices after the party*.

My teeth chattered. At first, when Moria had taken the throne, everyone had assumed that spring would come. That was the entire fucking purpose of having a queen on the throne. We waited for the warmth, for the thaw, but Moria wasn't sitting her cute little ass down on that stone.

The thing was, like any good tyrant, Moria knew that if people were happy and comfortable, she'd lose her grip on power. She needed their rage and fear, or they might start to question her legitimacy. *Hang on a minute, why are you queen...?*

If people were comfortable, they might welcome Torin back again if he returned. They might forget to be angry at the demons, and she needed them desperately united against a common enemy—one only she could defeat.

Only by the constant threat of an attack by the Unseelie could she exert this control, so when people asked her why they were still freezing in their beds and why the cold gnawed at our bones, she still had her scapegoat. The demons were to blame, along with every traitor who might support them.

I turned back to the spluttering fire and knelt, rubbing my hands together and breathing on them for warmth. Aeron had brought me one other amazing treat: he'd managed to smuggle a single book out of the castle library, an eighteenth-century Gothic romance called *The Cursed Monk*. For something written centuries ago, it was surprisingly dirty, and I wondered if the subject matter had been on purpose. Aeron was, after all, something of a monk himself, sworn to chastity. It was hard not to think of some of the dirtier passages in the book as what might happen if he finally let that vow go.

The creak of the door turned my head, and snow swept into the room around Aeron's fur-clad figure. The cold breeze slipping into the room stung my skin, and he turned to close the door. "I brought you back bread and cheese."

My heart swelled at the sight of him, braving the icy temperatures just to make sure I could have a sandwich.

Aeron's expression had become haunted, and I wasn't sure I wanted to know everything he'd seen by the castle.

"You need to be careful, Aeron. How are you getting this food without people seeing you?"

He handed me a paper-wrapped parcel, and I pulled out the frozen block of bread to warm it by the fire.

He sat down next to me on the hearth, stoking the fire with a stick, the dim firelight warming his cheeks. "It's not just me, Shalini. There's a small network of people who don't trust the queen, those loyal to Torin because they loved him. Those who know she could have ended this winter a month ago. A resistance of sorts. People are starving now, and some believe her story that it's all the demons' fault, but she's losing her grip on them. She's not doing what a queen is supposed to do. And the more she's losing her grip, the more she retaliates with force."

I swallowed hard. "What's she doing now?"

He stared into the fire. "She has a dragon called the Sinach, and she's using it to hunt people. Then she burns them. She wants us to think she's a female King Caerleon. He left piles of bodies in his wake."

My stomach dropped. "Oh."

He leaned back, sitting cross-legged before the guttering flames. He looked exhausted, and I wanted to wrap him up and keep him safe here. But it wasn't in his nature to hide out in a cabin while his kingdom was being destroyed.

"This cold," he added, "is starting to feel less like a calculated political strategy and more like revenge. I think she's furious at us. Her sister died, and none of us really cared or noticed. We all thought Milisandia was missing, but we didn't look into it. And then it turns out the king everyone loved so much was at fault."

"You still don't know what happened?"

He shook his head, staring into the flames. "Whatever his reason, I know it was a good one. I know him. Maybe she was as cracked as her sister. I don't know. Maybe it was an accident." He slid his gaze to me. "I know he has sent assassins into the Court of Sorrows to kill Queen Mab and the royal family as revenge for what she did. He had one of Mab's sons killed. I know he's not allied with them. It's hard for me to believe he managed to survive there at all, that Queen Mab didn't have him slaughtered immediately. But I can only imagine she's keeping him alive just long enough to torment him as brutally as possible."

I shuddered. "Well, Modron didn't show us everything, did she? Just what Moria wanted." I warmed my hands by the fire. "If they find their way back to Faerie, could Torin reclaim the throne from her?"

"He doesn't have any magic." He raked a hand through his hair. "Moria has stationed soldiers around his throne, preventing Torin's loyalists from finding a way to fix it. If he returns, he won't have any power to fight with." He turned to look at me, his eyes glinting with firelight. "I don't understand how they ended up in the Court of Sorrows. How well do you know Ava? Do you trust her, even though she's Unseelie?"

"You're all just fae to me." I nudged him. "Are the Seelie really that much better? Because right now, we're cowering in the frozen forest hiding from a queen who wants to light people on fire with her dragon."

He cocked his head. "Fair point."

A sharp longing twisted through my chest. "Aeron, do you know what I would give to take you to a dive bar in my hometown? I was so desperate to get out of there and see Faerie. Ava warned me it wouldn't be all butterflies and rainbows, but I had to see it. Do you know what I would give to just watch a basketball game with

you in a bar? With beer? I don't even like basketball."
My voice held a ragged, hysterical edge.

His features softened. "When this is over, you can
take me to your dive bar."

"Have you ever had a chili dog?"

He stared at me like I'd started speaking in tongues.
"Absolutely not."

"Tuesday nights, they're half-price at the Golden
Shamrock. I don't think I appreciated how exactly
amazing they were until now. A hot dog with chili and
melted cheese..." My mouth was already watering. "I
know people criticize Americans, but who else would
have come up with that genius? It is genius, Aeron." I
think I was shouting.

Outside, a roar like an avalanche rumbled over the
horizon, and when I glanced out the windows, snow was
shaking off the boughs. For a moment, I wondered if I'd
caused it with my loud enthusiasm for chili dogs. But in
the next moment, a dragon's shriek sent a jolt of fear
through my bones.

My heart fell.

I wanted to sneak under the covers and cower—
because let's face it, I had no dragon-fighting skills—but
Aeron gripped me by the elbow.

"We can't stay here. He'll burn the cabin down."
Aeron pulled me toward the door so quickly, I nearly
lost my footing. The moment I was outside, the cold
stung my skin. Luckily, I never took my cloak off.

Outside in the snow, I turned to see the dragon
swooping lower through the skies, its scales gleaming
under the winter sun—stygian black blending to a deep

maroon at the tail, the colors of soot and dried blood. It swooped above us and unleashed a gout of fire that arced into the gray sky. Heat seared the air, and icicles shot from their branches into the snow around us. As the dragon circled, Aeron pulled me north. I ran through the snow, the air smelling of dragon musk and the scent of burning oaks.

I felt as if a serpent had coiled in my chest, stealing my breath.

As Aeron urged me on, the snow melted into the thin leather of my boots and stung my toes. His grip on my wrist was iron tight, and I knew I was slowing him. But my muscles felt leaden, shaking. The panic swallowed me whole until I could no longer understand what Aeron was saying to me.

The dragon swept in an arc above us, then unleashed a stream of fire on the trees to the south. The trunks exploded into flames, a forest blazing like an army of giant torches. A wall of fire erupted before us, cutting off our access.

Aeron swerved and yanked me in the other direction. My body vibrated with fear. Dimly, under the wild panic of my thoughts, I could only hope that Aeron had a plan.

Behind us, the dragon's wings beat the air, and it circled again, fanning the flames with its wings, the sound a thunderous rhythm that blended with the roaring in my ears, drowning out all my thoughts. Snow whirled around us, mingling with cinders.

I was too out of breath to ask where we were going

and if there was a plan at all. Our feet crunched over the snow, and the dragon let out another roar.

And yet, we were still alive. The dragon could have killed us ten times over.

Why did I have the disturbing feeling that it was herding us exactly where it wanted us to go?

27

AVA

I crept through the enormous tunnel, its walls made of mossy blue roots and floors covered with lichen. Curling black vines snaked over the rounded walls with leaves of claret. As I tiptoed over the ground, my heart was a wild beast.

Beneath the castle, my eyes adjusted to the dark, and my heart thrummed in my chest. Shadows flickered around me, dancing across the wooded tunnels like unquiet spirits.

Through the gnarled roots beneath my feet, I felt the vibrations of fae moving somewhere nearby. When I closed my eyes, I could see them: a group of soldiers moving quickly, heading right for me. Of course, the disruption I caused when I freed myself must have alerted the entire palace, though I don't imagine they'd suspect I was choosing to go deeper into the castle itself.

I went still, and the sound of horns blared through the air—the Unseelie alarm.

I scanned the passage around me until I found a large, dark crevice in the indigo tree roots. I nestled back into the oaky fissure and called the boughs and vines to cover me, cloaking me in shadow.

As the sound of footfalls grew closer, I held my breath. Shielded by plants, I watched the group of guards thunder past me, heading for the cell where I'd buried Morgant in stone.

As soon as the soldiers disappeared around a corner, I let the vines slip away. I broke into a sprint, eager to put as much distance between myself and the cell as possible.

When I reached a narrow spiral staircase, I rushed upward. I needed light and windows to orient myself so I could figure out which way was west. But as I climbed, it didn't take long for my muscles to start aching. I was desperately dehydrated, energized only by adrenaline.

On the first floor, the bluish tree bark melded into stone of the same color. From behind a column, I peered out into the hall. Shadows gathered beneath the towering arches of the corridor. People bustled around, moving between columns under the soaring stone vaults. On this floor, diamond-pane windows stretched to the ceiling on my left. Outside, light streamed through the red leaves, staining them with coral and gold. At the far end of the corridor, a distant pinprick of rose gold light angled through the windows.

My delirious brain snagged for a moment, trying to decide whether the sun was rising or setting. But I was pretty sure it was evening now, the light casting the ruddy flush of sunset on the cold floors. So that was west.

Twilight, when the veil between the worlds grew thin and shadows flickered between the living and the dead. Almost, I imagined, I could smell Torin's oaky scent and hear the velvety timbre of his voice.

Loneliness carved open in my chest, the feeling so painful, I nearly lost my balance. I sucked in a deep breath and tried to sharpen my focus.

With the western light pouring in, I knew where I needed to go. But I couldn't get to the far side of the hall with all these people bustling about. The alarms still blared, and most of these people would be hunting for the escaped prisoner.

From my hiding spot in the stairwell, I gripped the stones, scanning the hall for a route to the other side. What I needed was a diversion.

I knelt, pressing my fingertips to the arboreal floor beneath me, and closed my eyes. I envisioned the entire castle, the blue stones that seemed to rise from gnarled roots and the ruby-flecked branches that curled around it protectively, like a mother's embrace. In my mind's eye, I had each of the boughs mapped out. A rush of power thrummed through me as I felt the entire castle in the grip of my magic. I controlled this place now. I breathed with it.

To the north, I envisioned one of those enormous midnight limbs shifting just a little, then smashing through the windows on that side.

The castle floors shook, and the sound of shattering glass echoed through the halls.

My magic vibrated up from the tree and into my body. Distantly, I felt the vibrations of the breaking glass. With the tree's shift, poppy-red leaves rained down outside, and the stone halls filled with the sound of commands barked in the Unseelie language, directing soldiers, I assumed, toward the tumult.

Chaos reigned, which sent a shadowy thrill through me. As anarchy gripped the castle, my own thoughts quieted.

After everything they'd done to Torin and me, a vicious part of me wanted to leave this place in ruins. I wanted to rip the tree free of the stones that burdened her, to bury the queen in a pile of rubble.

But I had to exercise restraint. My work wasn't done here until I had Torin's body.

I slipped back into the stairwell, leaning my head against the cool stones. Shielded in here, I tuned into the castle's vibrations, and my heart started to race at the rhythmic marching that pounded through the stone. The oncoming footfalls of armored guards rushing closer, steel-clad bodies clanging through the halls. My breath caught. If I hesitated too long, I'd be dead.

I knelt once more and brushed my fingertips over the rough bark, letting my mind slip into the tree's world, feeling the life it drew from the rays of the setting sun. With a rush of magic, sap surged through its veins, dripping off its leaves. I drew the boughs closer to me through the southern wall, and they smashed through the nearby tower windows, shattering glass.

When I peered out into the hallway, Mab's soldiers were scrambling, drawing their swords as sap and glass rained down. What did they think they were going to do with their swords, kill the tree? With a curl of my lip, I summoned the tree branches to twine around the soldiers, yanking them out through the shattered windows. Their screams filled the air, along with the coppery scent of blood.

The hall was nearly clear now, but footfalls pounded up the stairs from below, coming right for me. I held my breath, and the tree breathed for me.

With my fingertips touching the floor, I compelled the tree to exhale until the air filled with pure oxygen—enough to make a man's head spin, to make him stagger around like a drunk. When the first Unseelie soldier dragged himself up the stairs, gripping the walls, all it took was one kick to his chest to send the entire troop tumbling backward down the stairwell.

The tree exhaled my breath. Still, I was starting to feel light-headed. When I stood, euphoria clouded my mind.

Steadying myself on the doorframe, I was relieved to see the hallway was still clear. Only a single woman moved in my direction now, a little slip of a thing. She looked pale, terrified. Dressed in a delicate white dress and a flower crown, she stepped gingerly over broken glass and sap, which glittered like garnets in the flaming rays of sun. The world was a bloody and beautiful place, nowhere more so than in the Court of Sorrows.

I stepped back into the stairwell and held my breath, waiting until she was inches from the doorway.

With a flick of my wrist, red-leafed vines curled around her neck and mouth, and I dragged her into the stairwell as she kicked and bucked. A dark survival instinct unfurled within me, and I tightened them a little more around her neck until her eyes closed and her body went limp. I had no idea if I had enough control to suffocate someone while keeping her alive. But when faced with my own death, I'd take the chance on a stranger's. When her muscles went slack, I released the vines and looked down at her with a twinge of guilt.

She looked about forty, delicate of frame, with black hair and tattoos on her cheeks. She could be someone's mom, I supposed. Her chest still rose and fell, soothing my nerves. That was one less thing to keep me up at night if I managed to get out of here. In the stairwell, I undressed, peeling off my filthy prisoner's clothes. With a hammering heart, I pulled on her white dress, then adjusted the flower crown on my head to hide my copper horns. I shoved her unconscious body into the corner of the stairwell and made a half-hearted attempt to cover her with my clothes. I pulled her shoes off, too, and they nearly fit, just a size or two too large.

With my new disguise, I started toward the western end of the castle. Broken glass crunched beneath my stolen shoes. I moved west toward the light, hurrying toward the Tower of Dusk.

It was only a few feet away now—

Someone grabbed me by the hair, yanking me back.

"Here she is," he snarled in my ear. "Queen Mab has been looking for you. She wants to throw you off the tower."

Already, a blade was at my throat, pressing against my skin.

28

AVA

At the mention of Queen Mab, fury slid through me, a rage so hot it made my legs shake, a wrath sharp as thorns that would set me free.

I saw it in my mind as it happened. Behind me, a vine shot through the fae's skull. His muscles went limp, and he slumped to the floor. I whirled to find two more Unseelie standing there, mouths agape. Hardly had the words formed in my mind, hardly did I dare to admit to myself the monster I could become. Flaming violence, hot as a forge, burned all rational thought out of me. My thorny vines carved through the two other fae, severing their heads from their bodies.

Blood spattered around me and on the new white dress.

My body shook. *I am death.*

The first fae I'd killed was unrecognizable, his face destroyed beneath long, silvery antlers. I pulled my gaze from the other two, trying to block out the screams of the soldiers trapped in branches outside.

Shaking, I turned to the stairwell.

What was I capable of?

Maybe the people here in the Court of Sorrows should have asked themselves that before they decided to find out. Maybe they should have considered that before they locked me in a prison and forced me to kill my lover. Maybe all this blood and the screams were *their* fault.

By the time I reached the upper levels of the tower, carnage danced in my thoughts. From the stairwell, the tower room glowed with fiery light.

I stepped through the archway into the Dusk Tower itself, and the light seemed to shift, darkening to periwinkle and violet, streaming through windows.

My breath caught at the sight of three enormous silvery wolves that sat protectively around the figure in the center of the room. A fire burned in a stone pit before her, illuminating the stooped woman and her wolves. A pewter-blue veil covered her face, and it hung down over the silver fabric of her dress. She sat still as stone. The only parts of her that were exposed were her pale, wrinkled hands and the enormous silver antlers that jutted from her head. I had the distinct impression that I was trespassing in a place I didn't quite understand.

One of her wolves lifted his head, narrowing his eyes at me, and let out a low growl. A shiver snaked up my spine.

A flicker of movement caught my attention. There was no glass in the soaring windows, just the open air and the vines that snaked in from the outside. When I took another step into the tower room, the vines twitched.

"Isavell," the woman murmured.

The name lit a spark of recognition in my mind. I'd been called that before. "I need your help. Please. I want to know how to get out of the Court of Sorrows."

"Is that what you call our kingdom?" She spoke without moving, and I had the unnerving sense that her words were coming from inside my skull.

I breathed in sharply, frustration burning like an ember inside me. "Please tell me how to get back to Faerie."

"You will return to Faerie in the Avon River. There, in an abandoned temple to the ash goddess, you will find a mirror hanging from the wall, one that can open a world by naming it. " Little sparks from the fire danced in the air around her. "East of the castle along the river. That is where the temple stands."

I closed my eyes, so relieved I could cry. But an unsettling feeling shivered up my nape. This felt too easy. "Why would you help me escape?"

Her head arched back sharply, and her wolves bristled, baring their canines.

"I only foretell the future," her voice boomed. "And nothing happens in this castle without the queen's consent. Everything occurs as she intends. Your own sense of control is only an illusion." The flames rose higher before her.

I stared at her, and despite the growing fire, a sense of dread chilled me down to my marrow. "So nothing I decide actually matters."

"You have another question for me."

My breath had gone shallow. "Where do I find Torin's body?"

"Do you burn for him? Does he burn for you?"

Not the answer I was looking for. "Where do I find his body?"

"You will find him in the throne room."

"They left him there? Why?"

"I foretell the future, not the past," she hissed. "That is where you will find him. And her soldiers come for you now. If you do not leave at this very moment, they will capture you. And if you don't eat or drink soon, you will die."

My lip curled. "I thought it didn't matter what I did because the queen controls everything."

"She will throw you off the tower."

My heart skipped a beat. I felt the vibrations moving through the stairwell, the clanking of armored guards hurrying up the winding stones.

My gaze flicked to the open window, where the vines hung inside, clinging to the stones. When I held out my hands, the indigo vines unfurled, snapping around my wrists. They lifted me into the air. I landed against the wall with bent legs to cushion the impact and crawled out the window onto the side of the tower. The night wind rushed over me, whipping my hair into my face. Protectively, the plants slid around my waist, a harness of claret leaves.

Under the darkening night sky, I crawled down the tower's exterior until I reached the floor beneath it, then lower to the third floor.

My thoughts snagged on what the crone had said—that ultimately, Queen Mab was in control of everything happening here. But what was I supposed to do with that knowledge? And who knew if it was even accurate? All I could do was keep moving forward.

I moved east across the castle's surface, avoiding the windows.

When I glanced down at the earth far below, my heart skipped a beat. Holy *shit*, I was high up. Dizziness blurred my thoughts. The old crone had been right. If I didn't get water soon, this would all be over.

Midnight vines carried me across the castle's face, moving me lower toward the floor with the shattered windows. Beneath me, some of the armored guards still dangled from the wreckage.

They kicked in the air, flailing and screaming. I aimed for an opening as far as possible from the trapped soldiers. The vines lowered me down, then lifted me in through the shattered window. My shoes crunched on the glass, and I broke into a run.

I stumbled through the halls toward the throne room with a rising sense of dread spreading through me like poison.

Because—gods, I wasn't sure if I wanted to do it. I wasn't sure if I could handle seeing him dead. The horror of it all might shatter what was left of my fragmented mind, and I was already turning into a monster.

And yet...there was that feeling again, that his presence was here, the raw, masculine power of the Seelie king. I kept thinking I could smell him, that I couldn't leave here without him...

My nostrils flared as the scent was gone again, replaced by a sharp sense of loss.

And something else now, a sharpness in my belly. The scent of cooking vegetables and the pungent smell of coal curled through the vaulted corridors. When I breathed in, I smelled food. Something else, too. Burning coal, melting steel. But it was the food I needed.

As I rounded a corner, moonlight slanted in through shattered windows. Flame-colored plants climbed cobalt walls, and a few burning cinders floated through the air. My legs were shaking uncontrollably. The crone had been right. I was absolutely desperate for water, and I wasn't sure I could make it through the rest of this castle without it. I'd never make it back to Faerie with Torin's body unless I drank. If only I could feast off light itself as the tree did.

I followed the scent of food until I arrived at a kitchen. It was the size of the throne room, and I peered around the corner. I spotted a great hearth, eight feet high and made of the same bluish stones. A black metal pot bubbled in the center of the hearth, a cauldron of sorts that emitted the most delicious scent. I didn't feel a normal sense of hunger anymore, but rather an incandescent survival instinct that screamed at me. I would collapse soon without food and water.

Unfortunately, though the rest of the castle had emptied out, the kitchen was bustling with servants, all of them dressed in aprons and white caps. Cooks were chopping vegetables, hurrying around with sacks of flour. My gaze snagged on a pile of carrots that I very much wanted to snatch, but a large man with a wheel-barrow was ambling closer to me.

I darted back into the hallway and waited until he emerged, pulling the wheelbarrow behind him.

He froze as his eyes took in the bloodstains on my dress, but thorny blue tendrils were already around his throat, silencing him. His wheelbarrow slammed to the ground, and I snatched a steaming piece of bread, so hot it burned my fingers. With my other free hand, I grabbed a pitcher of water from inside the doorway, and I was off again, searching for a quiet place to eat and drink, clinging to my new treasure like some kind of raggedy scavenger bird. Behind me, the vines slid together across the hall, shielding me.

I didn't stop moving until I found an open archway in what looked like an empty temple. Near the entrance, I found a dark alcove overgrown with plant life. I nestled down in the corner and peered out into the temple to make sure no one was around.

On the far side of the flagstones stood an altar with a fireplace in the center, flanked by columns. A temple to the ash goddess, maybe, spitting burning cinders into the air. Gleaming swords jutted from the arched rock above the flames. From the smoldering forge, smoke curled.

Tucked in my corner, I put the pitcher to my lips, drinking the water deeply. My muscles unclenched as I slaked my thirst. Never before in the history of water had anything tasted so amazing. Water dripped from the corners of my mouth as I chugged it.

Only after drinking half of it did I realize it wasn't in

fact water, but ambrosia. I ran my tongue over my lips, savoring the sweet flavor. Shit. I could easily down the whole thing, but it would make me drunk, fast. My body already hummed with the seductive magic of its effects, the air around me seeming to caress my skin and the delicate silk of the dress.

I forced myself to stop drinking the ambrosia and bit into the hot bread, closing my eyes at the rich flavors. After a few bites, I slowed down so I didn't make myself sick.

I inhaled deeply, breathing in the scent of burning oak and charcoal. Embers wafted through the air in burning motes. The ambrosia was making me feel at one with everything around me, the castle itself formed from the earth, with the hot metallic scent of melting steel. The words *Love is a forge* formed in my mind like a red-hot beacon.

It was time to find Torin again, and the euphoria of this ambrosia might help steel me mentally for the shock of seeing his corpse.

But as I chewed, I felt the subtle vibrations through the floor, the echo of footfalls through the hall. From the shadows, I held my breath, watching as a woman draped in gray crossed into the temple. I kept out of view for a moment, then turned to see her stoking the flames on the altar's forge. I peered out to see her bathed in rosy light, the sword hilts above her illuminated with dancing orange hues.

She reached for a piece of steel, heating it in the fire, and grabbed a hammer to start shaping it. The sound of clanging metal echoed around me. But my thoughts turned back to the sword hilts above her, and it took me another moment to realize why.

My heart raced at the sight of one particular sword, one with an obsidian hilt. The Sword of Whispers belonged to the Seelie king, and I wasn't leaving here without it.

In moments, my vines snaked around the priestess, wrapping about her neck and putting her to sleep. I dropped my bread and gingerly stepped over her body.

I had to climb on the altar, heat searing my skin, to reach the sword. The hilt was hot to the touch, but not enough to burn me.

When I gripped it, I heard the voices of gods whispering around me, and the rich voice of Torin booming through the corridors.

My heart skipped a beat.

Was I losing my mind, or was that actually his deep voice echoing from the hall where I'd killed him?

I broke into a run.

❦ 29 ❦

SHALINI

The frozen air stung my throat, and my lungs felt seared with ice. A small part of me thought that I should yell at Aeron and tell him to go on ahead of me, but even if I could muster the courage to do that, I didn't have the breath to shout.

I stole a quick glance behind. The dragon circled overhead, herding us toward the castle. Every time we tried to veer off course, the fucking monster would light up the path with incinerating heat. The world around me was half glacier, half firestorm.

Aeron turned to me, and I'd never seen him look scared before. His eyes were open wide, his face pale. He wrapped his arms around me protectively.

"We can't go any further, love," he said through ragged breaths. "That thing is trying to force us back to Moria. Maybe she wants a trial."

I clung to him, my heart thundering like a stampede. I didn't think there was any way out of this. Aeron's use of "trial" seemed like a euphemism—one last act of kindness from him to keep hope alive until my last breath.

But we both knew that Moria didn't plan to let us live.

A roar rumbled over the horizon, and the dragon swooped overhead, unleashing a firestorm behind us, the heat scorching the air. With a snarl, Aeron grabbed my arm again and pulled me along with the frantic desperation of a dying man.

My toes stung in the icy snow.

What the fuck was my life right now?

I could hardly piece together a coherent thought, just panicked, fragmented wisps about how it was better to take our chances with an evil queen's justice in the future than to burn alive. Could there be a worse death than burning alive? I had a disturbing feeling I was going to find out here in Faerie. The world smoldered behind us. In front of us, it gleamed with ice.

The dragon's fire forced us closer to the castle, and smoke clouded the air around us, making me cough. Ashes mingled with snow, and the sharp-towered castle came into view, along with a legion of soldiers in silver armor. White sunlight gleamed off them as they marched forward, the intensity nearly blinding.

My thoughts went quiet.

I couldn't breathe anymore, the smoke stinging my lungs, the forest smoldering behind us. My brain teetered on the knife-edge between panic and survival, and panic was winning, making my limbs heavy. As I slowed, Aeron lost his grip on my arm.

I don't know if it was exhaustion or fear, but my body simply wouldn't move anymore, my muscles locking.

I slammed to my knees in the snow. Aeron whirled, gripping me around the ribs, like he was going to carry me to safety. And as much as I loved him for it, I knew we had nowhere left to run.

"I'm sorry!" I shouted at Aeron.

Guilt pierced me. If I hadn't been here, Aeron would have found a way out.

Shouts rang out as the silver-clad soldiers descended on us and ripped Aeron away from me. His panicked eyes were locked on me as I felt the boot on my back and found myself facedown in the snow. Rough hands captured my wrists in freezing iron shackles, then clamped one around my throat.

When the soldier yanked me up again, I felt as if my arms would be pulled from their sockets.

I shivered wildly, trudging on through the snow. The soldiers led us to the castle. And as we got closer, a sharp tendril of horror wound through my chest.

Cages hung from the castle walls on long iron chains. In one of them, I glimpsed the pale, shivering figure of Princess Orla. She must be freezing to death.

I stared at her, my eyes stinging. I wondered if she'd been screaming, and when she'd stopped.

The other cages? I had a horrified feeling that they were empty, waiting for us.

30

TORIN

The queen had made me a throne of sorts of thick, barbed foliage and blood-hued leaves that bound me to a stone.

And today, anarchy reigned in the Court of Sorrows. From my spiky little throne, I'd listened to the sounds of shouting and screaming. Breaking glass. I felt the acrid miasma of panic sweep through the castle. I smelled blood on the air.

I had no idea what was happening, but I liked it.

I flexed my biceps and forearms, trying to weaken the plants. The queen's dark tendrils came alive at her command and ripped my skin whenever I tried to break free.

Propelled by sheer rage and determination, I'd ripped through them four times so far, trying to get to Ava. Each time, the fucking things would score my flesh with bloody lacerations. And each time, I'd be captured again within minutes, strangled with spiked ropes of plants, and dragged back to the throne. The vines were everywhere, dark as bruises flecked with red. And the queen controlled them all, living nooses that sprawled around me. I'd grown to loathe the sight of them.

With every successful escape, the number of soldiers standing guard grew. Now, there must be around thirty of them, staring at me, fingers twitching at the hilts of their swords. Even as chaos ripped apart the castle, the soldiers stood guard, trapping me here.

Still, I was certain I'd break free again.

It had been worth it every time. In brief moments of escape, I'd managed to kill thirteen of her soldiers, and in my most bored moments, I would fondly remember their deaths. In fact, the highlight of the past month had been the one moment when I'd managed to steal one of their swords. For several glorious heart-beats, I'd felt like a god again. I'd felt alive, like I once more held the Sword of Whispers. Euphoric, I'd carved through the heads and bodies of seven of her soldiers, slaughtering as many as I could, until the winged maniac queen had returned with her prison of vines.

I had no idea why the fuck I was still alive. Initially, sure, I'd understood. She'd commanded her idiot son Morgant to heal me, and she'd set me up here like a broken statue, a triumphant display of her conquered Seelie king.

But how many weeks had passed now? Surely six?

Bruises covered my arms, and the queen's scarlet-flecked vines scored my skin. Bizarrely, the queen had left the stains on the floor where Ava's sword had pierced my heart, a burgundy smear across the moss and stone. It was all part of her pageantry, a display of power.

But what had they done with Ava?

She'd promised that if Ava killed me, they would let her go. That had been her oath. That had been the entire reason I'd thrown myself in front of Ava's sword, so she could return to her normal life as if she'd never met me. As if I'd never dragged her from the safe world of the humans into the brutal and bloody world of the fae.

But as the days wore on, I started to doubt Mab's word. Somehow, I could sense Ava's presence still here, a breath of life in a barren world.

Sometimes, I imagined I could hear her, smell her. Right now, I felt her presence moving closer.

Mere fancy? Perhaps, but I shouted, "I'm here!"

But where the fuck was the queen as someone smashed and shattered their way through her home? Because she controlled every little thing that happened here.

My heart started to race, and I ripped at the plants, not caring that they were shredding my skin. But the soldiers were not looking at me, and not a single one of them noticed. They drew their swords and stared down at their own feet.

And while they were distracted, it was the best possible moment to kill as many of them as I could.

I must be delirious, though. Because now I could have sworn that I heard the Sword of Whispers speaking to me from the other side of the hall.

❧ 31 ❧

AVA

From a leafy alcove, hidden from view, I peered into the hall. Queen Mab had a small army guarding his body, at least two dozen.

I could easily hang each one of them, except my magic was no longer working.

Shielded from view, I'd been trying to gain control of the dark, purplish vines that hung from every column and wall in the great hall. But it was as if another, sinister mind already controlled them. When I tried to seep into the consciousness of the plants, I felt a dark and unsettling power already there, a feeling that set my teeth on edge.

But I supposed I didn't have to stick to the easy plants. Every stone here was alive with the magic of the forest, with the power of the life-giving tree. And maybe there was another, less obvious way to get these soldiers out of my way.

I glanced down at the flagstones, my gaze landing on the tiny sprigs of weeds growing between the cracks,

fragile, with delicate leaves. I compelled them to grow
—taller, larger, winding around the feet of the soldiers.
They slithered upward like hands rising from a grave,
grasping to drag the living beneath the soil with the
dead.

My gaze moved to a man with long silver hair. His
white wings beat the air wildly. My weeds crawled up
him, a tourniquet of roots, and pulled him to the floor,
trapping him. They slipped around his belly, his ribs,
and his wings, restraining them. The fallen soldier called
out for his queen.

Swords clanged to the ground as the weeds
dragged soldiers to their knees. Every time they
hacked through a plant with their swords, another
would grow in its place, a cocoon of vegetation wrapping around their thighs, pulling their swords from
their hands.

My concentration was broken by an attack on one
of them, hands that gripped a soldier's skull, snapping
his neck with a sickening crack.

As the soldier fell to the ground, my gaze lifted to
the face of the most beautiful fae I'd ever seen, and the
world went still.

It was Torin, moving and breathing, looking for all
the world like a god of vengeance with his blazing blue
eyes and battle-battered body. Ribbons of blood
streaked his arms and his torn white shirt. My heart
clenched tightly.

Was I drunk on ambrosia?

For a moment, I couldn't move. From the shadows, I
stood immobile, hardly breathing, while he wreaked his

vengeance on Mab's soldiers. Molten heat cracked through the ice beneath my ribs.

Dimly, I was aware that I was shouting his name as I burst free from my hiding spot, gripping his sword. And as I ran toward him, Torin turned to see me, and our gazes met.

The smile on his lips was heartbreaking in its beauty. With his deep blue eyes locked on mine, he staggered back, away from the soldiers trapped by my weeds. My blood throbbed in my veins, pounding in my head. I leaped over the soldiers, slamming into Torin's iron chest.

Gently, he pulled his sword from my hand, then wrapped his arms around me, holding me tightly. I pressed against his blood-soaked chest, feeling the thunder of his heart under the thin white material of his shirt. I slid my hand up, feeling that beautiful heartbeat, his warmth.

His voice rumbled through his chest. "Ava. I've been looking for you."

"Morgant healed you." It came out as hardly a cracked whisper. There were, of course, a million other things I wanted to say, the powers I'd developed and the havoc I'd wreaked. The plan to get out of this place, to find the mirror in the abandoned temple. But my thoughts were a wild tangle of words that I couldn't quite unravel, not when I was lost in the euphoria of his perfect, living scent. The feel of his body against mine made the rest of the world melt away, his muscles moving against me as he tightened his arms around me.

He kissed the top of my head. "I've been trying to get to you."

I was clinging to him as tightly as the tree branches around the castle walls. He seemed so amazingly tangible and concrete, and I never wanted to pull my arms from him.

And even as I melted into him, a dreadful thought slithered its way into my mind...

Why did the queen want him alive? Why order Morgant to heal him?

Grim ice crept over my heart. *Nothing happens here without the queen's consent...*

As if hearing my thoughts, Torin's muscles went rigid, and he pulled away from me, his gaze flicking over my shoulder.

He held out his hand to me protectively in a signal to stay back.

Did I need protecting now? I'd left a trail of gore in my wake.

Slowly, I turned to see the queen.

On the other side of the trapped soldiers, Queen Mab waltzed through the hall. A crown of ivy and jewels rested on her head, and her white hair draped over a fur cape. She arched an eyebrow as she looked down at the weeds that trapped her blue-uniformed soldiers.

"I see you didn't let Ava go, as you promised." A quiet threat laced Torin's voice.

The queen stopped walking just on the other side of the line of soldiers. "I didn't say *when* I would let her go. Or whether or not I'd throw her off the tower first. And I believe I made another promise, didn't I? That if you went to see the Lost Unseelie the night before the tournament, there would be consequences."

My gaze flicked up to the vines above her, but I couldn't entwine my magic with their life force, not when another magic already possessed them.

"You see, Lost One?" She radiated light. "You're not the only one who can control the vegetation around us." Mab smiled, her teeth white as bleached bones. "Of course I wouldn't kill Torin swiftly. I did mention castrating him, I believe, and slowly crushing what remains of him in a tree? Isavell, do you know what he did to my son?"

I swallowed hard. This wasn't a question I wanted to answer, but Torin did.

"I never sent my assassins after your sons. I sent them to kill you."

"My sons would give their lives to protect me, and I them. That is the burden of love, I suppose. But you haven't known the exquisite pain of losing a child. You've never known the pain of feeling another's death like it was worse than your own. I've done it twice."

She started to step gingerly closer to her trapped soldiers, and as she did, one of the thick, purplish vines from the walls shot out, straining for Torin's sword.

He swung his blade through it, then the next, and the next. A new horror was dawning in my mind. The queen's magic mirrored my own.

But I didn't have time to dwell on this connection between us because she was sending her thorny weapons after me now. Torin pivoted, and the Sword of Whispers hacked through them, one by one. He wouldn't be able to keep up this relentless attack forever.

I still felt as if frostbitten stones encased an infernal power in my chest. If only I could unleash a torrent of power, I could wrest control from her.

I took a step back from Torin, trying to think clearly with my heart slamming against my ribs.

In almost every living thing around me, I felt the stain of her poisonous magic. It tinged the living fibers, except those strong, thorny weeds wrapped around the soldiers. Mentally, I still controlled them, and I could compel them to stretch toward her. Long, grasping hands that reached for the queen.

She sauntered further into the hall, turning back to look at us. "Oh, I'm afraid that isn't enough. But Isavell? I wanted to tell you about what his parents did. They promised our families would meet. They promised we'd trade between kingdoms, after all these years. That we'd share magic and food, unite against the growing threat of mortals. And I never assumed a fae royal would lie. *We* don't lie here. But it was an ambush. When I saw them bring in the severed bull's head, I knew I'd been betrayed. They demanded that I lift the curse of frost. Except it wasn't the Unseelie who cursed them, was it?" Her voice grew louder. The smile faded from her face, and fury contorted her features. "The Unseelie aren't responsible for the frost in Faerie," she roared. "That is your own fault, Torin."

Her fury was like a toxic fog in the room, making my legs shake. A wrath that could be matched only by my own.

I cocked my head, tuning out the noise and the chaos around me, until all I felt was the flagstones beneath my feet and the phantom breeze rustling the leaves of my weeds.

I closed my eyes and commanded them to grow, to burst from the cracks. A raw, primal power tumbled from my body, magic so ferocious that it sent molten cracks racing through the ice in my chest. Beneath me, the stone floor itself burst open with the force of the unfurling plants. The weeds ripped through the flagstones, tearing through the floor beneath our feet.

I felt myself plunging, stones and dust raining around me, until I landed hard on the wooded floor below. Beneath my back, the gnarled roots of the tree pressed against my spine, and above me, steely muscles wrapped in a ripped and blood-soaked shirt. Torin arched his body, covering me like a shield, taking the brunt of the falling stones that tumbled around us. Enormous, sinuous plants surrounded us.

Warmth streamed through the dust, which covered his dark hair, his eyebrows, his eyelashes. When I looked over his shoulder, I could see the hole my plants had ripped in the floor, at least twenty feet across.

The queen and I agreed on one thing: we would give everything we had to protect those we loved.

I reached up to touch the side of his face for a moment, and the corner of his mouth curled in a faint smile.

But this was our chance to escape. Torin reached past me, grabbed hold of the sword nearby, and pulled me up from the floor. Around us, soldiers were starting to shift and push off the fallen stones.

Torin started to run in one direction, but I grabbed his hand to still him for just a moment.

I quickly surveyed the network of oaky tunnels around us. Through the tree's living network, I knew which tunnel led to a moonlit night.

"This way," I whispered, breaking into a jog. The dusty air clouded my lungs. Down here, shadows devoured the dark tunnel.

"Was that you?" Torin asked quietly. "Controlling those plants?"

My breath was ragged in my throat, but I tried to answer anyway. "It seems I have magic after all."

We let the unspoken question hang in the air, the one about my magic being disturbingly similar to Queen Mab's.

If we got close enough to the exterior walls, I could try to shift the enormous roots around, making an opening for us, though it wouldn't be the subtlest way to escape.

"Why did you jump in front of my sword?" I asked sharply.

"She promised to let you go."

"She doesn't lie, but that doesn't make her trustworthy, does it? She has workarounds."

"Ava." His deep voice rose just a little too loud. "We didn't have many options."

He was, of course, right, but I found that I still carried a hot flame of anger for him. As though he'd abandoned me out of malice and not to save my life.

The hollow, lonely part of me didn't seem to know or care about the difference, only that I'd been left behind.

"Torin, I think I can get us out of here. I found Cala, the Veiled One. There's an abandoned temple to the ash goddess by the river. East of the castle, she said. There's a mirror in there, and it can take you wherever you want."

The words were tumbling out of my mouth now, and I knew the effort to speak was costing me speed, but I had to tell him anyway. For some reason, if I didn't make it out of the Court of Sorrows alive, maybe he could make it home.

"They love the ash goddess here," he muttered. "Love is a forge," he said in a mocking tone.

As soon as the words were out of his mouth, he looked behind us.

He lifted a finger to his lips, and I felt it—the vibrations of the soldiers running for us. I whipped my gaze back over my shoulder, and my stomach twisted at the sight of torches bobbing in the air, running for us at a speed I could no longer match. Months in captivity hadn't exactly made me strong.

But what I did have was the power to hide.

I grabbed Torin by the arm and pulled him into a crevice behind me, an opening formed from several large roots intertwined. With my magic skimming over my skin, I widened the gap in the roots, forming an archway large enough for both of us.

I pushed Torin into it, catching a surprised glint in his eye. Then I backed against him and summoned a curtain of vines to hide us. Torin's hand slid around my waist, a powerful forearm around my abs, his fingers just above one of my hipbones. This close to him, I could feel his muscles flexing with tension behind me. Clearly, some of that ambrosia was still pounding hot in my veins, because Torin's closeness was wildly distracting, and his earthy scent wrapped around me like a caress. Through the fabric of his shirt, his heart beat against my back. As the soldiers ran closer, I let my head rest back against him, just in the crook of his neck.

He lowered his head a little, as if to whisper something, but the soldiers were close, and he didn't say a thing. Still, his breath warmed the side of my face like sunlight on the tree's canopy. When his thumb swept over my hip in a slow, absent caress, I closed my eyes and melted into him.

Bloody hell. How could he be so sexy at a time like this? I never wanted to let him go, never wanted an inch of space between us again.

I had to let him go, though. When he returned to Faerie and found a new wife—

An icy crack spread over the embers in my chest.

Best not to think about that now.

Best to simply think about trying to live. Best to think about getting out of the Court of Sorrows with our bodies and our minds intact.

When the soldiers' footfalls went quiet, I felt Torin's muscles flexing behind me. He leaned down and whispered, "I missed you, changeling."

"I'm going to get you out of here, Torin," I whispered back.

"Are you saving me?" A hint of amusement laced his deep tone.

The thing was, yes, I was saving him.

I pushed out past the veil of vines and led Torin into the dark corridor.

We walked for a few more minutes until I could feel the tree's roots bathed in moonlight. Freedom lay just on the other side of these roots.

"Here," I whispered to Torin. "Watch for falling debris."

My body buzzed from ambrosia as I brushed my fingertips over the gnarled roots. With my hand against the bark, I felt the wind rushing through the leaves of its boughs.

The world around us rumbled, and soil and dust shook from the ceiling until the roots shifted and parted, and a vault of stars spread out in the world outside.

As soon as a large enough gap opened in the roots, Torin grabbed my hand, and we ran out into the night. I breathed in the fresh, sultry air of the Court of Shadows.

Euphoria and Torin's blinding smile lit me up.

Out here, the air rushed over my skin. We only had to get to the river, to find the ruined temple.

My gaze landed on the paddock, where the horses stood, still and calm under the moonlight, oblivious to the chaos in the castle.

In the distance, a red glow lit the sky, a spark of ruby against shadows. It took me a moment to understand.

The volcano was erupting. Tonight, the goddess of ash was alive with fury.

We made it about twenty feet in the grass before I heard the groan of the tree shifting behind me. My stomach flipped.

With rising dread, I turned to see the queen's dark vines snaking out from the stone walls.

The breath left my lungs.

I had only enough time to call out a brief warning to Torin before the vines wrapped around my waist, tight as a noose, and yanked me off the ground and into the sky.

❧ 32 ❧

SHALINI

I stood before the stage in a hall I'd never seen
before, listening to the murmurs of the crowd
around me.

My teeth chattered uncontrollably. It didn't feel
much warmer in here than it was outside, and cold iron
bound my wrists behind my back. I glanced to my left,
my chest clenching when I saw Aeron. His blond hair
hung before his bowed head, and he wasn't even looking
at me now.

Behind me, a row of armored soldiers gripped
swords. Above them, grotesque figures of giants were
carved in the stone over the hall entrance. Between the
giants stood scales of justice. Because that would be
today's performance, right? Inspired by the aesthetics of
justice. Just not the actual concept of justice, I was sure.

This place was called the Guild Hall, and I was
pretty sure that its soaring ceilings were designed to
intimidate, along with everything else in its design.
Aeron had told me that the Guild Hall was where the

city guilds met to discuss their business, but it was also where important trials were conducted—such as treason trials.

A blood-red carpet stretched from the back of the hall to the stage. Narrow stained glass windows stretched to the ceiling, and chandeliers cast wavering light over the people crammed into the hall to watch us condemned—and we all knew the outcome already. This didn't end with me walking free and bringing Aeron back to a dive bar.

Aeron met my gaze, and a muscle twitched in his jaw. "We'll get out of this," he said quietly.

He was being kind, and I nodded, pretending to believe him.

The only way I could stay sane right now was to vividly imagine my little apartment at home and the Golden Shamrock. In this situation, my world of fantasy was not the fairytale world. It was a beer-stained bar with mediocre nachos. That was my heaven. And I would keep that comforting world alive in my mind as long as I could.

When Moria crossed onto the stage, her dress trailing over the red carpet, I knew we were in for another show. Her burgundy hair tumbled over a snow-white cape, and her crown gleamed on her head like icicles.

"It pains me," she began, "that we must continue to burn out the scourge of treason from our kingdom. But we are still starving, still freezing here in Faerie. Because even with a queen, my magic cannot compete with the curses that the Unseelie and their allies hurl at us. Here, in Faerie, the Unseelie have wicked agents doing their bidding. Consorting with Torin after his betrayal." She strode across the stage like Lady Macbeth, gripping her stomach, as though it weren't a load of absolute bullshit.

She whirled dramatically to face us, and I wondered how, exactly, the legal system worked in Faerie. It didn't seem we were going to be afforded the courtesy of legal representation.

As she droned on about treason and secret demon spies, Aeron lifted his head. His jaw tensed, and ferocity gleamed in his eyes.

"Everything she's saying is a lie," he snarled. "King Torin has not betrayed us. You have betrayed us by refusing to sit on the throne." He glanced at me, his eyes burning. "I have been with Shalini for weeks. She's no more a spy than I am a princess."

My heart swelled at his attempt to defend me, but I knew there was no point. Aeron's defense was cut short when soldiers yanked him by the arms and dragged him out.

Panic gnawed at my ribs. I called his name as he was taken from the hall. A hand was clamped hard over my mouth, and I was forced to look at the queen. I struggled against my attacker, my arms burning with the strain of having them wrenched behind my back.

Queen Moria's lips were a thin red line. "Are you quite finished with your little temper tantrum?" she asked. She lifted her eyes to the ceiling, and her maroon irises glistened. "When I was a child, if I did anything naughty, my father, king of the Dearg Due, would give me time to think about what I'd done, time spent outside the castle in a small cage. There, under the taunting gaze of the peasants, and in the freezing cold of winter, I learned the value of obedience." Her gaze roamed the crowd again, her eyes gleaming. "He wanted me to be strong, like King Caerleon in the old days, the strongest leader of the Seelie. And while I was out there, growing strong, only my older sister would come to help. She secretly fed me and brought me water. She brought me a cloth to wash with to try to preserve some of my dignity. And where did that kindness, that softness, get her? The king buried her under the frozen earth."

She turned to face us again, and tears streaked down her cheeks. For the first time, I thought her display of emotion was actually real. "In this world," she went on, "women cannot be weak. People expect us to be soft and pliable, and when we are, they crush us in their fingers, like a child mashing a flower. That is why an Iron Queen stands before you, as strong and as ruthless as a king." She raised her fist, and her cheeks went pink.

"Only I can protect you from the demons who want to harm you. Only I can protect you from the demons who want to starve your children. Only I have the mettle and the strength of spirit to do what is required, even if what is required is ugly. Only I am willing to do the dirty work because I know what happens when women are weak," she shouted. "I learned that from my sister." She turned, pacing across the dais. "She was the only person I've ever trusted, ever loved. And all of you forgot she existed."

Her voice echoed off the frozen arches high above us, and she seemed to realize she was going off script. She turned back to us, her eyes wild. "I wasn't able to protect her from King Torin and his wicked ways, but I will protect you. I will not make the same mistake again."

I could feel it around me--the energy of the crowd that drank up every word she said. Every eye I caught seethed with hatred.

I bit the finger that clamped over my mouth. I needed at least a minute to defend myself, to explain, to try to convince them that Aeron and I had nothing to do with the kingdom freezing.

Soldiers took me away, and I screamed at the crowd that Moria could sit on the throne and end all of this. She could bring the spring. She had that power. But no one was listening to me, and the soldiers dragged me outside more roughly than they had before. My mind swam with panic, and I could hardly breathe.

The mob was shoving me, jostling me from side to side, and I wondered if I would even make it outside to the cages, or if they were about to beat me to death right here on the stone floor, but the soldiers closed in around me. I was grateful for their temporary protection, even though I knew they were only keeping me alive long enough to hang me in an icy cage so I could die in public, a warning to others.

My fear rose to a roar in my mind until I felt myself almost separating from my body. I felt it as if it were happening from a distance to someone else—a poor woman shoved through the halls, outside into the icy air. A little broken doll pushed into an icy cage. I knew she could feel the stinging cold on her skin, but I didn't feel it myself. Distantly, I heard the sound of chains scraping against stone as they raised the cage up the dark castle walls. Here, she would freeze as a warning to others, a message to keep the kingdom in line.

Only when the chains stopped moving against the stones did I slam back into my own mind again, cold horror stealing my breath. A biting wind whipped over me, tearing at my hair.

A fae could survive out here for maybe a week or two, but a human like me? I didn't think I had long at all.

At least they'd taken the handcuffs off, and I folded into my cloak as much as I could, trying to protect my face and hands under the thick wool.

From a cage above me, I could hear Aeron screaming my name.

AVA

The queen held me aloft in thorny coils, my feet dangling inches above the castle's stones. With her powerful magic, she'd tightened them around me, binding my arms to my chest. Fear raked its claws through me. The queen's power was stronger than mine, and I wasn't sure we'd ever get free of this place. Panic pressed against my ribs.

I whipped my head around, looking for Torin, but I saw no signs of him.

Washed in silver, Queen Mab looked victorious. Her son, Morgant, stood behind her, his muscles and clothes shredded by my prickly vines, blood streaking down his body. His dark wings hung still behind him, and he held Torin's sword. His amber eyes locked on me, his chin lowered.

The night wind toyed with the queen's hair as I struggled against her cage of brambles. My breath heaved in my lungs as the queen prowled closer.

"I was trying to tell you something, Isavell, but you

ripped the floor out from under us."

"That's my name, then, is it?"

As she drew near, I could see that she wasn't feeling quite as victorious as I'd first thought. She held her chin high and her back straight, but her mouth was tight with tension. And close up, I could see the tightness of her hunched shoulders.

The queen was scared. But what was she afraid of? My gaze flicked to Morgant, and I read in him the same rigid posture, fists clenched and veins popping on his forearms.

"Before I throw you from the tower, you must know what happened." Her voice faltered a little. Was she scared of me?

The corner of her mouth twitched. "We were supposed to bring our families and discuss a future alliance. Torin's mother proposed an engagement between our heirs. I'd always wanted my Unseelie heirs on the throne of Faerie. Of course, I accepted," she said sharply, like I was reprimanding her for her decision. "But then they asked me to remove the frostbitten curse from the kingdom." She bared her teeth. "It wasn't my curse to remove. That was Modron, the one who looks back. She's the one who loathes the Seelie."

"What are you talking about?"

"No one wanted her around," Queen Mab said, ignoring my question. "Can you blame them? The woman was a poison, spilling everyone's secrets. Long ago, the king banished her from court, and she unleashed the frozen mantle of winter on the kingdom. She sent the Erlkings and the dragons from her home in the woods to torment the Seelie. They must kill her to lift the curse. It has nothing to do with me."

I clenched my teeth, scanning the shadow-drenched battlements for signs of Torin. "Why are you telling me all this?"

"At the banquet, the Seelie queen had taken my child, pretending to fuss over her," she hissed. "The queen passed her to a nursemaid to hold. Someone brought out the severed head of a black bull. A barbaric threat, isn't it? I tried to run for my daughter, but the Seelie king froze me in ice, and I watched as the nurse-maid murdered my heir before me. Smashing her against the rocks. So when I cursed the Seelie royal family, believe me, they bloody deserved it."

I stared at her, no longer understanding at all. "They killed your daughter?"

She raised an eyebrow. "Apparently, the nursemaid was a master of illusion. Maybe she couldn't stomach the orders her king issued. Because here you are, Isavell. Alive."

I'd suspected it already, but hearing it out loud had a dizzying, disorienting effect. Nausea rose in my stomach. No wonder I'd left a trail of blood in my wake, and why killing came so naturally to me. An actual monster had given birth to me.

The wind toyed with the queen's white hair.

Did she know that the full force of my magic was so close to the surface now? That I could almost taste the cinders on my tongue? Before, she'd been stronger. Now? My magic was a raging river of fire beneath cold rock, and it was ready to erupt.

Love is a forge.

I inhaled deeply, seething. Was this what she thought love was? "So, this is the welcome you give to your own child whom you mourned as dead? Locked in a dungeon? Beaten? Starved? My real mother took care of me."

Her eyes flashed. "Your human mother left you weak."

Morgant pulled his gaze away from me, and I sensed that he wanted to disappear into the shadows.

As I stared at him, the pieces slid together in my mind. He hadn't known who I was until Mab ordered him to heal Torin. He must have had questions after that. That's when he began bringing me soap, telling me the clues I needed to learn to survive.

Queen Mab narrowed her eyes. "This isn't what I wanted, Isavell. I wanted an Unseelie heir. A daughter with magic. With wings. Because without those things, you are not my heir. True, you've managed to summon a little magic. You have done a good job of destroying my home."

I raised an eyebrow. "I only did what the tree wanted. It wants to be free of these stones. From your suffocating court."

"You think you know my home better than I? This tree *is* me. The castle is a child I hold in my arms. I guess no one ever told you that motherhood can be a terrible burden."

I sucked in a sharp breath, my heart twisting. Maybe Chloe left me "weak," but she'd never treated me like a burden.

My anger was threatening to suffocate me. "What do you want from me?"

"I want an heir who isn't broken, Isavell, my daughter. And all those deaths mean nothing if the Unseelie don't get what we deserve—the kingdom of Faerie."

A door in the tower opened, and three soldiers dragged out Torin by his wrists, coiled tightly in manacles of thick foliage. His gaze met mine, his pale eyes mournful.

"Let him go," I snarled.

A dark smile curled her lips. "I don't want to make my child scream, but a queen does what she must. Ava, what I do next will hurt me more than it will hurt you."

My stomach plummeted, and I looked at Morgant. His eyes seemed to search mine. Pleading. His words rang in my head...

We all have wings in the royal family. Some are just too stupid to use them.

"You have blood on your hands already." For just a moment, she lowered the vines until I was within her reach, and she lifted her hand to touch my cheek. Her eyes glistened. "You are my daughter, and this will hurt more than the others. But I ask myself sometimes— what is one more death when I'm already haunted by a sea of blood in my past? When it is all for the glory of our realm?"

I gritted my teeth. Flaming tongues of my trapped magic licked at the ice in my chest, melting it away.

"Torin's death," she cooed, "will not weigh on my soul at all. He did, after all, murder my son. I am going to suffocate him."

I slid my gaze to Torin once more, feeling my soul scorched. The queen's vines crawled over his neck, wrapping around his throat. Terror ripped through me as I watched them tighten, cutting off his air. His eyes went wide, and panic pierced my chest.

The monster queen had given birth to me.

"Then throw me off the tower, Your Majesty," I yelled. "You've promised to do so since I first met you."

My heart slammed against my ribs.

"Very well, then." Mab's expression was grim as she flicked her wrist, and the vine shot out into the windy night, high above the rocky earth. I gasped, and the vine unfurled.

The wind whipped at me, the ground surging closer.

As I plummeted, time slowed. In the hollows of my mind, I saw Torin, a child at his own coronation after his parents died. His expression was far too serious for a boy of his age, his little brow furrowed.

The wind yanked at my hair as I fell, and my memories flickered past me: Chloe making me hot oatmeal for breakfast, the sharp loneliness of her funeral. Shalini laughing so hard that she snorted. The day I'd met Torin in the Golden Shamrock...

The way he'd looked that night in the cabin when he'd told me about his mom.

The cold rock in my chest cracked open, and molten magic exploded at last. Hot tingles raced down my shoulder blades.

Searing power burst from my body, and my wings sprang free, tearing through the thin dress. I caught my breath, exhilarated.

The beating of my wings was instinctive, an innate part of me. I hovered just a few feet from the ground, close enough to see the dark blue pebbles on the path and the clouds of dust formed by my beating wings.

My thin, dark wings pounded the air behind me, and the muscles shifted and flexed against my shoulder blades. Like a heartbeat, they pulsed rhythmically, automatically. The feeling of the wind rushing over the delicate bones in my wings sent euphoria racing through my blood.

My heart slammed hard against my ribs, and my body blazed with power. Never in my life had I felt this strong.

I looked up and saw Morgant, hovering in the air above me, arm outstretched. Inches from me. I stared at the prince, the wind tearing at his white hair. He'd been there, ready to catch me.

A crooked smile curled his lips, and he handed me Torin's sword. "You need to get out of here, Isavell. Take your Seelie king to his home before anything happens to him."

I breathed in a shaky breath. Was he really letting me do this?

Pounding my wings against the air, I raced up to the castle's battlements. My magic sizzled through my limbs as I soared above the tower, taking in the view of the queen. With a growl, I seized control of the vines and commanded them to slither around her, a coffin of vegetation to trap her in place. As the plants slipped toward her, she bared her teeth.

With a flick of my wrist, I pulled the vines off Torin,

freeing him. He gasped for breath, his hands going to his throat.

I flew up and wrapped my arms around his waist. He did the same, his forearms locked tightly to me.

I breathed in the scent of him, the earth and woods mingled with his blood, and carried him into the air. The effort of lifting him nearly kept me rooted to the battlements, and pain shot through the top of my wings as I took off. The wind whipped over us as I carried him over the wall, and Torin's weight dragged us down to earth.

I could fly now, but my wings weren't made to carry a large, muscular man. I angled them to slow our fall, hoping for a smooth landing.

I didn't achieve that. We landed hard in a tangle of limbs and wings, the ground battering us.

I winced and looked for Torin. Streaked with dirt and blood, he arched an eyebrow and shot me a lopsided smile. "Graceful."

"Let's get to the horses, Torin."

I bit my lip, turning back to the castle. I could rip it apart. I could use the tree to pull it stone from stone and bury every Unseelie in there so I wouldn't have to worry about a single person following us.

But I had no idea how many people I'd be killing, and the queen's haunted eyes blazed in my mind. I swallowed hard.

I only needed my brother to keep her bound long enough for us to escape.

❧ 34 ❧
AVA

The horse's hooves pounded hard against the rocks, kicking up dirt. We'd been riding for hours.

After we'd landed beneath the castle, my wings had disappeared again. Now, I leaned back into Torin. He held me tightly as we rode east, his arm an iron bar around my waist.

After all that time, those weeks in the cell, replaying his death in my mind until I'd nearly gone mad, it was hard to believe he was really here with me. Tangible behind me, solid as the earth beneath us.

A month of darkness, and now I felt as if the sun were lighting me up from within.

Even after several hours, my heart hadn't slowed its unrelenting hammering. The wind slid over us, carrying with it the scent of molten rock and ashes.

I sighed. "If I go home to Shalini's apartment, what do you think the chances are that I'll find Aeron there, too?"

"Quite high, I should think. Assuming Orla is ruling in my absence."

I bit my lip. "What do you mean?"

"Only the monarch of Faerie can grant someone permission to leave or return." His deep voice rumbled from his chest. "And I haven't been there to grant permission."

"So, if I wanted to pop by for a visit, I'd need to ask you first?"

"Ava, my love." His voice sounded husky, ragged. "You won't be able to visit Faerie. The curse doesn't work here, but it will in my kingdom. You can't be around me in Faerie."

I felt as if shards of glass pierced my chest. What I understood the most right now was that I wasn't ready for this to end. "Sure."

"But if you return home, Ava, and you realize that you want someone to drive a sword through Andrew's throat, please send word to me, will you? I do believe I can murder him without consequences."

"Thanks. Pretty sure I can do my own killing now." My voice sounded small, and a heaviness weighed on my chest. "Did you hear what Mab said? She said some bitter Seelie crone is the reason you're all cursed. Modron—the one who looks back. She said if you kill her, the curse would be lifted."

"Do you believe her?"

I took a deep breath. "Mab is a terrible person. But I really don't think she lies."

By the time we reached the ruined temple by the riverside, morning rays pierced the leaves, igniting them with the first blush of dawn. Flecks of honeyed light danced over the ruined stones of the temple, columns of stone and a crumbled roof open to the sky.

Torin tugged the horse's reins, slowing her to a halt outside the temple. He dismounted first, then gripped me around the waist to lift me off.

I stared down at my bloodstained, dirty body and took a quick plunge into the river, washing off the grime, the blood, and gods knew what else. I drank a few palmfuls of its clear water. I'd never take water for granted again. But I didn't have much time to waste here, so I stepped out again.

Hope lit me up as we crossed into the temple. At the far end of the truncated columns, an altar stood. Just as Cala had said, a mirror hung above an empty forge, beaming with morning rays of light. My chest unclenched as I stared at it. At last, I'd be freeing Torin from this place.

I turned back to him, his perfect features gilded by morning light. Only now did I have the space to think about what this would mean, and a lump rose in my throat. This would be the last time we'd see each other. Or at least the last time we'd touch, until sometime in the future when we no longer felt the incandescent heat of love.

"Go on," I rasped. "Just say the name of the place you want to travel to."

Torin turned to the mirror, hands planted on either side of it. My heart cracked, and I sucked in a deep breath.

"You should go first." He turned back to me.

I shook my head. "Go." Because there was one more thing I wanted to do, and I wasn't sure that he would approve.

He brought his hand up to my cheek. "This is the last time I can touch you, Ava. I know we need to leave here, but I just need a little more time."

My heart started to race, and I tried to sense the vibrations of oncoming horses or soldiers through the soil. I didn't feel anything.

"Of course, I've thought you were beautiful since the first time I met you," he said, "but it changed into something else when I saw you in the tournament, letting Eliza get hits in on you just to save her honor. You hardly knew her, and the Seelie hadn't given you the warmest welcome...that was the moment I knew I was lost for you. And I should have stopped it then. I should have ended it all, called off the marriage."

My throat was tight. "There's no point in punishing yourself for decisions you made in the past, Torin. All we can do is move forward. We're both alive, and that seems like a miracle right now."

"I can't leave you without kissing you one last time." A jagged edge of sorrow cut through his voice.

He leaned down, lips hovering over mine. He slid one hand into my hair, threading it between his fingers. He pressed his lips against mine, and my back flattened against the cold stone wall.

One last time...

The words hummed through my heart like a bitter-sweet song. A final kiss, a final embrace.

His tongue darted in as the kiss deepened, and

desire swept through my body. His primal power, warm and vibrating, skimmed over my skin, and I had to drink it up because this would be the last time. The loss of him pierced my chest, and I wanted to devour him whole.

River water dampened my body, and every inch of me felt alive, kissed by the rich forest air. I was acutely aware of every place the wet dress clung to my skin.

With one hand in my hair, his other moved to my waist. The way he kissed me with an exquisite heat, like he wanted to memorize my lips, told me he was as heartbroken about our parting as I was.

Slowly, he pulled away, his blue eyes smoldering with the possessiveness of a king. "I wish I could take you with me."

I reached for his tattered shirt, unbuttoning it. Was this really the last time my fingertips would trace over his chiseled abs and the whorls of tattoos on his skin? "Torin, so do I. You have no idea."

Even as sorrow twisted through me, my desire for him coiled off my bare skin like steam.

Gently, he pulled down one side of my dress, exposing my breast. He reached up, caressing me and making my nipple go rock-hard against his palm.

He lowered his mouth to my throat, licking the river water off me.

I tried to memorize his scent as I breathed it in, the mossy, magical scent of an enchanted forest. This was the last moment his primal, earthy magic would twine around me. I needed to memorize the feel of him, the smell of him. Because when he left, I'd be living in a world of shadows.

I arched my back, my breast pressing into his palm. Every one of my sensitive nerve endings burned with a startling truth: that I was his, and he was mine. Curse or not, we belonged together, joined by a bone-deep connection. And the idea that this was our last moment together was impossible to bear.

One hot, lazy kiss after another scorched my throat where his lips met my skin. He moved at an indolent pace, holding back, but I could feel the desperation behind every searing kiss. The way his fingers went tight on my body, the rigidity of his muscles. The Seelie king was warring for control over himself.

I arched my neck, resting my head against the temple wall. He was the most beautiful man I'd ever seen, and liquid desire pulsed in my core. I threaded my fingers into his dark hair, committing the feel of it to my memory.

How could I let him go after all this?

I wasn't sure that I'd ever felt truly alive until this moment. Every inch of my skin ached for his touch, and I savored the brush of his lips against me, trying to etch each moment on my heart for all time. "You know we belong together, right?"

"Yes." The word sounded torn out of him against his will.

His hand moved from my breast to my waist, his movements frustratingly languid. Especially frustrating since we could be discovered at any moment, and if Torin were captured again, it would break me.

"Torin, I don't want this to end," I breathed. "But I don't want them to lay a finger on you again."

"I can't rush with you. If this is the only time we can be together..." He gripped me tightly, his words trailing off. As if we had all the time in the world, he raised his face and slanted his lips against mine, giving me a sensual kiss.

My body lit up.

I craved his hands on me, and a hollow ache built at the apex of my thighs. I reached for the top of his pants and slid my fingertips beneath his waistband. He inhaled sharply.

"Dress. Off." A jagged note of desperation tinged his husky voice, and he started to pull it off me.

Under the dress, I was completely naked and slick with desire for him. A little spark in the hollows of my mind was aware that we might have to leap through that mirror at any moment, and I'd be making the trip back home in the nude. But the majority of my mind didn't care at all, and every stroke from Torin incinerated my rational thoughts.

Torin's eyes swept down my body, and he went rigid as if he were seeing me naked for the first time. His eyes, usually so cold, blazed with heat. His jaw flexed, and I sensed he was losing the battle with his tightly leashed control. "Ava." His husky voice had a pleading sound. "I wanted to take my time with you, to remember, but..." He trailed off again, inhaling deeply.

He clamped a hand on my hips, rooting me against the dew-kissed stone wall, exactly where he wanted me. With his free hand, he stroked me between my thighs, his touch excruciatingly light. His restraint was faltering because when he touched me where I was wet, he let out a low growl. Heat radiated off him, and he held me in place firmly with one hand.

Every inch of my bare skin felt exquisitely sensitive, aching for him. As two of his fingers slid into me, molten pleasure lit me up.

The Seelie king was enjoying my body, dangerously turned on as I was. He was stoking my lust into a wild, primal state.

I opened my thighs wider for him. I breathed deeply, my bare breasts heaving and flushed.

He stroked me with light circles, teasing me until my core was coiled tightly, desperate for release. "Torin," I whispered, "I need more of you."

"I knew someday I'd have you moaning my name, changeling." Despite the danger, despite his obvious arousal, it seemed nothing would hurry him. He teased me, delighting in the pleading words tripping off my tongue, until at last, he stroked me over the edge, and a shudder rippled through me. My climax had me moving against his hand, gasping his name. My fingers were tangled in his dark hair, and I slowly unclenched them.

Breathing hard, I unbuttoned his pants, freeing his hard cock. Goddess of ash, I'd sensed it before, but now I knew for certain that fae men were built differently in every way.

More frantic now, he reached under my ass, spreading my thighs wide as he brought my legs up over his hips. My back pressed against the wall, and he paused at my entrance. My hips rocked against his tip, then slowly, carefully, he pushed into me. One inch at a time, he moved inside me, eyes locked on mine. A slow thrust in and out, with a tenderness that bordered on reverence. My fingernails traced over his back, up into his hair, and I pulled his face closer to mine.

"Ava." My name on his tongue was a hoarse groan that lit my blood on fire. "I would tear my own kingdom apart for you if it meant we could be together." He pressed his mouth against mine in a devouring kiss.

He would tear his kingdom apart for me...

These words wrecked me. Destroyed me. Because I never expected to hear them from him, and my love for him flooded me.

He moved slowly in me, a deep stroke that sent pleasure rocketing through me. I raked my hands down his back, urging him to move faster, deeper. His tongue swept mine, and his hips moved against me, body moving and rolling exactly where I needed him. He drove into me again and again, and firelight scorched my thoughts. At last, the pleasure of release ripped through me, and I clenched around him, arching my back, fingernails digging into him. As he climaxed, he whispered my name with a desperation that broke my heart. Watching the ecstatic look on his face, his eyes closed, I shuddered against him with aftershocks of pleasure.

His muscles relaxed, and he leaned against me, catching his breath. Another long kiss, drawing out the pleasure. When he pulled away, he stared into my eyes.

"Ava, you have made me thoroughly undone in every possible way. I am returning to my kingdom a ruined man. But with you, I don't think I have a choice. You're a command I can't refuse."

"And yet, we're never going to see each other again."

He heaved a sigh. "That's to keep you alive."

I swallowed hard. "The curse doesn't work here. How do you know it will work in the human realm?"

"Because there would be only one way to test it, changeling. I died for you once, and I would do it again...I'd rip through the realms to get to you again. But I will not put you at risk."

Our bodies glowed with morning dew, and we slumped against each other, muscles limp. He reached up for the side of my face and kissed me again, softly. A worshipful kiss.

We had to leave now before it was too late, before they found us, but neither of us seemed to want to be the first to let go.

❦ 35 ❦

AVA

Pearly, coral dawn streaked the sky.

Torin picked up his sword, and I pulled on my damp dress, squeezing some of the water out of it. As I did, I felt the distant vibrations of hooves pounding through the forest trails.

My heart sped up, and I smoothed out my dress, the fabric still stained from other people's blood. "Torin." I tried to make my voice sound calm and even. "You have to go now. *We* have to go now."

He turned back to me for just a moment, then pressed his forehead against mine. One last kiss, a brush of lips against mine.

"They're coming, Torin."

He couldn't meet my eyes anymore as he turned away from me and back to the mirror. Framed by silvery coils, it hung above the empty forge. Torin touched the glass with his fingertips. He inhaled a deep, shaky breath, his voice hoarse. The moment he finished saying *Faerie*, silvery light exploded around him, so bright I could hardly see. I shielded my eyes. Magic vibrated over my skin, sizzling in the droplets of river water on my body.

When I opened my eyes again, Torin was gone, sword and all.

I stared at where he'd just been, feeling like my chest had hollowed out. My emotions flitted between relief that he was safe and barbed emptiness at his absence.

A tear rolled down my cheek, and I wiped it away with my palm. Why did it feel so hard to breathe?

With a shaking breath, I stepped closer to the mirror and swallowed.

The thing was, I couldn't have Torin entirely in control of whether I could come to Faerie again, could I? He was hell-bent on self-sacrifice to atone for what he'd done to Moria's sister. I trusted him with almost everything, but I didn't trust the man to look after himself properly.

Here before me was a magical tool that could open the realms, that could create portals between worlds. I couldn't just leave it here. So I clenched my teeth, and I punched the glass in the lower left corner.

As soon as the pain shot through my knuckles and the shards cut my skin, I realized the stupidity of not picking up a rock to break the mirror instead. But what was done was done. A crack splintered the mirror in the left corner, and I pulled off a triangular shard.

Now, the vibrations of the oncoming soldiers were growing louder, closer. I held the fragmented mirror in my hand, and I stared into the remains of the looking glass on the wall. The magical surface shimmered and rippled.

With a racing heart, I called out the name of my city. Pale light erupted around me, and I felt myself falling, gripping tightly to the shard of the mirror as I tumbled through a void. I landed hard, two bare feet on the pavement. I may have put my dress back on, but I'd left the stolen shoes back in the Court of Shadows.

I staggered, trying to get my balance, and my ears rang with a strange rushing sound. A cool breeze whipped over me.

Disoriented, I blinked, looking around.

I stood in the center of town by the bus station. Dawn was breaking over my city. A bus rolled out of the terminal, starting and stopping, releasing little black clouds of exhaust.

Newspapers tumbled across the street, buffeted by the wind. How did the magical Unseelie mirror choose this bus station? I suppose it was the center of town, and it was our main public transportation.

My thoughts trailed off.

An elderly woman with plastic bags on her feet was pushing a shopping cart full of cabbages in my direction. She scowled at me, then muttered, "We don't need your kind around here."

I reached up to touch my horns and found they still jutted from my head. At least I didn't have the wings out.

When I looked down at myself, I was wearing a white dress soaked in river water and other people's blood, and it was pretty much transparent on me. Dirt caked my bare feet, and I held a sharp shard of mirror that could probably be considered a weapon. In short, I looked like a living nightmare.

My stomach rumbled, and I glanced at the McDonald's across the street. Holy shit, that would taste amazing right now, but I didn't have money, and they'd probably call the police.

I started walking. From here, it was about a mile to my old apartment, but that was where Andrew lived. There was no way I would show up looking like I'd had a nervous breakdown. Like I'd fallen apart, unable to handle the shame of the nude photos he'd shared.

It was only another mile more to Shalini's place. I broke into a run, hoping to get back there before any police officers stopped me with awkward questions. The sidewalk felt cold and grimy beneath my bare feet, and I tried not to think about what I was stepping on.

Gods, I missed Torin already. My mind kept flicking back to the feel of my fingertips on his chest, the glorious smell of him.

As I reached the emptier streets closer to her apartment, I slowed a little to catch my breath. The only people out this early in the morning were a few joggers who studiously avoided my gaze.

Don't look at the half-naked lady.

Once, I'd enjoyed running through the streets for fun. Now? I don't think I'd go back to it. What was the point of jogging when you could actually fly?

At last, I turned onto Shalini's street, and my stomach clenched.

Great ash goddess...

There they were, dressed in tidy gray Lululemon outfits, practically matching: Andrew and Ashley. Out for a morning jog.

I stopped walking, practically freezing in place. Ashley grabbed Andrew's arm, and her face went pale.

I knew I looked like an absolute monster right now.

Why did this encounter feel more horrifying than a month in the Unseelie dungeon?

I winced and gave a slight wave to Andrew. Unfortunately, the happy couple now stood between me and the entrance to Shalini's apartment.

I cleared my throat and pointed at the gate behind them. "Just going to Shalini's." I really didn't want to get closer, to have them inspect the absolute state of me and ask why I was covered in blood.

Andrew's nose was wrinkled, his eyes narrowing like he couldn't quite believe what he was seeing. "Ava, what happened to you? The gossip columns said you had a nervous breakdown after you were dumped. Is that, like, a psychotic break?"

My jaw clenched. "Is that what they said?"

His gaze darted to the top of my head. "Was it the horns? I didn't know fae had horns." His lip curled with obvious revulsion. "Did they cause the breakdown?"

Ashley's blonde hair was pulled into a ponytail so tight it tugged at her features. Still gripping Andrew's arm, she cocked her head, her forehead wrinkled. "Are you...*okay*?" Her voice sounded unnaturally high-pitched, and her words were slowly enunciated, like she was speaking to a confused child. "Should we call someone to come get you?"

"I'm fine. I can't really divulge what I was doing," I ventured. "It's fae stuff. Magic. Top secret. You wouldn't understand." I didn't realize how insane that explanation would sound until the words were already out of my mouth. "Never mind," I said sharply.

"What are you holding?" asked Andrew. "Why are you...where are your clothes? Where are your shoes?"

"It's not really your business, though, is it?" I snapped.

"You nearly ruined my life, you know," Andrew said sharply. "Everyone was sympathetic to the poor dumped fae woman. I got fired."

"So you sold nude photos of me." I inhaled deeply. "You know what? I really don't care anymore. About any of this."

He shrugged, his cheeks turning pink. "But maybe people should know what you are really like. Why I couldn't be with a fae. Maybe then they would understand and have some sympathy that I just wanted a normal life."

I narrowed my eyes at him. "You know, Torin really doesn't like you."

Andrew's lip twitched. "He's not your boyfriend, though, is he? They said you're not actually marrying him. They said you disappeared after he turned you down at the altar." His gaze swept down, taking in my tattered state. "Ava, you should really get some help."

For a blinding, incandescent moment, I could see myself running up to him and ramming the shard of mirror into his shoulder. Not enough to kill him, but enough to make him deeply regret every decision he'd ever made up until this point.

But I was in the human world now. And here, we didn't just stab people. In fact, I liked that about this place. Right?

I had at one point, anyway.

I clenched my teeth and hurried past him on the sidewalk.

As I left the two of them behind, I reached the black, wrought-iron gates outside Shalini's apartment, gates that were just for show, because I'd never seen them locked. I cast my gaze around the courtyard garden of begonias and asters, thinking how tidy it looked compared to the Court of Sorrows. Nice and civilized.

I stood outside the apartment's brick exterior and pushed the buzzer to her apartment.

I waited a few minutes, my chest tightening a little bit.

As the breeze nipped at my skin, I hugged myself.

I suppose she could have stayed in Faerie?

If she wasn't in her apartment at six in the morning, then she probably had stayed in Faerie. But was it by choice? Had the entire kingdom frozen over when Torin left without a queen? I had no idea, but a nauseous feeling was starting to climb up my gut.

I pushed the buzzer of another apartment—then a second one, until at last someone answered, sounding annoyed and groggy. "What?"

"Sorry," I said, in the best imitation of Shalini's voice. I turned my head away in case they had a camera view. "It's Shalini. Can you just buzz me in? I forgot my keys." Without another word, the stranger buzzed the door open, and I pushed through the heavy wooden door.

I climbed the pretty tiled stairs to her apartment. I didn't have a key, of course, but what I did have at this point was an insane lack of patience and the heightened physical strength of a fae.

After knocking several times and calling her name through the door, I kicked the door three times—hard —until the wood splintered just above the doorknob.

When I'd created enough of a gap, I shoved my hand through the splintered wood and unlocked the door from the inside.

As soon as I stepped in, the scent of trash and mold hit me hard. I cleared my throat with a growing sense of unease. When I stepped into the kitchen, I dropped the magic piece of mirror onto the table.

There, I found a box of donuts, completely overgrown with fuzzy gray and green mold. My nose wrinkled, and I dumped them in the trash.

I should probably eat, I supposed. I opened her cupboards and pulled out a box of Cheerios, then filled a glass of water from the sink.

At the kitchen table, I ate like a toddler, shoveling dry cereal into my mouth. As I chewed, my mind ticked over the possibilities of what could have happened.

Shalini must have known that I had disappeared, and she was the most loyal friend I'd ever known. Maybe she didn't want to leave Faerie without finding out what had happened to me. Maybe, when Torin returned to his kingdom, he would send her home.

She'd run back here, relieved, maybe with a new boyfriend in tow, and we would hug each other and drink wine and tell each other about everything that happened in the past few weeks. Months? How long had it actually been? Somehow, it felt like years and hours at the same time. I washed down the dry cereal with cool tap water. *Holy shit.* Had I never realized before how amazing tap water tasted? Tap water was the nectar of the gods, and you could have it whenever you wanted it. It was the one thing I still liked about this place.

When I'd filled my stomach and drank as much as I wanted, I headed over to Shalini's bedroom. As she was my best friend, I didn't think she'd mind if I borrowed some clothes.

I pulled open her drawers and fished out some dark leggings and a long-sleeved shirt, then stepped into her cream-tiled bathroom.

I turned on the shower, letting the steam fill the room. As the shower heated, I felt myself slip into a daze, listening to the comforting hum of water pounding against the tiles. I pulled off the bloodstained dress and shoved it into the trash. Naked, I stepped into the shower, and the hot water pounded my skin. I grabbed a bottle of liquid soap and scrubbed myself. Dirt from my feet swirled in the drain, a tiny whirlpool of mud.

What was Torin doing right now?

I came out of the shower smelling like vanilla and

civilization. I towel-dried my hair and pulled on the clean clothes, then crossed into the living room to drop down onto the sofa. How long would it take for Shalini to come back once she realized I was here?

I bit my lip, staring into space. She would come home, wouldn't she? With Torin's permission, she could go in and out of the different realms. But worry nagged at the back of my mind.

I cleared my throat as my nervous thoughts grew louder. I really had no idea what happened after I left the kingdom. Torin wondered if his sister had taken over, but who knew? Maybe no one took over and they all starved. Maybe Moria took over, or the bitter hag who cursed the place.

I stood and started pacing. How long was I going to wait before giving in and using that magical piece of mirror?

A male voice, tentative and worried, pierced my thoughts. "Hello?"

My head snapped up, and I looked at the door.

Someone, Shalini's neighbor, I presumed, stood in the doorway, a man dressed in a light blue button-down shirt with closely cropped brown hair. "Is everything okay here? It looks like there was a break-in. I'm sorry —who are you?"

I rubbed the knot in my forehead. I needed people to leave me alone. And it seemed like I'd forgotten how to behave normally in the Court of Sorrows, because I muttered those words out loud.

"Are you supposed to be in here?" he asked.

"I'm Shalini's roommate," I said. "Her new roommate."

"She hasn't been here in a while," he shot back, staring nervously at my horns.

I really wished there was a way to shut the door, but I'd broken it too much.

I prowled closer to him across the room. "Your help isn't needed here." I bared my teeth with a snarl. "And I'd advise you to leave well enough alone. You don't know what might happen to you if you cross a Dark Cromm."

I heard the echoes of my brother in my threat.

The stranger turned white as milk, and he pivoted to hurry down the stairs.

❧ 36 ❧

TORIN

The portal ejected me onto a cold stone floor. Icy light filtered through a mullioned window, and a marrow-deep chill was in the air. I was back in my castle, for some reason, in Orla's room. The mirror had sent me here.

Orla herself was not here.

As my eyes scanned my sister's room, a shiver of dread snaked up my spine. It was even colder than it had been when I'd left, and the air carried a faint scent of smoke and sulfur. Was the desolation of this place because of my forced separation from Ava?

No, that wasn't it. Screams pierced the stone walls from outside. The normally serene stillness of the castle was replaced with a sharp tension coiling through the atmosphere, dragging cold claws over my skin.

I went still. A voice wended through the air, one I recognized.

Orla's voice.

From somewhere, she was calling my name. Had she

felt my return? If she'd left the kingdom, nearly died, and come back again, I thought I would feel it in my blood.

But her screams...

Up here, the castle felt empty, haunted. My breath misted around my head in a frozen fog. I crossed into the corridor. Darkness crept over the walls, even though it was day. Deep gray shadows writhed over the stones.

I gripped the hilt of my sword. Today, the castle felt like a tomb of rock.

The Sword of Whispers sang to me. *You are death. You are the frigid isolation that comes with the last breath.*

The walls exuded a malign presence, and I didn't feel welcome here anymore. My magic hadn't returned to my body, which meant my throne was still shattered. Here in Faerie, I felt like a hollow king walking through these corridors, divested of the power that had once coursed through my veins.

When I heard the distant pounding of soldiers' heels on the stones, I slipped back into the shadows of an empty bed chamber. I needed to see who the soldiers served before I engaged them, to find out if I was an enemy in my own kingdom. With the Sword of Whispers, I could cut them down in a fight, one by one. The blade sang in my skull with every breath I took, hungry for blood.

But this wasn't the Unseelie fortress. These were my soldiers, part of an army I'd commanded. I probably knew half of them by name, even if I was now an interloper here. I couldn't just murder everyone.

As I stood behind the door, I thought of how I'd felt

with Ava pressed into me as we'd hidden in that alcove, her hips moving back...the only spark of warmth in this nightmarish atmosphere was the idea of Ava at home, safe from the ruthless world of the fae into which I'd dragged her. Right now, she was probably curling up in a comfortable bed, her belly full of warm food.

From behind the crack of the door, I watched the soldiers troop past. My heart skipped a beat as my gaze landed on the sigil of the Dearg Due royalty: white, spiky whorls over venous red.

Moria? Had she wrested control from Orla? But if she had control, it didn't explain the icy chill of winter that spilled through the kingdom. A queen could bring spring just by sitting on the throne.

So what the fuck had been happening here while I'd been gone?

When the soldiers marched around a corner, out of view, I stalked out once more.

I heard it again—Orla calling for me, her voice traveling through the glass windows from the east. I broke into a run until I reached the east wing, and the sounds of screams from outside pierced the narrow windows. Worry clawed at my thoughts.

This place was ancient, built long before anyone had developed the concept of windows that swung open, so I used the Sword of Whispers to smash through the glass. Leaning out into the gnawing cold, I peered at the sheer black drop-off of castle walls below me.

Horror and revulsion hit me like a fist to my throat. Chains shot down the side of the wall, holding up icy cages that dangled just above the snowy ground. They swayed a little in the glacial winds. I remembered reading that King Caerleon had done this to some of his enemies.

I counted ten cages in all.

From far below, Orla's voice floated in the wind.

I clenched my jaw, making fast mental calculations. I could try to fix my throne and regain my power, or I could run through the castle and approach the cages from below. But the castle was enormous. Moving around inside for long periods of time risked my imprisonment and death at the hands of the new monarch. And then, Orla would live out her last moments freezing to death in the cage.

The other option...the other option was simply to crawl down the chains with the Sword of Whispers and get to Orla directly. They hung on the eastern wing, which had no portcullis or gate. I didn't see any soldiers patrolling below. Why patrol a locked cage?

I let out a long breath, and it formed a cloud around my head, freezing in the air. The safest option for Orla's survival was for me to go straight for her. Right here. Right now.

A gust of frozen wind whipped over me, and I crawled through the shattered glass, my sword in my hand.

A few shards lacerated my palms and legs, but I ignored it. Just like I ignored the frostbitten wind that whipped at me.

Snow whipped at the skin exposed through my tattered clothes. I didn't have a sheath for my sword, so I carried it in one hand and used my legs and my other arm to crawl down the chain. The icy stone walls stung my bare feet. The frozen chains stuck to my fingers, so every minute or so, I switched hands. I rappelled down the side of my own castle, slammed by snowy winds.

When a roar rumbled behind me, dread made my stomach tighten. Slowly, I turned to see a black and red dragon swooping through the skies.

On the dragon's back was a woman in red, her burgundy hair streaming behind her like a bloody banner.

Moria. Ava had warned me she was terrible...I just didn't think it would be quite this bad.

The creature unleashed a gout of fire, hot orange against a sky the color of cinders.

A new horrific thought took hold.

In the old days of King Caerleon, he'd dabbled in evil magic. Specifically, he'd used a black and red dragon called the Sinach to light his enemies on fire. And here she was, a reincarnation of Faerie's worst tyrant—King Caerleon in a dress.

I moved faster down the chains. At any moment, the Sinach could turn on this wall of cages, melting the chains, melting me, broiling the prisoners alive. My muscles had started to freeze up, but I forced myself to move as fast as physically possible.

In the biting cold, I thought I was losing skin from my fingers as I scaled down the frozen chain. I'd made it a few stories now, and I looked below me. From this distance, when I looked at the cages, I could actually see an arm jutting from one of them. This was an arm that I recognized, so thin and delicate, the pale skin turned blue with the cold.

Anger flooded me.

Orla called my name again, sounding agonized. This time, I shouted back to her, "I'm coming, Orla." I couldn't help it. I needed her to know I was trying to get her out of this hell.

When I glanced over my shoulder again, Moria and the Sinach were soaring closer.

Orla's cage was just to the right of the chain I'd climbed down, and I was desperate to get to her first.

When I was twenty feet above the nearest cage, I let go of the chain and jumped. I landed hard, the shock of it sending a judder through my legs. The cage rocked with the force of my fall, but I steadied myself on top of it. From there, I leaped another ten feet through the frozen air to Orla's cage.

I glanced down at the ground below us. It was only about fifteen feet to the snow. "Hold on," I shouted into the wind.

I leaned over the metal edge, peering in. Orla lay huddled and frozen, without even the small mercy of a cloak. Snow dusted her eyelashes and clung to her hair. Her lips had turned blue.

"Torin," she said, "Moria has gone mad. She's using the dragons, she's using Modron. She's trying to kill us all. She's convinced the army that you're working with Mab."

It wasn't as if I needed to hear anymore.

I swung the Sword of Whispers to carve through the lock. The rusted door swung open, creaking on its hinge. "Can you jump out?" I shouted against the wind.

She nodded, shifting to the entrance of the cage, her body shivering violently.

"It's about fifteen feet below you, Orla. You will land in the snow, and then you need to find your way to the woods. I'll help you as soon as I can."

For Orla, this leap would be more difficult than for the others. She couldn't see the ground. But Orla always did what she had to without complaining.

She threw herself from the cage and landed hard in the snow, tumbling. In moments, she was on her feet and running for the forest, the wind whipping at her dress.

I leaped to the next cage, where I recognized the deep voice of Aeron.

"Torin," he shouted, "they will kill you."

I leaned over the side of the cage, the frozen metal stinging my body through my clothes.

My blade carved through his lock. I barked at him to go after my sister. He jumped from the cage, whirling to face me, and pointed to another cage to my right.

"Shalini," he shouted.

And with a sharp pang of horror, I realized that Moria had trapped a human in one of these cages, someone who could easily die from frostbite.

With a thundering heart, I leaped to her cage and hacked through the metal of her lock. Her door groaned open, and Aeron called her name again and again, his voice wild. I peered into her cage to see her shuffling, half crawling toward the open door. Her body looked rigid with the cold under her cloak. She practically fell out of the cage and into Aeron's open arms. He carried her like a bride toward the forest, following after Orla's footsteps.

I crouched, ready to jump to the next cage, but something stopped me. From around the corner, a line of red-clad soldiers marched, archers among them. My heart pounded like a war drum as I watched them kneel in the snow, arrows aimed at me.

I wasn't sure of many things at this point except that I'd been shot with arrows far too many times recently. Of that, I was completely certain.

One of the soldiers barked out an order to shoot. I braced, waiting for the arrows to fly.

Only the punishing wind hit me. Maybe, in this hellish landscape, they understood that their new queen did not have their best interests at heart.

"You know me!" I shouted into the snowy wind. "I am your king. And whatever has happened while I was trapped in the enemy lands, whatever they said about me, you must know who I really am. That I have always done my best to protect Faerie, to keep you all safe. Some of you served with me for years. And it was never like this when I was king, was it?"

My gaze landed on a man with blue hair and bronze skin whom I recognized. "Lonan! Your family joined me for dinner to celebrate the birth of your youngest sister." I pulled my gaze to another, one with golden curls whose family owned a cattle farm. "Malo, I helped negotiate the conflict between your family's farm and the neighbor's when their fence was crumbling in your fields."

Overhead, the Sinach swooped lower with Moria on its back. She was maybe a hundred feet above us in the air.

The creature unleashed a flaming stream beneath iron-gray clouds. The soldiers looked over their shoulders at the burst of flame, and the tension in them sharpened into talons.

I raised my sword. "I still hold the Sword of Whispers. The old gods have still blessed me as their chosen king. The Unseelie Queen Mab trapped me in her kingdom against my will, and I fought tooth and nail to return to you."

On top of the Sinach, Moria's crown gleamed like brutal shards of ice. She bellowed into the storm.

The dragon whipped back around, arcing even closer, and the poisonous miasma of fear spilled through the air. The Sinach pounded his wings, now only twenty feet behind the soldiers. From its mouth, a scorching burst of flame blasted the snow behind them.

One of the archers loosed an arrow, and I blocked it with my blade. The second arrow, too. The soldiers were terrified of the dragon and doing as their queen commanded, and how could I blame them? No one wanted to burn to death.

My blood roared in my ears.

With a reign of terror, Moria had an iron grip on this kingdom. As the dragon unleashed its flames, the arrows kept flying until I could no longer block all of them. One of them slammed into my gut, another into my bicep. The pain ripped through me, and the force of the second arrow knocked me off the cage.

I slammed down hard into the snow, my spine jolted by the force of the fall onto ice. And as my soldiers clamped chains around my wrists and my throat, they whispered apologies to me. They whispered that they didn't know the truth, that I could be a demon lover, for all they knew, but I could hear the doubt in their voices.

It had always been cold, but this—the Sinach, the cages, the palpable terror—this was a living nightmare.

They dragged me across the icy snow, hoisting me into a cart. I grimaced at the arrowheads ripping at my flesh.

As the cart took off, bouncing over the frozen earth, I felt every jolt. Not exactly the welcome I'd hoped for.

Where the fuck were they taking me?

AVA

I stared at the piece of the mirror. I'd hardly moved in the past hour.

One thing I'd learned in the Court of Sorrows was that I had to be ready to escape at any moment, and that sense of urgency was skittering up my spine. With the fragment of mirror, I dropped down onto Shalini's sofa.

I waited, staring into space at the ash gray of the human world.

On a table by Shalini's windowsill was an aspidistra plant, its leaves withered and browned in her absence. My muscles tensed. I felt its thirst, its isolation, the nearness of death. Cocking my head, I summoned life back into the plant, and the magic sweeping over me felt like warm sunlight on my skin. The plant beamed with golden light, and its leaves shifted to green again.

I stood and stroked a fingertip along the waxy leaves. A very human choice for a plant, a tame, civilized choice.

But Shalini had a wild side, too, which was how she'd ended up in Faerie in the first place.

Next to the plant, a green book lay on the table. Under the crumbles of dead leaves, I read the gold lettering: W.B. YEATS.

I dropped back into the sofa and flicked through the pages. My gaze landed on a poem, and my heartbeat started to pound.

"Faeries, come take me out of this dull world,
For I would ride with you upon the wind,
Run on the top of the disheveled tide,
And dance upon the mountains like a flame."

My blood pumped hot. I was meant to dance upon the mountains like a flame.

We, the fae, were tempered in the fires of a mountain goddess, forged to race through the star-flecked skies. We were not born to be civilized.

We were not born to eat fucking Cheerios.

And I could never stay here without knowing if my friends were okay. After everything I'd been through, I was never taking anyone's safety for granted again.

Torin had told me that as long as his throne was shattered, he would have no power whatsoever. So when he returned, was he returning as a king? Or had someone usurped him?

Given what I knew about the fae—that we were ruthless and vicious—I had a strong suspicion it was the latter.

I didn't have a lot to my name right now, but what I did have was an insane lack of patience and a burning determination to keep my loved ones safe.

Wildly, I rushed to Shalini's closet and plucked out her warmest winter coat and a pair of knee-high boots.

Fully dressed, I glanced into the piece of mirror and shouted the word *Faerie*.

TORIN

Icy manacles bound my wrists, and an iron collar clamped around my throat. I looked down at the blood streaming from my body, the arrows jutting from my flesh. The blood had frozen on my clothes.

My soldiers had chained me to a post in the center of the stone amphitheater. Thick ice and snow covered the ground beneath my feet.

Moria and Modron stood where I'd once presided over the duels during the trials. How long ago had it been since Ava had won in this arena? It felt like centuries. At the thought of her, grief carved me open, a cold sense of loss that I'd never see her again.

Was this it, then?

The cold gnawed at my skin, and the shadows seemed to grow thicker around me, dancing over the ice like frozen spirits. When I died, I'd be severed from the people I loved.

Dazed, I scanned the amphitheater, my gaze roaming over the crowds in the stone seats. Anger whispered over my skin. This was to be a public execution of a conquered king.

On the stone platform, Moria wore a deep burgundy cloak that matched her hair and long white gloves. A smile curled her lips.

Modron was by her side. The crone was dressed in a cloak the deep gray of smoke. My thoughts snagged on what Mab had told Ava—kill Modron, and this would all be over.

An icy wind swept over the stadium, carrying gusts of snow. No one had told me yet how I would die, but I imagined it would be more creative than freezing to death. Up there with some of the threats Mab had already delivered, no doubt: eviscerated, castrated, or sealed up in an icy tree. Humans may have created beautiful art, but the fae were immensely creative when it came to methods of killing.

Seelie poured into the stands, dressed warmly in furs.

Moria pulled up her burgundy hood. Gracefully, she stepped down from the dais and crossed the snow-swept arena. I watched her, pierced by a seething hatred as she strode across the ice, the wind whipping at her cloak. If I had my magic, this would be over in minutes.

She stopped a few feet in front of me, flashing me a smile that made my blood run even colder.

"Are you going to freeze me to death, Moria?" I asked. "Is that your plan—show everyone that the king no longer has any power?"

She blinked fluttering her long eyelashes. Under her hood, her crown glinted like ice in the dull light.

"Oh, no, my dear, you're not going to freeze. That's what you did to my sister before you buried her in the temple. Freezing is too good for you. I want you to die terrified, screaming, and completely out of control. I want you to die gripped by real horror."

I know she wanted me to ask her what she was going to do, to beg for my life, but I wasn't about to, because she would never grant it.

She gestured at the crowds filling up the stands. "They're here to witness what I will do to a demon lover. They'll see the lengths to which I'm willing to go to protect the kingdom from those who would starve them."

Wrath stole my breath. This was why she'd let the kingdom grow colder. It was much easier to get away with tyranny when your kingdom was at war. All she had to do was blame it on the traitors.

"You won't last as queen," I said. "They will see that you're forcing people to suffer. They will find a new queen, one who will give them the spring they need."

She stepped closer to me, her wine-colored lips by my cheek as she whispered, "But Torin, this is all your fault. I've helped them to understand that."

"Why are you doing this, Moria?" Violence laced my tone.

She leaned back, her smile fading. "You may no longer call me that. The correct term is *Your Majesty*."

Something gleamed at her hip under her cloak, and anger heated my chest at the sight of the Sword of Whispers. She was already a tyrant, but that sword would turn her into a completely unhinged monster.

"Why am I doing this?" she hissed. "Because you took the only thing I loved from me. My father raised me to punish my enemies. He raised me to be strong like King Caerleon and the powerful kings of old."

"Caerleon wasn't strong. He was a paranoid, blood-thirsty sadist, and that is exactly where you are headed."

"His court was respected." She glanced back over her shoulder. "I have a new friend, though, Modron. She was very lonely, you know. It was just her and the river for centuries. And now she has me." She turned back to me with a coy smile. "She can control the river, you know? The Avon. She can make it swell."

Ah. She planned to drown me. Less creativity than I'd anticipated.

When Moria smiled this time, she let her fangs out and licked one of them. "In the old days, the Dearg Due drank blood. But that's considered vulgar these days, isn't it? Our society has become so soft." Her brow furrowed. "I was meant for this moment. This is written in the stars. This is why I went through hell as a child. This is why the gods cursed me with the agony of losing the only person I loved. It was all for this moment. This is fate, Torin. All of this has made me strong."

No, it's made you demented.

She turned away, climbing the stairs once more.

While I tugged on my chains, she gave a speech that echoed over the stones of the arena. One full of propaganda, all about how I loved the demons and how I'd been conspiring to destroy my own kingdom. Apparently, I'd been seduced by a wicked minx, one with horns, half animal.

As she spoke, workers were sealing up the tunnel entrances to the arena.

My thoughts slipped back to Ava. No matter what happened here, at least she was safe. With that knowledge, I could die happily enough. Orla, too, had a chance to survive. Aeron would look after her. That was the best I could hope for, wasn't it, to die with the hope that the people I loved were safe?

I closed my eyes, thinking of Ava sleeping soundly in a warm bed. When she'd slept next to me in the Court of Sorrows, she'd snored ever so slightly. I could picture her chest rising and falling. The image made my chest ache.

A great crack of stone pulled me from my vision, and I sucked in a sharp breath as frigid geysers burst from the stones around me and river water flooded the arena. Streams erupted around me. Murky water poured in from every part of the amphitheater, freezing my feet.

Modron chanted with a strange, ecstatic look on her features. Wisps of dark magic curled from her body and into the charcoal skies.

Cold water gnawed at my skin until my toes went completely numb. Overhead, the dragon swooped beneath the stormy sky, and murmurs of fear ran through the crowd.

Moria's voice pierced the air. "The Sinach will help to execute this traitor. Only when the demon lover lies dead, when his treason is burned from the earth, will spring return to our land."

When the dragon landed on the stone dais by her side, I felt my gut tightening. The cold didn't scare me, no, but fire was another matter altogether. My freezing body had started to make my thoughts slow, as though even my brain were encased in ice. Mentally sluggish, I couldn't quite piece together what was happening. What was the point of the river water if she planned to use the Sinach?

The water was up to my waist now. Did she want to burn the top half of me?

When she barked out a sharp command, my heart skipped a beat.

On the stone platform, the Sinach reared, unleashing a stream of flames into the water. The arena seats erupted in screams. No one wanted to see this.

Slowly, through the fog of my freezing brain, I put the pieces together. She wasn't going to drown me.

She was going to boil me alive.

The mirror dropped me east of the castle, and I immediately realized three things: one, the magical fragment had not come with me; two, wearing Shalini's coat had been one of the best decisions I'd ever made because it must be negative twenty here; and three, this place had turned into an absolute hellscape.

And that suggested that Torin did not, in fact, have his magic back.

Dread whispered through me. On the east side of the castle, cages hung from the walls with prisoners trapped inside. A few of the cages hung open, but most of them contained people, frozen and half dead. Bile rose in my throat. If Torin's throne were intact—if his magic had returned to him—he'd never allow this.

I scanned the cages desperately, searching for Shalini. No sign of her. A glimmer of good news.

In one of the cages, a woman crawled to the bars. Snow crusted her black hair and her pointed ears. "Help me," she rasped. "We're here because we were loyal to the king. Please help me."

"Who rules here now?"

"Moria. She took the king. She took him to the amphitheater." Hysteria barbed her voice. "Help me, please."

Horror hit me in the gut. "To the amphitheater? Why?"

"I don't know!" she shrieked. "Let me free, and I'll be able to think more clearly."

I breathed in a sharp, icy breath, feeling as if my thoughts were splitting in two. I could either race to the amphitheater now or I could try to fix his throne. If I returned to him the awe-inspiring power of a Seelie king, he might be able to save himself.

I stepped back in the snow, keeping Shalini's hood over my horns.

When I glanced to my left, I glimpsed two soldiers marching in the distance. Their maroon uniforms gave them the appearance of drops of blood against a white landscape.

Wasn't that Moria's favorite color?

Distantly, I heard the mournful wail of a banshee twisting through the air. Cleena, maybe.

A shudder snaked up my spine. Someone was about to die.

I looked up at the cages once more and summoned life from the frozen earth. It was much harder to make things grow here than it had been in the Court of Sorrows. In Faerie, a thick crust of ice covered the land, trapping the living world beneath winter. In the hollows of my mind, I connected to the plants beneath the soil, feeling their struggle to break free of the ice.

I closed my eyes and thought of the flames of the ash goddess that danced atop the mountain in the Court of Sorrows and of the seductive heat of the Unseelie kingdom. I thought of Torin kissing me deeply in the abandoned temple of the ash goddess. *Love is a forge...*

I clenched my teeth, my fingers tightening into fists. Vines were hammering at the ice, struggling to break free.

I opened my eyes. Plants burst from the wintry earth, whipped upward, and wrapped themselves around the cage doors.

With a flick of my wrist, the vines pulled open the rusty iron doors. I dropped Shalini's warm coat in the snow for one of the victims and freed my wings. They burst from my back, ripping Shalini's shirt, and I soared into the air. Soldiers heard the noise of the cages opening and came running.

Swooping around to the northern side of the castle, I flew through the open portcullis, then beneath the towering ceilings.

Shouts rang out behind me, but I was moving quickly, and the throne room wasn't far from the front gate. Behind me, a few archers unleashed arrows, but they flew harmlessly past.

My wings pounded the musty castle air, and I swooped into the throne room. A sheen of ice and frost gleamed off the stones, and a shiver chased down my spine.

Five soldiers dressed in black furs guarded the thrones, swords at their hips, but as in the Court of Sorrows, little weeds grew between the cracks in the floor. The soldiers ran at me, but I summoned thick, spiky vines. The vines snaked around the guards, and their swords clattered on the floor.

Locked within the ropes of plants, they shouted for backup. From behind, an arrow zipped past me, too close for comfort.

I whirled around. Zooming in on the little weeds by the door, I summoned them, bigger, higher, until they wove together to form a barrier to shield me from oncoming arrows.

With a hammering heart, I flew above the fallen soldiers and touched down behind Torin's throne. Winter light poured in through stained glass windows, washing the shattered throne in deep shades of gold and blue.

Brushing my fingertips over the frigid stones, I envisioned the shattered throne coming together. Warm magic skimmed over my body, kissing my skin.

Slowly, roots grew between the fragments, pulling and knitting them together. Magic hummed and buzzed up my spine, making my heart race and my body glow. Piece by piece, the throne came together, the roots tightening, burrowing into the stones until it was half stone, half root, like Mab's castle. Like an Unseelie throne...

Moss grew between the cracks until at last, a living throne stood, slightly misshapen but intact.

On the other side of my plant shield, soldiers hacked at the barrier.

I pivoted, my wings carrying me into the air. With a boot through the stained glass, I kicked my way out into the winter day. Glass shattered around me in shards of colored light.

A frozen wind whipped at me as I swept outside. On the wind, I heard the sound of screams. I tuned in to the noise, adrenaline sparking through my nerves.

What horrors was Moria unleashing?

39

TORIN

The dragon's fire blasted onto the water. At first, it felt like a warm bath, a relief from the ice. My toes thawed, and my muscles relaxed. Then, it became a punishing bath, the kind of bath that Ava enjoyed. The water grew warmer until it felt like how I imagined a volcanic lake. With Modron's magic, it reached my shoulders, coils of steam twisting around me in a thick fog.

I grimaced, bracing for more heat. But just as I thought it was about to scald my skin permanently, icy power ripped through me. My ice magic surged through my veins, and strength pumped through my blood. My thoughts swam with wild euphoria.

When my throne had broken, the loss of my magic had felt like losing one of my senses. Now, it crashed back into me with a sharper focus than ever before. The power of it was almost overwhelming, vibrating through my bones. Cold magic spilled from my body, cooling the steaming river water.

Had the gods blessed me?

I snapped the chains that bound my wrists, keeping my hands hidden under the water. The moment Moria realized I was free, she would circle over me with the Sinach and set me ablaze.

Mist billowed around me. Once the water reached my neck, I ripped off the collar that bound me to the pole.

I dipped under the murky surface, sending icy currents out from my body. I swam through twisting streams of muddy river water—some currents surging with heat, others chilled by my magic. But with ice and dragon fire mingling together, the heat was bearable.

When I was close to the dais, I rose from the water and exploded with frost. Glacial wrath poured from my body. This was my kingdom, and I would protect it from these monsters, from the nightmarish shadows encroaching on it.

The Sinach roared, breathing fire onto me, but I blocked it with ice. A brutal stream of hoarfrost burst from my chest, extinguishing the dragon's flames. Frost rippled over the creature's scales, and it recoiled.

Moria leaped onto the creature's back, and the Sinach took off into the skies, maroon-black scales gleaming with ice. As I climbed onto the dais, I searched for Modron. The old crone had already disappeared. The spectators in the stands were running, searching for exits.

The Sword of Whispers echoed inside my skull. I needed to get my hand on its hilt.

I raced down the exterior stairs of the amphitheater,

following the Sinach on foot. I ran barefoot through the snow, but the cold no longer touched me.

I raced through the wind in my tattered white clothes. To my left, dark, bare trees lined the snowy fields, the castle a small shadow against the white expanse.

I pumped my arms, legs burning with exertion. Snow kicked up around me as I sprinted. I could run fast, but not nearly fast enough to keep up with the Sinach.

What had happened to give me my power back? Aeron, perhaps.

I didn't have time to mull it over because Moria and her Sinach were circling again, the dragon's frosted scales gleaming under the dull winter sky. Like King Caerleon, she'd try to burn me to death.

Except now I wouldn't be so easy to kill.

The Sinach approached, scorching the earth with consuming fire. I countered with a plume of frigid air that doused the flames. The Sinach's dark wings beat the air, and he opened his mouth to roar, his fangs glinting in the dull winter light.

Another incendiary burst from the dragon's maw seared the air, but my magic crackled up my spine and erupted from my chest. Frost raced along the dragon's scales, turning them white and glazed. The Sinach's movements grew jerky and uneven.

Moria turned her dragon away from me, heading back to the castle. I followed her on foot again, feet pounding in the snow.

As I raced toward the castle, I spied a figure with black wings like a moth's. My world tilted.

Ava, my love, what the fuck are you doing?

৯ 40 ৯

AVA

The world below was a sea of white interrupted only by the line of bare trees to my right. Icicles hung from their dark, spiked boughs.

As I flew, my mind snagged on what Cala had said. *Nothing happens here without the queen's consent...*

If that were true, how had I escaped at all?

Except the queen had told me quite clearly what she wanted, hadn't she?

Slowly, the puzzle pieces slid together in my mind.

Everything that happened in the Court of Sorrows had been under her control. The imprisonment, the duel, the rules about not seeing each other on pain of a horrible death, the many promises to throw me off the tower...

Every single thing that had happened there had been a test, with the specific purpose of discovering if the queen could get what she wanted.

The sound of distant screams sent fear prickling up

my nape, interrupting my thoughts. Every inch of this place, every rock and slope of snow, every sharp blade of ice—it all exuded menacing brutality. When I'd first arrived for the competition, Faerie had seemed sinister. Now? The cold, rocky earth breathed violence.

The scent of sulfur and ash floated on the wind. And from the direction of the amphitheater, a monstrous form swept through the skies. An icy shiver danced through my nerve endings.

A dragon soared beneath the steely clouds, wings beating under a wintry sky. Perched on its back was a figure dressed in crimson, a smear of bittersweet nightshade against ink and bone.

My stomach plummeted. My plant magic, though amazing, was not the best defense against an actual inferno of hellfire. And with the thick layers of ice like a tomb over the earth, I needed to stop and concentrate to rip vegetation free.

I flew toward the cover of the skeletal trees. As I turned, the dragon soared closer, scorching the air with a blast of solar wind that singed my exposed skin and wings.

A tendril of panic twisted through my gut as I careened for the trees, angling my wings for speed but sacrificing control. I landed in a tumble of wings and limbs and snow. Pain shot through my wing bones, and I winced. But there was no time to nurse my wounds because the dragon was hurtling toward me.

Fear ignited my thoughts like lightning.

I lay at the edge of a forest, bare, black trees jutting like antlers from the white earth. This was my army, the trees, my soldiers. As the dragon swept closer, ready to breathe another stream of fire, the sharp boughs swept out above me like hands reaching for the dragon. Icicles dropped into the snow as the branches shifted, and the tree limbs twined around the dragon's throat.

The monster crashed to the icy ground, the force of the impact shaking the earth. A cloud of shimmering snow puffed around the dragon, frosting it. Snow dusted my body.

My blood roared with the predatory thrill of a hunter bringing down prey, and the trees formed a cage around the dragon.

In the puff of snow, I'd lost track of Moria.

I stood, wincing at the pain from my bruised wings. Winter kissed my skin.

The dragon lay only about fifty feet from me now. The creature was facing away from me, but if I didn't put enough distance between us, the monster might turn and ignite me with flames.

I flexed my wings, once, twice. My plan was to fly close to the trees to avoid the dragon, but with my injured wings, I wasn't sure I could do it.

Each time my wings thumped the air, a sharp pain burst through the left one. The snow whipped at my face, and I gritted my teeth, trying to fly higher, faster. I made it a few feet off the ground, but one wing felt weighted down, and my flight was uneven and meandering. Desperately, I wanted to get to Torin. Had I given him his power back? I hoped so. And what if Moria had already killed him? After all, she was flying *away* from the amphitheater, like she'd just finished the job.

A storm of dark, frantic thoughts whipped through my mind. I absolutely could not lose him again.

My heart stampeded in my chest as I struggled to lift off, tears stinging my eyes—until my gaze landed on another figure joining the fray. In the distance, through the whorls of snow, I spotted someone dressed in white rags streaked with blood. My heart cracked at the sight of Torin running barefoot through the snow, a tiny figure against the vast white landscape. The relief of it made hot tears spill down my cheeks.

But before I could make my slow, uneven flight closer to him, a hand clamped tightly around my ankle, and Moria ripped me out of the air.

I landed hard on my back, wincing at the excruciating pain running through my wing bones. Fear climbed up my throat. Now I *really* wouldn't be able to fly away from her.

As her eyes locked on me, she bared her fangs. Frantically, I tried to push up on my elbows, but in the next moment, her vampiric fangs were tearing at my throat. Terror spiraled through me as a corrosive toxin spilled into my body, making my muscles lock. It burned, eating at me from the inside.

My gaze swiveled to the dark trees above us. I summoned one of the branches. It reached through the air, a jagged, beckoning finger that curled around Moria's waist and plucked her off me. My hand went to my throat as the poison pulsed through my blood.

Moria snarled, struggling against the branches. My blood dripped down her body to the snow, spattering the white as she wrestled with the bough twisted around her. "Demon!"

Dazed, I tried to stand. Scarlet droplets fell to the snow from the wound in my neck, and I wasn't sure I had the strength to stand for long.

"It is my job," Moria yelled, "to protect my kingdom from demons. People think a woman like me can't do it? It is my job to show them that I can. My Sinach! Burn the traitors."

My chest tightened.

Where it lay trapped, the dragon reared its head. I staggered back, bracing for fire, but it wasn't looking at me.

The dragon's glowing red gaze was on Torin.

I shouted his name and tried to take flight again. Pain spiked through my wing, and I fell back onto the snow, dizzy from blood loss.

The dragon's fire roasted the air, a searing heat that I could feel from here, but Torin met the blast with an icy gale that ripped across the frozen landscape. His magic stung my skin. My teeth chattered, and my hands pressed into the snow—two red handprints against the pristine white. Blood spilled from my ripped throat.

Moria tore free from the branches, screaming for Modron, her voice ragged with hysteria. Leaning into the bitter wind, she pulled her cloak tight and headed for Torin.

I needed to fight her—Torin couldn't fight two monsters at once—but I could hardly stand. Dizzily, I staggered to my feet again.

And yet, my magic was powerful. I should be able to heal myself. That's what Morgant had told me.

I touched my ravaged throat and closed my eyes, envisioning the starkly beautiful face of my brother, the healer and bone crusher. Maybe I couldn't heal others like he could, but I should be able to heal myself. My vision blurred.

I looked down at my palm smeared with blood and snow and pictured Morgant's magic on my back. When he'd pulled the infection from my shoulder blades, it had felt like warm water trickling down my skin. As I recalled the feeling, magic crawled over my skin. Slowly, strength pulsed into my muscles, and the skin at my throat closed.

In my mind's eye, I saw the gnarled blue tree where I was born, its boughs burdened by the weight of the castle.

It had all been a test. Mab had wanted to make sure I was strong enough to kill my enemies. Love was a forge—viciously painful, but it made us stronger nonetheless.

I burn for him.

Power coursed through my blood as the gash in my neck healed and the pain in my cracked wing ebbed.

I searched the snowstorm for Torin, and my heart went still in my chest. Moria had leaped on top of him, her fangs sunk into his throat.

❧ 41 ❧
AVA

The dragon bellowed, trapped in dark boughs. I cut its roar short with another coil of trees and vines that snapped around its throat, clamping its jaws together.

My wings pounded the air. They were still sore and cracked, but they'd healed enough that I could force myself to fly. I folded them behind me, angling them to glide through the gale. The winter wind carried me, and the freezing air stung my lungs with every breath.

With adrenaline surging, I touched down behind Moria.

Torin's blood stained the snow, and I yanked her off him by her hair. She whirled to face me, her bloody fangs bared and her body glistening with blood. With the force of a Dark Cromm queen, I slammed my fist hard into her throat. She fell backward, flat into the snow. Torin tried to sit, but blood spilled from his throat.

I tried to summon a vine from the frozen earth to

wrap around Moria, but the plants were trapped beneath the ice. Moria gripped her throat, her eyes bulging as she struggled to breathe.

"Torin," I screamed through gritted teeth, "the ice!"

His eyes flashed with understanding. Pale blue magic skimmed across the landscape, and the ground began to rumble. Holding his bleeding throat, Torin split the ice, and a great crevasse opened in the earth, revealing the dead grass four feet below.

Clutching her throat, Moria tumbled into the hold and onto the frozen grass. I stepped to the edge of the ice and peered down at her. She was still gasping for breath.

"Demon," she croaked.

My thoughts went silent, my mind a haunted, quiet midnight, until a single incandescent thought lit up the darkness: *kill the queen.*

Moria tried to lift herself from the chasm, the Sword of Whispers gleaming at her hip. Time seemed to slow as an ancient power skimmed over my body, one that smelled of the forest and fresh grass. My body vibrated with life, and my skin buzzed. And when my chest had filled with a golden light, I arched my back and flung my magic at the queen.

A spiked, thorny vine raced from the grass, impaling her through her ribs. I exhaled a long, shaky breath, staring at my work.

Moria's body hung suspended in the air above the ravine, her blood dripping over the frosty grass.

Shadows whispered through me. Mab hadn't wanted

to release me until I was strong enough to kill the monsters. And now?

I was a monster.

I whirled, my pulse roaring at the sight of Torin's lacerated throat. He'd sat up in the snow for a moment, but he was losing blood. He slumped to the ground, and I knelt beside him, clamping my hand over his throat to stanch the flow.

Torin had taken a sword to the heart for me, and I could risk freezing at his touch.

"Torin," I shouted, holding his throat, "you're safe from her. Moria is dead. Use your magic to heal yourself."

He met my gaze for a moment, and electricity passed between us. His cold power skimmed over me, but it didn't freeze me. I kept my hand on his throat, feeling the cool thrum of his magic pulsing along my skin.

As he healed himself, Torin's jaw sagged with the realization that we were touching. He replaced my hand with his. "You touched me. Ava," he said sharply, "you shouldn't even be here. I told you not to come."

I swallowed hard. "The curse is gone, Torin."

He stared at me. "How could you possibly know that?"

"Because Queen Mab told me what she wanted. It took me a little while to put it all together, but it all makes sense now."

The earth trembled again, and shadows seemed to lengthen around us, growing thicker. Above us, the iron-gray sky seethed and writhed, churning with storm clouds.

A roar rumbled over the horizon, and from the clouds of white snow, a dark figure stalked closer, a shadow against a landscape the color of bleached bones. Her cloak swept around her lanky body like dark smoke, and her hood obscured her face. She swept closer to the tree line, disappearing into the forest, but I could feel her malign power from here.

Modron was hunting us. "What did you think would happen?" she shrieked. Her voice sounded dissonant and layered, like ten agonized people screaming at once. "What did you think I'd do when the Seelie exiled me? When King Finvarra had enough of the truth? Did you think I would go quietly?"

Torin stood. His throat was healed now, a dark red line all that remained of his wound. He staggered over the snow to Moria's corpse and took his sword. Whispers echoed through the air, a haunting sound, like a chorus of the dead.

Torin gripped the hilt of his sword. We stood separated from Modron by the crevasse.

Unease crept up my spine at the sound of a deep rumbling beneath the earth, like a volcano erupting.

"You should get out of here," Torin called out. "Fly."

"Not a chance. But I'm going to see what's happening."

My bruised wings pounded the snowy air, and I lifted into the skies for a better view. As I carried myself up higher above the tree line, fear spread through my chest.

From the east, where the Avon River flowed, a tsunami was coming for us, roaring over the snow and consuming the forest. The wave was seventy or eighty feet high, a tower of murky water that would kill everyone in its path.

I couldn't breathe. That monstrous wave would drown us all. It would sweep through the villages, flood the castle. It would carry away every house and farm in the kingdom.

My mind flickered, electrified with panic as I tried to figure out how to stop it.

"There's a tsunami coming, Torin," I shouted. "We need a bigger crevasse. Circle it around the castle, the city. We need city walls."

He acted without question, and the ice split with a loud crack, as if a great god were carving an arc around the city and villages.

I dropped onto the grass beside him. "It's less than a mile away. If we work together, I think we can build a wall faster."

I scanned the white landscape but could no longer see Modron. Still, I could feel her magic flowing across the ground.

I pressed my boots into the snow, feeling my connection to the earth. The heartbeat of spring pounded far beneath my feet, and light beamed over my body, a pale gold that spilled from my limbs and fingertips, warming the world around me.

My body vibrated with power, a molten heat that cracked beneath the cold surface. Grass, plants, and roots burst up from the soil, weaving together and shooting toward the heavens.

As my wall grew, Torin sent ice racing over it, making it rock solid. It was several feet thick, a barrier of ice and spring that rose to the stormy skies.

I am the Dark Cromm heir, forged in the mountains of the ash goddess, and I will protect those I love.

My mind erupted with an ancient power like flames dancing on the dark rocks, a night sky tinged red with fire. Miles of twisting vines and brambles shot from the earth as power thundered through my body. I wasn't Ava anymore. I was a vessel of the ash goddess.

A circle of life rose around the city, and Torin's ice glazed over the plants, filling in cracks. The magic of Seelie and Unseelie intertwined, as it had in the old days. The image of Mab kept flickering in my mind as plants encircled Faerie. I'd told Torin we belonged together, and here was the evidence.

Spring swept through me, a current of warmth.

As we finished our work, my body trembled, depleted of strength. Nauseous, I tried to stop myself from shaking.

Torin turned, scanning the snowy horizon.

"Modron." He spat out her name like a curse.

My gaze flicked up, and I saw her emerge from the forest. She was trying to slip away like smoke in the wind. Torin stalked after her.

As he did, the tsunami slammed into the walls, sending a shock through the snowy ground that knocked me to my hands and knees.

I turned, my heart frantic as large cracks began to

appear in some of the ice walls. Reaching deep within, I called forth more magic, filling the holes and cracks with moss and roots.

Water rumbled against the walls, making them shake.

I turned to see Torin open another crevasse ten feet in front of Modron.

He didn't need to ask. We knew each other's rhythms now, and I knew what to do. With the last steamy hiss of my magic, I summoned a wall of brambles, trapping Modron.

She stumbled as her path was blocked and whirled to face us. "All I ever did was tell the truth," she bellowed, her voice carrying across the snow "But the Seelie prefer to live with lies. Isn't that right?"

The whispers of Torin's sword echoed through the air in a haunted symphony. He carved his blade through Modron's neck, and the deep gray cloak fell to the earth, empty. Only her head remained, rolling on the snow. I stared at the gruesome sight, clutching my stomach. My reserves of magic were completely spent, and exhaustion burned through me.

I knelt in the snow, and Torin dropped his sword and ran to me. He wrapped his arms around me, and I leaned against him.

"The walls," I muttered against his chest. But even as the words were out of my mouth, I could feel the thaw in the air. The warmth kissing my skin wasn't just from Torin. The sun slid from behind the clouds.

"Her magic is gone," said Torin, his voice husky. He

scooped me up, carrying me toward the castle. "The wave is receding."

I lay against Torin as rays of light gilded the white landscape and gleamed off the icy walls. I glanced above me, watching the dark storm clouds thin and the sky bloom with blue. Our icy walls began to glisten.

"Where are you taking me?" I asked, listening to the rhythmic pounding of his heart.

He breathed in. "Our enemies are dead, my love. The Seelie live for pleasure, not war. And with that in mind, changeling, I have been dreaming for a long time of feeding you apples in my room."

✣ 42 ✣
AVA

I lay entangled in Torin's sheets and took a deep, shuddering breath. I'd been asleep a few hours, I think, and I'd dreamed of Torin jumping in front of the sword. I'd dreamed of my fall from the tower, but with wings that never burst from my back. And then I'd dreamed of Moria, her body dangling limply from that vine, the blood spilling out beneath her.

I shuddered, bringing my gaze to the sun-drenched glass ceiling above Torin's bed. Apricot light streamed through the leaves of the tree in his room, dappling everything with coral.

It was all over now, wasn't it?

At least, I hoped it was. Worry scratched the surface of my thoughts. I still had no idea where Shalini had been when the wave hit. My throat felt tight.

I rose, my gaze sweeping over the apple tree that grew in the center of his room. Torin had carried me in here, and he'd told me to eat as many apples as I'd wanted. Instead, I'd simply fallen into a deep sleep tormented by nightmares.

I plucked a cherry-red apple from the tree and bit into it. The taste exploded on my tongue. Gods, this was heaven. Torin said he thought the tree had been dead until we'd killed Modron.

I crawled back into his bed, eating my way through the apple. When my gaze flicked up to the glass ceiling, my heart jolted with joy at the sight of the sunset once more. I'd never seen it this gorgeous in Faerie.

As I was finishing my apple, Torin opened the door to his room, flashing me a lopsided smile as he took off his shoes. "You're awake."

My pulse raced. "Did you find Shalini and Orla?"

"Both of them, in fact. And Aeron. He was leading them to a cabin in the woods when the flood hit, but they were within the boundary of our walls."

I exhaled a long breath. "Are they okay?"

He slid into the bed next to me, sunlight washing over him from above. "They will be, but Moria hung them in cages. They need time to recover."

My eyes widened, cold fury crackling through my chest. "Shalini, too? What the fuck did Shalini ever do to anyone?"

"Nothing, of course. It's just that she was your friend, and thus a demon lover."

I supposed it was a good thing the person I wanted to murder was already dead. Saved me the effort. "And she's fine?"

"She had some frostbite, but I healed it. In a way, she seems better than Orla. Orla was in the cage longer,

I think. She seems very rattled by the whole thing." He ran a hand through his hair. "She keeps talking about the cold like she can't get warm."

I shuddered, shadows flitting through my thoughts. "It must have been horrible. Can I see Shalini?"

"She's sleeping, but soon. Of course." He slid into the bed next to me. Sunlight slanted in through his ceiling, lighting up his features with dabs of gold.

I turned to lay on Torin's chest, and he stroked a finger down my lower back. I licked my lips, and they tasted of sweet, tangy apples. Light warmed my skin, and I felt as if I fed off it, just like trees.

My muscles throbbed with exhaustion. After I'd burned all the power from my body, strength was slowly seeping back into my limbs. Still, I wanted to sleep for days, wrapped in Torin's arms.

I traced my fingertips over the red scar at his throat. "See? I'm still alive." I arched an eyebrow. "No curse."

"I still don't understand." He caught my finger in his hand. "How were you so certain?"

I hadn't been one hundred percent certain, but I didn't need to mention that now.

I turned onto my back and nestled in the crook of his arm. "Mab told me several times that what she wanted was her heirs on the throne of Faerie. With us, she could get that." My mouth curved in a smile as I felt Torin's heart against my arm. For so long, I'd thought he was dead. I'd never take the feeling of his beating heart for granted.

"Yes...but why torture us, then?"

I sighed. "Everything that happened there was a

test. First, they wanted to see if I'd come as a spy. But really, what she wanted to know was whether you loved me, and if I was strong enough to be queen. You broke me out of the cell, and that suggested you cared about me. When they captured us again, they wanted to know if you loved me enough to make me queen. She issued the most horrific threats to castrate you if you came to see me. And you did it anyway. She *could* have stopped that from happening, I'm sure. She could have put us on opposite sides of the castle, guarded. But that was part of the test. She wanted to know if you'd risk your own life. Because if you would do that for me, maybe I could end up on the throne of Faerie. Even as an Unseelie, horns and all."

He arched an eyebrow. "The fight was to see if I would sacrifice myself for you. Did she care if you loved me?"

I nodded slowly. "I think she did, because they kept telling me the strength of Unseelie magic came from the pain of love. Maybe from the desperate anxiety of needing to keep loved ones safe. She wanted me to be strong. Without magic, without my wings, I wouldn't be a Dark Cromm queen. So, the next test was whether I was strong enough to be her heir, strong enough to take down my enemies, like we did today."

"Love," he said doubtfully. "Their version of love is twisted."

"It's not the gentle, comforting kind of love. They worship the ash goddess. Their love is a forge that burns them and everyone around them. It's the kind of love that makes a mother throw her child off the side of a castle to see if she can fly."

"Is that love?" Torin sounded disbelieving. "It sounds like Moria's father putting her outside in a cage to make her strong."

"Maybe." I sat up and stretched my arms over my head. "But she was a little girl, and I'm supposed to be a warrior. I still don't know if Mab wanted Morgant to fly after me to keep me safe, or if he did that himself. But I suppose nothing there happens without her consent, does it? It all worked out like she hoped, and she took the curse away. Now she can have what she wants, a Dark Cromm heir on the throne of Faerie."

"You're not going to convince me to be grateful to her."

"I wouldn't dream of it." A phantom breeze rippled over us, carrying with it the scent of apples. I licked my lips, considering another one. "Those apples are surprisingly addictive, Torin."

His pale blue eyes lifted to the tree that arched above his room. "Yes. They're called Blood of the Avon apples. They're bright red, named after the brutal battle of the Avon River between the Seelie and Unseelie centuries ago. We nearly wiped each other out. The apples hardly ever grew in our kingdom because of the curse. They need exactly the right temperature and sunlight, and the soil must be fed with blood. And if not, they grow up twisted and thorny."

"Hang on. What?"

He stroked his hand down my hair. "Ava, I think I know why Finvarra banished Modron."

I blinked, trying to rid myself of the image of Torin carrying a bucket of blood into his bedroom. "Because she was a living nightmare?"

"The legends were that once, the Seelie and Unseelie lived in these lands together. And among them lived a set of twins, old as the earth itself. Cala and Modron. I've also heard that King Finvarra had a taste for Unseelie women, and he kept giving his mistresses more favors. More land and titles. I think Modron told everyone his business. Showed them, even, what happened behind the king's closed doors. So Finvarra banished her, and a war broke out between the two factions."

"Aren't you directly related to him?" I asked. "A taste for Unseelie women must run in the blood."

"I don't have a taste for Unseelie women. Just you."

I wrapped my arm around his waist. "Do you think the Seelie will ever accept someone like me?"

"It will take time. Even I'm still shocked at the idea that the Seelie and demons belong together."

"You're never going to stop calling me demon, are you?"

"Sorry, changeling." A fingertip stroked up my horn, sending hot shivers through my body.

"I don't know if Seelie and demons belong together. But you and I belong together. I'm just not sure your subjects will agree."

"They will. When everyone understands the curse is gone for good, and that you helped save the kingdom, they won't care if you have wings or horns. People just want to feed their families and keep them safe. If we give it a few months, they will love you as I do." His eyes danced in the sunlight, and a wicked smile curled his lips. "Well, not *exactly* as I do."

A smile spread over my lips.

When I'd first arrived in this place, I'd thought them all ruthless and powerful as gods. And they were. But a person—even a fae—was like these Blood of Avon trees. They could be delicious and beautiful, even if fed on blood. But if you miss out on important elements that they need to thrive, they grow up twisted and thorny.

I swallowed hard. I'd heard how Moria had been kept in a cage. That Milisandia was the only person who'd ever shown her an ounce of kindness. Once her sister died, the rot began to set in.

I slid my fingertips under Torin's shirt and skimmed them over his tattoos. It was only this morning—just this morning as dawn broke—that I'd thought to never see him again. Before that, in the dungeon of the Court of Sorrows, I'd been certain his heart would never beat again.

And here we were, limbs entwined.

This was where I belonged. Here, in Faerie, the smoke rose from the ruins of an ancient war. Peace reigned, even if nightmares would plague us for a while.

The fae had been tempered in the fires of a mountain goddess to live lives that were wild and incandescent. But we didn't *need* bloodshed. The Unseelie lived for duty, the Seelie for pleasure.

And now, I was pretty sure I wanted nothing more than to indulge in the Seelie world.

But as I lay back in his bed, a familiar magic skimmed over my skin, the warm, liquid power I'd felt when my brother had healed me.

I rose from Torin's bed and crossed to one of his towering windows. Spring had blossomed outside already—within just hours, the snow had melted. The icy walls still stood, but they were fast becoming slush. Green grass spread out from the castle, and a carpet of bluebells strained for the setting sun.

But my breath caught at the sight of two dark-winged figures standing at the edge of the forest, their long shadows slanting over the grass. Twilight, when the worlds thinned...

Morgant and Mab stared at my window, washed in rosy light. My heartbeat sped up, and I felt as if I were looking at ghosts. I stared at them and lifted a hand.

In the distance, my brother waved back.

"What do you think you will do here, as queen?" asked Torin.

I turned back to him, my heart slamming hard. Flat on his back, he threaded his fingers behind his head.

When I glanced outside again, Mab and Morgant had disappeared. My heart clenched, and I breathed out slowly.

"Who says I plan to be queen here?" I asked, my voice shaking.

His lips quirked. "We do technically have a contract."

I pressed my hands to my chest. "That's so romantic. You also owe me fifty million, by the way."

He went very still. "You are staying, aren't you?"

As if there was any question. I climbed back into the bed next to him, feeling as if I'd just woken from another dream. "I suppose I could open my bar here. Chloe's? That's been my whole plan all along, really."

He brushed his knuckles along my bicep. "The Seelie king and his demon bride."

"We can get married, but at the wedding, I draw the line at sacrifices. We should fuck around bonfires and in the woods. I was promised this kind of party when I first got here."

A mischievous smile curled his lips. "At a wedding, changeling? Honestly."

"A Beltane wedding." I smiled. "Don't you remember promising me Beltane? *We fuck each other hard up against the oak trees,*" I began in my best imitation of his voice, "*rending the forest air with the sounds of our ecstasy. When was the last time you forgot your name? That you forgot your own mortality? Because that is what it means to be fae. I could make you ache with pleasure until you forgot the name of every human who ever made you think there was anything wrong with you.*"

He stared at me, his dark pupils dilated. The look he was giving me sent a hot electric thrill through me, and the power of his magic caressed my skin. "You remembered that word for word."

"It's seared into my memory, and I plan to have it engraved on your tombstone."

"Are you plotting my death already?"

"Just reminding you of what you promised."

"Who am I to tell the demon queen no?" He stroked

a finger lightly up one of my horns, sending a shudder through me.

He slid his hand into my hair, then pressed his lips against mine, capturing my mouth with his. The kiss started sweet, then deepened into something fiercer, hungrier. Desperate. As if we could sweep away the nightmares of death with the sensual magic of a kiss.

If anyone possessed that kind of magic, I was certain it was my Seelie king.

❧ 43 ❧

SHALINI

ix months later.

I caught my breath, my body wrapped around Aeron's. I nestled my head into the crook of his throat, inhaling the perfumed scent of the bath. Steam from the bathwater curled into the air, caught in the light from the window.

We'd moved into a new house not far from the castle, with windows overlooking Faerie's new gardens. Not overlooking the castle. I *hated* the castle, and I never wanted to see it again.

Beneath our window, roses grew along pebbled paths, and apple trees spread out in rows toward the forest. From here, I had a view of a breeze rustling the sunlit trees.

Aeron rose from the bath, water streaming down his finely cut body in rivulets. I'd never get sick of looking at him naked.

"You still haven't taken me to your dive bar, Shalini,"

he said. "Remember? You wanted to take me for chili dogs."

I rose from the bath and drained the water. "Well, maybe we don't need to go back to the Golden Shamrock. Now we've got Chloe's."

I grabbed a towel. Tonight would be the opening night of Ava's new cocktail bar—a first for Faerie.

Aeron dried his damp hair. "Doesn't it seem odd for the future Unseelie queen to open a tavern? In the castle, no less?"

I dried off my limbs, trying not to envision the icy castle walls or the icicles hanging from the iron bars in the cage where I'd been sure I would die.

I found myself staring out the window.

As if reading my thoughts, Aeron asked, "Will you be all right, Shalini, going back there?"

I nodded. "I think so. I can't miss her opening night. It's always been Ava's dream."

"To be a tavern wench."

I rolled my eyes, stepping out into our bedroom. Tonight was the first night of many that Ava would be hosting, hundreds invited at a time, until everyone would have the chance to be wined and dined by the future queen.

"I don't think it will be like a human bar. The idea, I think, is that it will be a way of inviting ordinary Seelie into the castle, to give them food and drink. It's to make them feel like part of its history. She's doing it for the people you called the common fae. The people Moria called 'peasants.'"

"I see." He strode into our room and pulled open his wardrobe.

"Ordinary fae without magic are the majority of your kingdom, and that's who she wants to impress. They've never been invited into the home of royalty like that before, have they? Unless it was as a soldier or servant. It's brilliant, really. And she has a lot of work to do if she wants Faerie to accept a queen with wings and horns."

"It does make sense. I just never would have thought of it. Our traditions are changing so rapidly here, it's hard to keep up." He smiled at me, droplets of water glistening on his skin, and kissed me on the forehead. "And that's a good thing, really, or I'd still be bound by my stupid oath of chastity."

⚜

MY GAZE FLICKED UP THE CASTLE WALLS, AND I FELT my chest tightening. In the echoes of my thoughts, I heard the dragon's roar.

Since I hadn't gone near the castle in months, I had no idea what I'd be walking into. I felt amazing, sure, in my pale gold gown with a slit up my thigh, but inside, I felt like I couldn't quite breathe. Dressed in a dark velvety suit, Aeron looped his arm through mine and stroked his hand over my forearm. "I'll be with you, love."

Thank the gods for Aeron.

Torches lit the path outside the castle, and I

followed a line of guests inside, most of them in ball-gowns or velvety formal suits like Aeron's.

We entered the castle. Torches on the walls lit the way, casting warm, dancing light over the stones and arches. As we walked through the hall, I swallowed hard, trying to banish the memory of being dragged in here, chained. I still hated it here.

But tonight, the whole place seemed transformed, and it helped me to relax a little. Blooming flowers snaked over the walls, and the air smelled alive with flowers.

Stewards guided us to an enormous, vaulted doorway with the name CHLOE carved in the stone, surrounded by etchings of vines.

Arm in arm with Aeron, I crossed through the doorway into a hall that was half stone, half open to the night sky. My breath caught as I surveyed the scene.

Red-tipped vines of indigo blue climbed stone columns and walls, and they flickered with tiny white lights. At the top of dark columns, fires burned like bright licks of volcanic flames against the night sky. Music floated through the air, and servants brought around trays with food and flutes of colored drinks. One of these nights, they'd be here as guests, too.

From across the hall, Ava caught my eye. She hurried over to me, a grin lighting up her face. Her skin glowed. "You both look amazing. Shalini, I'm so happy tonight."

"Ava." I clapped my hand to my chest. "This is much, much nicer than the Golden Shamrock."

She gave me a wicked smile. "But I am introducing them to chili dogs and nachos, and they *love* them. They think they're very sophisticated." She leaned in, whispering. "Don't tell anyone they're vegetarian."

I arched an eyebrow, whispering, "Since when did you become vegetarian?"

She shrugged. "It's an Unseelie thing."

Aeron plucked two amber cocktails off a tray and handed me one. "So this isn't really a tavern, then. You're not charging for any of this."

Her eyes widened. "No. We don't need the money. I just want people to have fun here for once. Also, honestly, I want them to accept me. And what is the best way to get people to like you?"

I nodded, raising my cocktail. "Free drinks."

Torin sauntered over to us, his hands in his pockets. He was beaming with pride over Ava's efforts.

Ava smiled. "That's how I ended up kissing Threesome Steve the night we met Torin. He bought me a margarita pitcher."

I narrowed my eyes. "I don't think that's quite what you're going for here, though, is it? Because that was creepier."

"Good point."

Torin pressed a finger to his lips, frowning. "Can we go back a moment to what you just said, Ava?"

Ava waved a hand. "The past is the past, and we are here to have fun. That is what the Unseelie do, right? We will dance and drink and love each other until our dying breath."

The word *dying* rang in my thoughts for a bit too long, but I inhaled and took in the faces of my beautiful friends. A fragrant wind slipped over us.

Nightmares still plagued me—the feel of the cold gnawing at my skin and the certainty that I would die. The dragon's roar and the scorching heat of its fire.

Sometimes, I still felt haunted by the memory of frozen ghosts twisting outside my windows.

But I was here now, arm in arm among the people I loved. With them around me, winter had started to recede again, the terror thawing—just as it had in Faerie.

ALSO BY C.N. CRAWFORD

A full listing of our books can be found on our website, and also on Amazon.

If you enjoyed this series, you might also enjoy Agent of Enchantment, a fae portal series.

Please read on for an excerpt.

EXCERPT FROM AGENT OF ENCHANTMENT

Excerpt from Agent of Enchantment

The fae lay on the ancient flagstones, candlelight dancing over his handsome features.

I had power over him now, and it intoxicated me. I was beyond taking things slow, beyond being careful. I was a fugitive, at the end of the line. I had very little to lose.

Standing below the towering stone arches of the ancient London church, I stared at him. Candlelight wavered around the nave, and high above me, thick shadows danced over the peaked vaults like malicious spirits. I took a deep breath, the battle over.

At least, I thought it was over.

As I drew closer, he seemed to rally, his lips curling into a grimace. With a roar, he leapt to his feet, charging me in a blur of movement. He moved impossibly fast, and yet to my eyes time seemed to slow down. His powerful arms swung like heavy pendulums, as if he were moving through a sea of honey.

Reflexes took over as I slid aside and let his fist pass me. Then, with both hands, I grabbed his wrist. Dipping my hips, I used his momentum to send him flying into a stone pillar. The crunch of his bones echoed off the vaulted ceiling, and dusty stone rained down on us.

The asshole had wanted to keep me in a cage, to torture me for fun. He wasn't going to see my merciful side.

With a dark smile curling my lips, I stalked toward him. A trickle of blood ran down his forehead, and he glared at me with his good eye. He snarled, a bestial sound—a predator, unused to being prey. As I came within reach, he tried to punch me in the stomach.

I slapped his hand away, then backhanded him across the face. His head snapped right, and he fell to the floor. I picked him up by the collar and hurled him at a row of pews. When he crashed into them, his body splintered the wood.

And yet he kept going, dragging himself up again, breath rasping.

This time I charged fast, intent on beating seven shades of shit out of him, but he was reaching for his boot. A knife? No. I recognized the familiar shape of a Glock 17, rising to point at my chest. My heart thundered. *Shit shit shit.* I dove, but not in time.

A gunshot echoed off the stone. Pain ripped through my side. Gasping, I fell back, clutching at my waist, my hands covered in blood.

He stood slowly, training the gun on me as I stumbled back, pain splintering my gut. The custom iron bullet seared me from within, and I fell to my knees.

Already the poison was spreading through my body, dizzying me. Quenching my magic. I gritted my teeth, mentally whispering my mantra. *Be prepared to kill everyone you meet.* Right about now, that wasn't working out so well for me.

His pale eyes flashing with fury, he pulled the trigger again, but it only clicked dully. The gun was empty. A small mercy.

"Well." He smiled wryly, walking toward me. "I guess I could always kill you the old-fashioned way."

I crawled away from him, gripping my gut, trying to block out the searing agony. "I should have known it was you. A fascination with power. Obsession with fear. You worship chaos..." Shivers wracked my body as the blood seeped through my fingers. "I profiled you all along."

"Mmm. Yet look where you are now, mongrel," he growled, eyes gleaming.

"Yeah, well..." I looked down at my blood-stained fingers. "I like to know that I got things right."

He kicked me in the stomach, right where he'd shot me. I gasped with pain, collapsing to my back, staring at the arched stone ceiling. Shadows writhed along the pillars, as if this place were cursed. And maybe it was—Smithfield, the vortex of slaughter. Moaning, I gritted my teeth.

The fae smiled, apparently enjoying my grimace of pain.

At the sight of his shit-eating grin, rage flared in me.

Fight, Cassandra. Always fight. If only there were some way I could use my remaining magic... I grasped around me for metal, glass, anything.

"No one to save you anymore." He knelt over me, running a fingertip down my chest. "No more tricks. No more magic. Just me and you. Do you know what I think I'd like to do? Break your ribs, one by one. I want to see the fear in your eyes. What do you think, profiler? Will I enjoy it?"

A line of blood trickled from my mouth. "I think you need a more pro-social hobby."

He leaned over me, his pupils black as coal, completely devoid of feeling. "Ready to die, mongrel?" he asked, pressing his knee on the gunshot wound.

I screamed.

"I'll take that as a yes." His fingers wrapped around my throat.

As if in a dream, I stared into his eyes. So soulless, so empty, that I could see nothing in them but my own reflection.

FIVE DAYS EARLIER

Despite my Special Agent training, I nearly got myself killed three seconds after leaving Heathrow airport. I could handle snipers, knife attacks, poison, bombs—just not cars driving on the left side of the road.

But hey, in my defense, I was a bit preoccupied with the serial killer case I'd been called in to profile.

Anyway, three steps into the road, and it was all screeching brakes, honking, and the words "stupid twat" and "fuckwit" piercing the air.

And I'd been thinking everyone in England would be polite.

As the red-faced man continued his tirade ("Watch where you're going, fucking dozy mare!"), I jumped back to the sidewalk, cheeks burning. I took a deep breath, forcing myself to focus. I was in England now. The land of Shakespeare, Chaucer, and—as I was quickly learning —inventive swearing. They drove on the *left* here, something I should really keep in mind.

Having oriented myself, I decided that maybe navigating my way to a bus in a foreign city in the middle of the night was beyond my capabilities right now.

I mentally scanned through everything I'd digested in my tourist guide on the plane: trains, the Underground, black cabs. Perhaps best to just get one of those. Supposedly, the black cab drivers were required to memorize the entire city, street by street.

I turned, catching a glimpse of the yellow *Taxi* sign by a long line of cabs. Pulling my suitcase behind me, I hurried across the crosswalk, back toward the terminal. As I hustled past the airport's gleaming windows, I caught a glimpse of myself: pale skin, rumpled blond hair, wrinkled skirt, and coffee stains on my white sweater.

Apart from the gloriousness of my favorite black boots, I looked like shit.

I reached the line of black cabs, and a bearded man rolled down the window, leaning over. "Taxi?"

"Yes, thank you," I said, relieved. "I need to get to the Bishopsgate police station."

"No problem." He smiled. "Hop in. I'll get your bags."

I let him put my carry-on in the trunk while I slid into the back seat. *At least some of them are polite.*

The driver got in, switched on the engine, and rolled into traffic. I relaxed into the soft leather seat.

I stared out the window at the dark West London streets. I was pretty sure we had a long drive ahead of us to the other side of London—the part called "the City." It was the old section of London, the part the Romans had encircled with a wall nearly two thousand years ago. The wall had fallen, but the ancient Square Mile still had its own governing bodies, separate from the rest of London. The Square Mile even had its own City police force.

My phone buzzed in my pocket, and I pulled it out. My stomach churned as I watched the contact name slowly scroll across the screen: *Under No Circumstances Should You Answer A Call From This Ballsack*, it read.

That would be my ex-boyfriend.

See? Brits aren't the only ones who can swear creatively.

I'm not normally the angry sort, but when I'd come home to find that my boyfriend had left open a dating site on my computer (username: *VirginiaStallion*), the swears had just rolled off the tongue.

According to a quick Google search, the Virginia Stallion had also been quite busy swapping dating tips on bodybuilding forums. Apparently, wearing a nicely tailored suit attracts the ladies, and Valentine's Day can be a nightmare when you're "banging three chicks on the regular." All things I'd learned in the past two weeks.

You'd think I'd be more careful about the kind of men I let into my life. Lesson learned for the future.

Scowling, I shoved my phone back in my pocket.

The driver glanced back at me. "Did you come from America or Canada?"

"The US. It's my first time here." I bit my lip. "Have you ever encountered the phrase 'dozy mare?'"

"Did someone call you that, miss?"

"Based on the context, I'm assuming it wasn't a compliment."

"I wouldn't pay it any mind, love." He turned onto a highway. "You working with the police at Bishopsgate? I don't imagine you came all the way from America to report a crime."

"Just doing a bit of consulting," I said. "Insider trading cases in the City. White-collar stuff."

A lie, and one boring enough that he wouldn't ask any follow-up questions. I'd become quite used to lying after a few years with the Bureau, though I still lacked the skill of the Virginia Stallion.

"Right," he said. "The financial district. You ask me, half those people should be in jail. Mucking about with the stock market and all that. Screws it up for everyone."

"Couldn't agree more."

My lies bored even me, but I wasn't about to expose the fact that I was here to profile London's most famous serial killer since Jack the Ripper. Plus, it creeped people out when I said I was an FBI special agent. And it *particularly* spooked them if they learned I worked for the Behavioral Analysis Unit, as a psychologist who profiled criminals. All of a sudden, people got jittery, as if I were going to unearth their darkest secrets just by looking into their eyes.

We lapsed into silence as the cab sped along the M4. As we drove further into the city, I began to feel a change tingle over my body, as though my senses were becoming heightened. Here, in the center of the City, the streetlights seemed to burn brighter, washing the streets in white light. On a road called Chancery Lane, we drove past squat Tudor-looking buildings, the colored lights from the shops on their lower floors dazzling off puddles on the pavement. No one lingered on the dark streets at this hour, but for just a moment, I thought I heard the buzz of a crowd of people; then it faded into the distance again.

A shiver rippled over my body. I'd never been to London, and yet I had a strange sense of déjà vu here. *Get a grip, Cassandra.*

The driver turned to me. "You hear about the new Ripper murders in the City?" he asked.

"I did hear about them. It freaked me out. Nearly canceled my trip," I lied. "You don't normally get many murders around here, do you?"

"Not like you do. We don't have guns. But these murders... I wouldn't advise walking around at night if I was you. From what I hear, they didn't even put the worst of it in the papers. The girls they found, they was..." He cleared his throat. "Well, I don't want to scare you."

"I'll certainly be careful."

I didn't need him to tell me the details—I'd been poring over them for the entire flight, and before that, in my BAU office back at Quantico. I practically knew the depth of each laceration by heart. Still, the cab driver's concern was cute, and I appreciated it. I was quickly reviving my "polite" theory of Brits.

A few days ago, the City of London police had persuaded me to fly to the UK. The London FBI overseas office was slammed with other work, the attachés delving into investigations of terrorism cases and election interference. None of them had time for a serial killer, but I'd made my career off these cases. I'd been researching serial killers for the Bureau for years. The strange details of this case had piqued my Unit Chief's interest—enough that he was willing to foot the bill. And the City Police wanted to meet me as soon as I arrived—a Detective Constable Stewart was waiting for me, even at this late hour.

I rummaged in my bag, searching for some makeup and my mirrored compact. I pulled out a rose lipstick and dotted some pink on to my pale cheeks in the reflection. As I did, something glimmered in my blue irises—a hint of rushing water, like a rolling river.

I snapped the compact shut. *I am losing my mind.* I obviously needed sleep, or water, or perhaps several Manhattans.

I rubbed my forehead. I was supposed to head straight to the station to quickly meet the detective, and the details of the case nagged at the back of my mind.

The driver looked over his shoulder at me. "Lots of papers to go through, I imagine. With your sort of work."

"Oh, you have no idea. I'd better go through some of the financials now, in fact." Diving back into my bag, I pulled out the case reports the police had sent earlier that week. I flipped through them, taking care to shield the gruesome photos from the driver.

Over the past month, three young women had been found dead in London. The killer had slashed their throats and abdomens open. And just like Jack the Ripper, he'd claimed macabre trophies: a uterus from one, a kidney and heart from another. From the third victim, he'd taken her liver.

So was this a Ripper copycat? The papers certainly thought so. The UK tabloids were already gleefully declaring "The Ripper Is Back!"

I wasn't so sure we were dealing with the same mentality. The killer was almost certainly inspired by the Ripper, but he was killing at a much faster pace.

Staring at one of the crime scene photos, I shook my head. I'd never understood why Jack the Ripper had gotten so much attention. He was hardly the worst, in numbers or methodology. Perhaps it was the name that had inspired endless horror stories. Or the fact that the lack of resolution provided fertile ground for wild conspiracies. Whatever the reason, no one could quite let it go.

My phone buzzed in my pocket, and I grumbled

under my breath. But when I pulled it out to glance at the screen, it read *Unknown Number*.

Tentatively, I swiped the screen. "Hello?"

"Agent Liddell?" It was a British man with a deep voice. A faint London accent, I thought.

"Speaking."

"I'm Detective Constable Gabriel Stewart. I'm the detective in charge of the serial killer cases."

"Right. Hi. I'm on my way to meet you right now." Gabriel was supposed to be my contact.

He cleared his throat. "I think you should come directly to Mitre Square instead."

I glanced at the time. It was past midnight. "Why?"

"There's been another murder." He paused for a moment as a siren wailed in the background. "Mitre Square is the location of the crime scene."

⚜

If I had any hope that the crime scene would be reasonably contained, it evaporated the moment I turned down the narrow covered alley leading to Mitre Square. Blocked by a line of police tape, a small crowd jammed one end of the passage, barring my way. One of the men seemed to be leaning against the wall, half asleep, and the entire passage smelled of piss and beer.

Pausing, I pulled out my phone to call Detective Stewart.

"Hello?" The detective answered almost immediately.

"Detective, it's Cassandra."

"Who?"

"Agent Cassandra Liddell."

"Oh, right! Are you close?"

"I'm standing just outside the crime scene perimeter in Mitre Passage," I said. "Do you want to let me inside?"

"Sure, just wait until Officer Holbrook comes over to you. Flash your badge, and he'll let you right through."

"Maybe I should be more discreet with all these spectators around?"

He went silent for a moment. "Good point," he finally said. "I'll come for you myself."

I hung up, gripping my suitcase a little tighter and scanning the crowd. For all I knew, the killer could be lingering around here to watch the action. It was one of those weird quirks of some serial killers, returning to the scene of the crime to relive it. I wasn't sure exactly what I was looking for, as his previous history suggested he wasn't overtly psychotic or disorganized. But it wouldn't hurt to memorize the faces for later. I looked at them hard for a long moment, imprinting the view in my mind. Satisfied, I relaxed and took a deep breath.

Despite the fact that half the people here were three sheets to the wind, I could sense an undercurrent of fear beneath their drunkenness. My guess was that whatever lay beyond in Mitre Square was sobering them up pretty fast.

In all honesty, it wasn't just that I could sense their fear. I could actually *feel* it, like a physical charge. And right now, it was building in my system.

As always, it started with my heart. It began pounding faster and faster, each beat thundering in my ears. My fingertips prickled with what felt like a delicate electrical current. Despite the chilly night breeze, my face flushed, heat waves rolling over my body.

The first time I had described this to my friends, they'd just stared at me. I'd assumed everyone felt this way occasionally. Sometimes you're hungry, sometimes you want to sneeze, and sometimes you feel like the emotional energy of the people around you powers your body like electricity. Right? *Right?*

Apparently not. This was not a sensation everyone experienced. This happened only to me. And after talking about it a few times, and getting very weird looks, I stopped mentioning it. Energy? What energy? Ha ha, the only energy I know is energy drinks. I'm totally like everyone else.

Whatever it was, it came from strong emotions. Going to a football game in my hometown was... intense. I'd walk out dazed, a grin on my face, and when someone asked me if I'd enjoyed the game that much, I would realize that I didn't even know what had happened on the field. I knew what had happened in the *crowd*. They were thrilled, or disappointed, or angry... and I felt it blazing through my body like a drug.

But no other emotion affected me like fear did. And right now, an undercurrent of fear flowed through me. It focused me, sharpening my senses. Any fatigue from the flight dissipated completely.

I began shoving my way through the small crowd, rolling my stupid suitcase behind me. As I did, I glimpsed a media van parked in the road. Damn it. Nothing hurt a serial killer investigation more than public fear.

I reached the police tape, staring at the horrific scene before me. Spotlights bathed it in white light. About seventy feet away, on the other side of the square, a group of people surrounded a woman's body. Even from here, I could see the crimson pool glistening on the cobbles beneath her.

Most of the investigators surrounding the body wore white overalls that covered their bodies completely, surgical masks on their faces. Shoes were covered with white sterile wrappers, and their hands were gloved in blue latex. Only their eyes were visible as they scanned the scene intently, documenting and marking evidence.

A tawny-skinned man approached, eyeing me. Unlike the crime scene crew, he wore a suit and a gray coat.

"Gabriel?" I asked when he got closer.

He nodded, and motioned me through. I raised the tape and stepped under it, then leaned my suitcase against a wall before turning to him.

He shook my hand, his grip firm. I found it difficult to pull my eyes from his face. Broad-shouldered and tall, he towered over me, and something about his hazel eyes drew me in. Plus, with his bronze skin and strong jawline, he kinda looked like a movie star.

His body seemed tense. "Agent Liddell," he said. "I'm glad you could make it."

"Call me Cassandra."

"Okay," he said, his tone cold. "Cassandra."

It didn't take a PhD in psychology to pick out the chilliness in his voice. I guess I had a few ideas why he might not be thrilled to have me there. For one thing, American law enforcement agents hadn't always done well with the British police. We tended to ignore their pesky legal systems and make our own rules. Plus, FBI consultants in general had a reputation of disregarding local expertise. And if all that weren't bad enough, he was probably terrified I was going to have a chirpy American attitude and say things like "good work, team," or force him to high-five at the end of the day.

"Come with me." He turned and walked away.

I followed him. As we drew closer, my mood darkened. I began to pick up the details—the red gash across her entire body, throat to belly, and the dark pool of blood beneath her. Lumps of flesh glistened under the lights. A woman stood above her, photographing the carnage.

"We can stop here," he said when we still stood twenty feet away. "It's intense, and I doubt you need to see it up close to profile the killer. We can provide you with photographs later on."

"Thanks for caring." I raised an eyebrow. "I think I can handle it."

I marched forward. When I reached the body, I crouched by a man who eyed me warily beyond a pair of glasses. I could have sworn I heard him mutter something about Americans under his mask, but I kept my focus on the victim.

Up close, bile began to rise in my throat. She was young, no more than twenty, her face full of pain and horror, mouth ajar in a voiceless cry, eyes staring emptily at the night sky. Her dark hair spread out on the pavement between her arms, giving the impression she was falling. The killer had torn her shirt, exposing the top of her ravaged body. A deep slice exposed her internal organs, or what was left of them. The glaring spotlights highlighted her white skin and bones, shockingly pale against her crimson blood. And as if that weren't bad enough, he'd mutilated her face, slashing perpendicular lines in her cheeks. Dread roiled in the back of my mind. Somehow, the marks looked eerily familiar, like something I'd seen in a nightmare, but I had no idea why.

I tried not to imagine what she would have felt in those final moments, but the images came anyway. The gash on her throat indicated that the killer was likely standing behind her, but her expression left no doubt— she had felt the hand that gripped her, the blade that cut her.

I could only hope that the shock of the attack had overwhelmed her, dulling the pain of the knife wounds somewhat—that her mind hadn't been able to process the horror of what was happening to her. I *hoped* most of the damage had been postmortem.

As my mind roamed over the horror of her final moments, I was almost sorry I hadn't listened to Gabriel. But this was important. This was the murderer's work, and I had to see it up close. This was his sadistic form of expression, how his mind worked. I pushed my visions of her death to the back of my skull, trying to focus.

A steady buzz drew my attention. Several flies roamed the open, bloody cavity. When a body was hours or days old, flies were valuable allies of the forensic team. A skilled investigator could estimate the time of death using fly and larvae samples taken from the body. But this corpse was fresh, and the flies were nothing but parasites, using the poor woman to feed their young.

I waved my hand to shoo the flies away. The coppery smell of blood overpowered me, and I quickly stood up. The flies returned, haunting the woman's wounds again.

I struggled with the desire to close her eyes, to soothe the tortured stare from her face. Somehow, that was what hit me the hardest: her eyes. Wide open and in pain. Maybe I couldn't feel her emotions on a visceral level, but they were written plainly on her face.

Stepping away from the body, I gritted my teeth, trying to picture the monster who would rip apart four young women like this. How many more would he kill before someone stopped him? Would I be able to help?

I was pretty sure I would. This was what I did best. I helped find men like him and put an end to their murder binges.

From the perimeter around the police tape, I felt the crowd's horrified energy, and it began to build my resolution. I wouldn't return to the US until we'd put this monster in prison.

"Are you okay?" Gabriel asked, handing me a pair of latex gloves. I took them and put them on, the synthetic material somehow reassuring.

"I will be," I muttered. "Looks like the viciousness is increasing."

"That was our impression as well," Gabriel said. "This one is the worst so far."

I looked around the small city square. There were no shop fronts here, just the back entrances of buildings, a fenced-in parking lot, and a tiny road. Still, it seemed impossible that he'd slaughtered her in the center of the city without anyone noticing.

"Do we have any witnesses?" I asked.

Gabriel shook his head. "No. A passerby found her at twenty past eleven. He saw no one near the body."

"Do we have an estimated time of death?"

"Yeah. Between eleven and eleven twenty."

"So he found her only minutes after she had been killed."

"Yes."

I frowned. "This doesn't make sense. Someone killed her and disemboweled her completely. It would have taken some time. How did he manage to do that without anyone noticing? Surely people must cut through here to get to the bars and restaurants I saw on Bishopsgate?"

"There isn't much light here without the spotlights. And most people out at this time in the City are likely plastered."

I looked around. The body was reasonably hidden from the nearby street, but anyone looking a bit carefully would surely have noticed it. "He must have been silent. And calm. This is... extraordinary."

"I agree. I've never seen anything like it."

"Any organs missing from the scene?" I asked, thinking of the previous cases.

"The heart, at least, but I'm not sure what else. We'll have a preliminary autopsy report tomorrow."

"Did you do a door-to-door? Did anyone hear anything?"

"We've only just found her," he countered. "And no one lives around here. Unless you wander further east, it's all empty banks and businesses at this hour."

I stared at the woman. "Do we have an ID?"

"Her name is Catherine Taylor," Gabriel said. "Nineteen years old. There was a driver's license in her purse, discarded by the body. We don't know if it's a coincidence yet."

"Coincidence?" I asked.

A sigh slid from him. "Jack the Ripper killed a woman called Catherine Eddowes in Mitre Square."

My throat tightened. Shit. Was he starting to mimic the actual Ripper? "The other victims weren't killed in places where the Ripper struck."

"This is the first that overlaps."

"And the other names didn't match the original Ripper's victims, right?"

"No. I imagine he is adjusting his signature as he goes along. But then, I'm no profiler, so perhaps I'd best leave all the complicated stuff to you."

I narrowed my eyes. Some British people were under the impression that Americans didn't understand sarcasm, and perhaps it was best if I just played along. "Right. Best leave it to the experts."

He stared at me for just a moment before the

medical examiner interrupted. "Detective. Can you have a look at this?"

Gabriel crossed to the body. As he quietly spoke to the man, my gaze wandered to Catherine's eyes again. What had gone through her mind in her final moments? Had she thought of anyone she loved, or had the pain overwhelmed her?

My fingers tightened into fists. I wasn't sure if it was my own past coming to the surface, the way it sometimes did at times like this, but I suddenly had an overwhelming desire to catch her killer and kick the living shit out of him *before* I put him behind bars.

Gabriel knelt close to Catherine's mouth, inspecting it.

I leaned over to get a better look. "What is it?"

"There's something here. It's shoved into her throat. Hang on..."

The man crouching by the body handed Gabriel a pair of medical forceps. Carefully, Gabriel inserted them into the victim's mouth, grimacing as the metal rattled against the teeth. He struggled with it for a second, before finally removing a small piece of paper, spattered in blood.

"What the hell?" he muttered.

Carefully, he unfolded it, and I peered over his shoulder.

It was a note, the cursive letters looping over the paper.

> The King of Hearts
> Tears minds apart,

Deep below the water;
From Bedlam's den,
He lures them in,
Like lambs led to the slaughter.

For just a moment I heard the sound of a rushing river, before the noise disappeared again.

I shook sensation from my mind.

Gabriel rose, frowning. "What's he playing at?" he asked, more to himself than anyone else.

Unnerved, I swallowed hard. "Jack the Ripper left notes, right?"

"Scribbles on a wall. Some tosh about Jews. But nothing like this."

"And this is the first time our current Ripper has left a note?"

He was still staring at the paper. "The first one."

"Well, if you want my input..." I stopped myself short. I needed to avoid coming off like a know-it-all, or I'd alienate him immediately. "Perhaps we can discuss this tomorrow morning. I'll gather a few ideas during the day, and I'd be interested to know your thoughts as well."

Gabriel nodded. "Right. I don't suppose you have an initial assessment?"

"I'd prefer to do a bit of research first. But the note and the gruesome display indicate that the killer seems to enjoy the attention of being the next Ripper. Maybe part of his fantasy revolves around the media and the police. The tabloid headlines might increase his obsession. And if so, maybe he'd want to see us working his cases up close."

I watched him carefully, interested if he'd get what I was implying. He stared at me for a long moment, before glancing over my shoulder, at the crowd beyond the tape. Then, he turned to the photographer—a middle-aged woman with a very expensive-looking camera.

"I want detailed pictures of the crowd," he said in a low voice. "Don't aim the camera straight at them. I don't want anyone to avoid the picture."

She nodded, pointing her camera at the blood spatter around the body. Slowly, she tilted the lens slightly higher, so that it would catch the people behind the tape. She took a few photographs, nudging the camera left and right. She knew what she was doing. And so did the detective.

I'd already committed most of their faces to memory—the two men with beer guts in cheap suits who probably had low-level positions in one of the nearby banks; the man in the white hat with track marks up his arm; the cluster of teens who'd convinced someone to serve them beer, at least one of them more interested in trying to get laid than anything else going on here. But photographs would make it easier for other cops to study the crowd after the fact.

From a far corner of the square, a man in a gray suit approached us, a serious expression on his face. "Detective Stewart." He nodded at Gabriel. I pegged him at about fifty, his hair silvery gray. He wasn't bad-looking, like a giant George Clooney. He was at least as tall as

Gabriel, and powerfully built. Standing next to them, I felt roughly the size of a young child. Was everyone in Britain a giant?

"Chief." Gabriel nodded at him, then motioned at me. "This is Agent Liddell from the FBI. Agent, this is Detective Chief Inspector Steve Wood."

"Oh, yes." DCI Wood's voice was deep, pure gravel. "The *profiler*."

He didn't sound thrilled either. It was becoming clear to me that the high brass had gone over everyone's head when they'd contacted the FBI. Still, he offered me his hand, and I shook it.

"So what are our preliminary findings?" he asked.

For a second I thought he was talking to me, but Gabriel cut in, "This murder is slightly different from the rest. More aggressive. More... public. And he left a note shoved in the victim's throat."

"Are we sure it's the same killer?" DCI Wood asked. "With the different MO—"

"The MO is the same," I interrupted. "The signature is different."

Damn it. I was doing that American thing.

The chief glanced at me. "Is that so?"

"Well, um, perhaps..." I blustered. *Ah, fuck it.* "The MO is the method used to commit the crime. In this case, cutting a young woman's throat with a knife is the MO. It's how he's killed all his victims. The signature is what he did later to satisfy his emotional needs. Mutilating her body postmortem—that's his signature. But this time he left a note. His signature has been modified."

"I see." He nodded slowly. "And what does a different signature indicate?"

It was a sensible question, but his tone clearly implied he thought I was full of shit.

"Serial killers modify their signatures constantly," I said. "They evolve and change after each murder. A different signature isn't unusual, but it suggests that his emotional needs may have changed."

He looked at Gabriel. "What are your thoughts, Detective?"

Gabriel shrugged. "I agree with her assessment so far."

The crime scene technicians were wrapping the body's hands with paper bags, and someone had rolled over a stretcher.

How long would it take to clean all this up? Would tomorrow's bankers stroll past the large stain on the cobblestones, not knowing why it was there?

As DCI Wood walked away, I nodded at the crowds. "How are Londoners handling the crimes?"

Gabriel frowned. "A mixture of fear and rage. They think it's a form of terrorism."

Irritation sparked. "It clearly isn't."

"For now, Wood is keeping the media in the dark, so they're creating their own narrative. Foreigners did it. That's the story."

I exhaled slowly. If Wood allowed this to continue, people could get hurt.

Gabriel stared at the body. Under his breath, I heard him say, *"The savage man is never quite eradicated."*

Surprised, I turned to him. "Thoreau. He's from my home town."

He seemed to study me for a minute, as if his curiosity had been piqued. "Where are you staying? I can walk you to the hotel."

"No need. I'm only five or ten minutes away—the hotel connected to Liverpool Street Station. And I don't imagine our killer will be striking again within the next fifteen minutes."

"Are you sure?"

"Gabriel," I assured him. "I'm an FBI agent. I can take care of myself."